I0940295

# Prophecy of Three
## Book One of
## the
## Starseed Trilogy

By Ashley McLeo

www.ashleymcleo.com



ISBN-13: 978-1-947245-01-3

ISBN-10: 1-947245-01-5

Dedication

For my husband Kurt.
The Starseed universe would not exist
without your help, patience, and love.

The Library of Alexandria 48 B.C. 1
Lily 2016 A.D. 7
The Emerald Isle 27
Brigit's Tale 39
Hecate's Daughters 54
Chance and Choice 77
A History of Witches 91
The Unbinding 108
Magic Lessons 121
A Change of Heart 134
Samhain 142
Alexandria 156
The Vampire Twins 165
Blood and Ash 173
The Tree of Life 186
In the Beginning 193
The Shadow Days 210

# *The Library of Alexandria 48 B.C.*

The knots in Hypatia's back wound tighter as memories of black smoke and lost knowledge flooded her mind.

The library was burning. Thousands of treasures flying toward the heavens reincarnated as ash and ember. Original works of Sophocles, Homer, and Euripides gone, and yet, Hypatia cared for only one. The one passed down through the centuries from woman to woman, witch to witch. She'd read it hundreds of times, recited every word and enunciated every syllable with care, should a disaster such as this ever occur. The one entrusted to her for safekeeping. The true secret of secrets and future of man.

She hardly felt the hot stones beneath her feet as she sprinted toward the volume secreted away in the quietest wing of the royal library. She was halfway there when the smoke began to lay siege to her body. Her muscles, strong from hours of dueling with her sisters for sport, strained beneath her will. Her skin screamed in protest with each brush against a flaming scroll or hot stone. A mere fifty paces away, Hypatia closed her burning eyes and began to navigate the long hallway and staircase blind. Her breath came like a reluctant lover, teasing her lungs before wrenching itself from her body. Years seemed to pass as she pulled herself up the steep stairs, and then suddenly, the floor flattened beneath her palms. She'd made it.

*I must be quick*, Hypatia thought, opening her eyes. Her heart dropped from its cage. The tower was not aflame, as she had feared. The fire was dying, having eaten its fill and moved on. Only layers of ash and gray ghosts remained in the inferno's wake. But how, when paces below the tower a fire devoured its prey with greed and glee?

The answer hit her: This place, the library's most isolated, least loved wing, had been the fire's birthing room. Her left eye twitched.

Someone knew of the treasure hidden here. They knew they would never find it. Not with a flock of dedicated librarians puttering about day after day. The enemy cared not for the sanctity of humanity's treasures. In their desire to destroy her ward, they had set aflame thousands of other works. Worse yet, they were still on the loose, shrouded in anonymity. But *she* had revealed herself.

How foolish! Based on the fire's point of origin, it was likely they had already suspected Hypatia as the keeper of the ancient text. Now she had eliminated any suspicions. What else could be so important that one would rush into flames? Only a matter of life or death.

Her heart chipped into smaller and smaller pieces as she examined the destruction further. Surviving scraps of parchment waved up at her like old friends from the wreckage. Half burnt symbols and illustrations, thoughts, entire worlds gone.

Hypatia's knees buckled beneath her, hitting stone. Her body and spirit cried out for mercy as she curled in on herself, relinquishing her weight to the floor, a sole mourner for the dead.

***

She woke in an unfamiliar room, cleaned and bandaged by familiar people.

Two days had passed since the fire. Hypatia's sisters-in-truth had ensured she survived the marks of smoke and flame by sitting at her side day and night. They whispered of conspiracy, arson, and murders in their coven. Each knew the secret Hypatia guarded, though none as well as she. None had ever bothered to commit even a single passage to memory, let alone the entire text, as Hypatia had done. There had never been the need, though there was now. They hatched a plan, knowing for all its flaws, it was their only option. Hypatia would rewrite the book as best she could from memory and place it under an enchantment only those long awaited could break. Hide it in space, guard it with time, and couple enchantment with prophecy. All before the ones responsible for the fire and deaths plaguing them came for Hypatia, as they were sure to do. Hypatia's sisters promised to provide protection while she worked. Lie for her, die for her if it came to it, but she must hurry.

And so, she did.

Three days she had been writing, teasing any detail she could from her memory. What if her scroll was the only surviving recollection of the past by the time those destined to save them arrived? If the past no longer lived as it did now, flying off the tongues of old women to young children eager to catch it. The threat was all too real. Hypatia had been as diligent as possible in her race against time, pausing only to sleep or when Octavia, her regular guard, brought food or news.

Octavia's assurances of peace within the magical wards their coven had put in place gave Hypatia hope. There had been no unknown visitors or lost wanderers seen in the area. Only Hypatia's family, friends, and library colleagues had asked after her. All had been told the same story: Hypatia was fine, embarrassed by her brashness, and intent on hiding her burned face and pride until they healed. She was sure to emerge soon, her sisters lied.

But then, maybe it was possible? She had not yet dared to hope, but now . . . she was close after all. Could she see her family once more before her enemies came for her?

Hypatia picked up the stylus and began writing with wild abandon, prying each detail from her memory and scribing it back into history. The curved reed mesmerized her as it danced in lines and swirls across papyri. Octavia dropped off breakfast, and still, Hypatia wrote.

Her hand stopped only as the sun rose high above the lighthouse tower. Eyes blurring and stomach clenching with hunger, she re-read the last line.

She'd done it.

The rush of blood that came with rising for the first time in hours dampened the sting in her legs. Spots swam in Hypatia's vision as she shuffled to the small table Octavia had set her breakfast on. She ate the stale bread and cold soup with gusto, washing it down with wine to fortify her for what came next: the part she had been dreading.

Amenia, the Alexandrian coven's high priestess, had reassured Hypatia after each of her many protestations that the enchantment, though challenging, was not beyond Hypatia's skills. Still, Hypatia had her doubts. She had never had a reason to bewitch an object into hiding. Nor had she ever bound an item to another being, much less beings yet to exist. When Hypatia had worried over the predicted length of time the enchantment should hold, Amenia assured her the words she'd woven for Hypatia would work. The tome would wait for the ones destined to fulfill the prophecy. The ones witches had awaited for centuries.

Hypatia had never been much good at reciting enchantments. There was no denying she would have liked more time to practice, more time for the spell to feel natural. When asked, Amenia admitted to having performed a similar spell twice in her fifty years. Yet she refused Hypatia outright when Hypatia requested the high priestess perform the enchantment in her stead.

"The volume knows you best. Thus, the spell will work best if you perform it," Amenia had explained with aggravating confidence.

While Hypatia rarely doubted Amenia's wisdom, right now with her nerves jangled and eyes half closed from exhaustion, the feat seemed impossible.

Perhaps a small nap for strength? Hypatia's dark eyes slid to her cold, neglected bed mat. Thin and lumpy though it was, at that moment Hypatia could not recall a more beautiful sight. *No doubt a rest would make the magic easier. Help it flow*, she thought, hope rising in her chest. *Yes, I'll lie down for a few minutes to gather my strength.*

***

A scream ripped through the night air, wrenching Hypatia from her dreams. Adrenaline tore through her as she ran to the window and gazed into a peaceful courtyard beneath a star-filled sky. *I've been asleep for hours! How could I have been so careless?* She whirled around to grab the sheets of papyri. Another strangled scream filtered heavenward.

That was close. Too close.

Her head whipped to face the door. A plate of steaming stew lay upon the table, its savory scent so fresh it had yet to cross the distance of her small room.

*Octavia*, she thought, rushing to the door to save her friend. The moment her hand clutched the latch she stopped. The ominous silence beyond her thin fortification registered in the sensible part of her mind.

Changing tack, Hypatia tossed the table and writing stool against the thin reed door. Her small barricade would not keep her pursuer at bay for long, but it only needed to buy her enough time to complete her task. She hoped they had not already managed to get past the wards her sisters had set in the alley.

Darting to her scribing slab, Hypatia seized the volume. *There's no time to glue together a proper scroll*, she thought. Quickly, she arranged the pages in order and wrapped them in the piece of goat leather she'd procured for the scroll's protective casing. A few loops of string around the crude codex bound it all together.

Hypatia laid the volume on her writing slab and rested her hand atop the leather. Trying her best to ignore the sound of soft, insidious footsteps approaching Hypatia began chanting the words Amenia had crafted.

"Seek your home.
A being foreseen,
A time unknown.
End my watch.
Go to thee."

In her mind's eye, a figure grew, and Hypatia's skin tingled with elation.

Though dressed as a man and large in stature, the figure's round belly proclaimed impending motherhood. The vision grew more detailed as three others materialized, hands clasped together in a circle around the mother-to-be.

*Good, she'll need protection*, Hypatia thought, as an insistent thrusting of reeds against wood sounded at her back. Committing to the image, the rest of the spell rushed from her lips.

"Hide in space.
Dissolve in time.
Become but myth,
In all but mind.
Seek those from whom,
Pure magic flows.
Offer them knowledge,
Hope, and voice.
Guide them home,
Give them choice."

A blue glow ignited in Hypatia's core, flew down her arms and out her fingertips, seeking refuge in the pages she had crafted. Through her palm she sensed heat, her magic, pulsing below the leather and string, weaving through the words. Finally, she whispered the prophecy, the plea to their saviors as reeds cracked dangerously behind her.

It was done.

Removing her hand, Hypatia saw the eddies of power she'd relinquished transmuting from the soft blue of her own magic to brilliant sapphire, fiery red, and finally a vibrant emerald green. Three colors, just as Amenia had said there would be. Hypatia watched mesmerized as the green light pulsed once more before dissipating into the book, sealing the prophecy.

A deafening cascade of furniture sounded. Hypatia glanced back to see a figure bathed in moonlight slinking over the threshold of her sanctuary. The man, if one could call him that, crept toward her like a cat, graceful and silent.

Hypatia sought his eye, a sliver of humanity with which to beg for her life. Instead, she saw the glint of a blade as it flew at her throat.

Blood shot from Hypatia's neck, leaving a testament to her life on the walls and floors. Her head grew slack, dipping to her chest, no longer able to hold its own weight. From her position of surrender, Hypatia watched as a river spilled from her. Streams of red flowed down her arms to the bony backs of her hands. Dimly she saw them trickle into creeks, following the fine lines of her fingers, before finally coming to rest upon the empty writing slab.

# *Lily 2016 A.D.*

Lily had always admired the stars' indifference. How they remained unaffected by everyday trivialities, great loves, wars, and falls of empires. They were simply there, not knowing or caring that humans prized their light, prayed to them during their darkest hours, even steered their entire lives by them. It felt safe to look upon them, non-threatening and obvious. It was a relief to know such steadiness existed when Lily's life seemed anything but steady.

She pulled her gaze down to the road. The Columbia River shimmered at her right. Its inky fingers glimmered and undulated east to west between Oregon and Washington, cocooned in the familiar peaks and forests of the Gorge. In her rear view mirror a sliver of light blue peaked over the horizon as the sun threatened the night.

Lily let out a sigh as her neck spasmed. Pain, once occasional and limited to post-race soreness, was now a familiar sensation. It had started over Christmas break as a dull ache creeping down her neck, claiming one vertebra at a time and knitting them together. From there it moved inward, settling in the shadow of her ribcage, occasionally radiating up and down her spine. Her anxiety about the mysterious aches and pains grew daily. They felt contradictory—as if something was trying to crawl out of her and sink deeper all at once. It made it hard to concentrate. Her last semester of college was nothing more than a blur.

As graduation day approached, it became difficult to believe Lily's senior year had begun happily. She'd performed beyond her expectations in her final cross-country season, and even managed to lead a relatively active social life—a small miracle, considering her preference for a hike in the woods over socializing. Most surprising of all, she'd had her first boyfriend.

Until a few months ago, Lily Whiplark had never been interested in dating, a quirk that seemed to baffle others. She figured ambivalence toward dating was bound to happen when you were raised in a commune where women ruled the roost and stories of past relationships gone acidic were no secret. She remembered wondering if she'd change her mind when she went to college. She hadn't. At least not until she met Liam.

He had been different. That much was clear upon their first meeting, when he'd rendered her powerless with his violet-flecked gray eyes and smooth baritone voice. She'd agreed to see him again later that day and promptly dissolved into him.

Lily had never met a man so perfect, so unlike any other guy her age. He didn't mind that she wanted to take things slow, that she never stayed at his place, or that she often kept her eyes wide open when they kissed. Even *she* thought that was weird. None of her neuroses phased him. After every perfect date Lily would collapse into bed like a lovestruck teenager, already obsessing about the next time she'd see Liam. Replaying the precise cadence of his voice as he dropped her off at her door: "Goodnight, Lily love."

Then, one day, Liam seemed to mind everything. He grew forceful, demanding answers and throwing allegations at her, each one more crazy and righteous than the last.

"You're hiding something. Rest assured, I'll uncover your secrets. You can't remain silent forever. You'll slip up soon, I can feel it. If you don't give them to me, I can force them from you," he whispered, right before Lily slapped his accusatory finger from between her eyes and ran out the door.

Her fear brought on the realization that she didn't like the person she'd become when she was with Liam. She'd transformed into one of the women she pitied, the ones who lost themselves in the men they were with. She'd never make that mistake again.

"Damn it," Lily swore, pounding the brakes as her Prius skidded into a turn identified by a Douglas fir tree decorated with ornaments. A box wedged in the back seat flew forward, nearly taking her shoulder with it as she brought the vehicle to a sideways stop.

*Argh! A thousand miles away and he's still a menace*, Lily thought, smashing the rogue box into the middle console before taking the wheel once more.

Lush greenery choked the narrow, pothole-riddled gravel drive, creating the strangely pleasing illusion of traveling down a funnel, as Lily drove the miles to the commune center at a snail's pace. The first of three iron fences that surrounded Terramar Commune had a reputation for sneaking up on people, and it had the dents to prove it.

Rena, the commune matriarch, considered lights on the secluded, treed drive an unnecessary expense. "Who's going to be visiting in the dark of night? We hardly get visitors in the day!" was her predictable rebuttal when the matter was brought up at community meetings.

As Lily dragged the third rusted gate over the uneven ground, she wondered why Rena insisted on keeping the three behemoths shut all hours of the day if no one ever visited. *Hypocrite*, she thought, pulling through and leaving the third gate open on principle.

*That's odd, all the lights are on*, Lily thought, turning into the driveway of a cabin with a cherry red door. *Hopefully Em isn't fighting insomnia again.* Emily would never admit it, but Lily knew insomnia was Em's code for battling her demons from a life years past and miles away. *Maybe she's up writing poetry again*, Lily hoped, pulling the keys from the ignition.

"Everyone else has equal claim to words during the day, but in the small hours, they're all mine, darlin', and I'll take 'em when I can," Emily would say on nights when Lily shuffled bleary eyed into the kitchen for a glass of water to find Em scribbling in her notebook.

The night air teased goosebumps up her arms as Lily exited the car for the first time in hours. The scent of damp, living soil flew at her and she inhaled deeply, savoring the nuances. Faint traces of rhododendrons, dahlias, and mint hung in the night air like secret admirers vying for her attention.

The red door swung open before Lily had even reached the stairs.

"Lawd, child! We weren't expecting you till noon!" Emily exclaimed, her hazel eyes crinkling as she pulled Lily up the steps by her arms and into a fierce hug.

Lily's body slackened as the pear scent of Emily's silver hair enveloped her. "I was too excited to sleep so I kept driving. You know summer solstice is my favorite! I didn't want to be late," she said, pulling an impish grin she knew Em couldn't resist to hide her half truth.

The *last* thing she wanted to do was bring up how her sleep was plagued by the feeling of dark, silky hair sliding between her fingers. That aromas of sandalwood and coins warmed in a hand lingered over her bed for hours, nearly as long as Liam's voice rang deep in her ears. It made sleep far less appealing. Only the fact that no one at the commune knew about Liam and their ill-fated relationship made the lie easier. That the relationship had devoured her completely for months, leaving little time for thought of friends or family, would have been enough reason for her family to dislike him. After their final encounter Lily had been too ashamed to reveal she had fallen for someone she'd so clearly misread. Liam was the only secret she'd ever kept from them.

Emily's eyes bore into her, as if sensing the lie by omission, before finally cupping Lily's shoulders and guiding her inside. "Rena's gonna be mighty displeased you didn't stop to rest, but truth be told, I'm right pleased you're finally home," she drawled in a voice that, despite having left the south decades ago, clung to its twang. "You look dead on your feet. Let's get you to bed."

Lily smiled at familiarities of home as they shuffled through the cluttered living room strewn with balls of yarn attached to half-finished projects. Countless books of poetry sat atop the old coffee table, a modern woman's shrine to George Chapman, Mary Oliver, Pablo Neruda, and Maya Angelou. Her chest loosened as they passed the kitchen with its small dining table and gleaming copper pots hanging from the ceiling. She'd passed many hours here, spilling her guts around the table that Emily referred to as the heart of her home.

"I've changed a few things since you've been home last," Emily warned, pushing open the door to Lily's room.

Lily's muscles softened at the sight of a welcoming sage green duvet, pulled back and ready for her to dive into. Dimmed amethyst lamps illuminated a colorful nosegay of fresh ranunculus. The once lime green walls were now a pleasant cream color adorned with black and white photos of Lily's family. A painting depicting an ethereal forest landscape hung above her bed, and a morsel of homemade caramel sat atop the pillow.

"You've been expecting me?" Lily asked, eyeing the turned down bedding.

"I had a feelin'." Emily Harp was famous for her intuition and knew when to heed it.

"I hope you don't mind I redecorated?" Emily asked, her tone uncertain. "Rena painted the picture. It's your homecoming gift."

"You've outdone yourself, Em! And the painting is absolutely gorgeous. I'll be sure to thank Rena tomorrow."

"Weeeel. There isn't a whole lot else to do when my soul doesn't want to sing. Plus that bright green color was hurtin' my old eyes," Em teased, giving Lily's shoulder a playful whack, before plumping a pillow one last time.

"Don't remind me," Lily groaned, as images of lime green walls dotted with posters of bands and celebrities she'd hung in a sad attempt to feel like a normal teenage girl threatened to override the serene scene before her.

"Alright, darlin', time for you to shut those pretty green eyes," Em ordered, as if Lily were still twelve. "I'm so glad you're home." She kissed Lily on the cheek before disappearing back down the hall.

"Night, Em."

***

Lily was ripped from sleep four hours later by an obnoxious noise. *What the hell*? she wondered, her head still foggy. It sounded once more, clearer this time. *That damn rooster*. Lily flung her face back into her pillow, though she knew it wouldn't help. She was awake and would remain so. Turning her head to the side, Lily spotted the caramel sitting atop the opposite pillow. She popped it in her mouth, savoring the buttery goodness rolling over her tongue.

*Now that's the way to wake up. I should convince Em to let me leave a bowl of caramels by the bed all the time.*

She stretched her body out long, reveling in the spaciousness of her queen-sized bed before dangling her feet over the edge gingerly. Her aches and pains had vanished. She paused, trying to remember if she'd had any nightmares, but none emerged in the light of day. *Well, isn't that something*, she thought, swinging her legs and stretching her arms without pain for the first time in months.

She pranced to the window and pulled back the thick, cream curtains. The lazy morning sun rushed in to warm her cheeks. *A perfect day*, she thought, taking in the view outside her window.

The woods surrounding Terramar were nothing short of magical. Large trees with spring green moss swimming up their trunks loomed high over the cabin. Weak morning light pushed through the foliage and mist to dance upon the undergrowth of mushrooms littering the base of each tree. A light breeze teased its way through the woods, its presence indicated by the faintest rustle of leaves marring the morning calm.

Emily's garden grew outside Lily's window and already boasted astonishing quantities of plump heirloom tomatoes, Oregon strawberries, lettuce, and wax beans. A fig tree planted twenty years before stood at the garden's edge. It was bare now, but Lily knew it would be heavy with deep purple fruit by summer's end.

Lily took her time in the shower, indulging in the homemade soaps and lotions made by Terramar residents. Last she heard, the boutiques in Portland were selling them at astronomical prices and still couldn't keep them in stock. She dressed in the first items pulled from her bag, which someone had helpfully set inside her door as she slept. *I could hardly have done better if I planned it*, she thought, examining her outfit of oxblood skinnies, a gray top, and navy ballet flats. She threw her wavy brown hair into her typical topknot and applied a single coat of mascara.

Em was placing a plate of warm scones on the table as Lily shuffled into the kitchen.

"Marionberry?" Lily asked. Her mouth was already watering at the thought of the commune's legendary marionberries embedded in one of Emily's moist scones. All crops grown on Terramar land ripened early. The reason why eluded commune residents (who admittedly never cared much to investigate) and baffled the handful of scientists Rena allowed to study the soil. Friends of the commune and a grocer in Hood River made regular trips to Terramar to buy plump, fresh fruit weeks before their own gardens would yield such treasures.

"Can't have you starvin' on your first day back, can I?" Em asked with a wink as she tended a sizzling skillet of Lily's favorite pulled pork hash.

*Thank god I love running*, Lily thought, claiming the largest scone without guilt. Her affinity for running had been fostered on the abundant dirt trails woven around their hidden community. It had given her a sense of strength and a small taste of freedom from her large, ever-present family. Time seemed to stop when her feet pounded dirt paths. More than once Lily found herself racing home in the dark unsure how she'd lost track of the hour. Surprisingly, her long absences didn't worry anyone else. Least of all Rena, who allowed her to run anywhere she liked, as long as she was on Terramar land. It was an easy rule to follow. Terramar extended for miles in all directions and was marked at its perimeter by iron fencing.

"Anyone stopped by yet?" Lily asked, spreading a liberal amount of butter on the soft scone. Dark purple berries burst and mixed with the yellow butter, creating a pleasing tie-dye effect.

"Lawd, have they! Richard, bless his heart, brought your bag in at dawn. Said he'd seen your car packed to burst on his run. He left the rest of your things over there." Em pointed to a tidy pile of boxes by the door. "I had to shoo Selma away once he told her you were here. You hadn't had nearly enough sleep and we *all* know how you get without your sleep," Emily finished, her eyes widening.

Bits of scone flew onto her plate and Lily clapped her hands over her mouth mid laugh. One of Em's nicknames for her when she hadn't gotten enough sleep had been "holy terror." The name usually got a laugh out of someone, though it was the first time that someone was Lily. Mountains of coursework, rowdy roommates, and the chaos of campus life had eradicated her adolescent quirk for ten hours of sleep. Though Lily saw no reason to inform anyone at Terramar of that. Better to catch up on sleep than be woken to feed the chickens.

"Then Rena popped in," Em continued, her eyebrows arched high over round hazel eyes. "I didn't tell her what time you got home, but she guessed it to be earlier than she'd like. Said she'd call on you later today. Performed an inspection of your car before leaving, of course," Em chortled, shaking her head as she turned back to the hash.

"Of course she did," Lily said, her tone unsurprised. "So when do we start prepping for tomorrow?"

Tomorrow was summer solstice. Every year the residents of Terramar went all out, throwing an infamous party complete with carnival games, food, singing, and dancing. The affair required weeks of planning, most of which Rena took on. For Lily, summer solstice had always been the most magical day of the year. This year would be no exception, as the celebration fell on her twenty-first birthday.

She would finally be allowed in the adult tent. The aged white dome was strictly for the twenty-one and over crowd and had been a source of extreme childhood puzzlement for Lily. One year she'd gone so far as to camp outside the tent and interrogate all who exited about the mysteries within. She made sure to pay special attention to anyone with rosy cheeks and loose limbs, courtesy of Hazel's infamous mead. To her annoyance, and Rena's great amusement, not one person slipped.

*Well, I'll find out for myself this year*, Lily thought, grinning into her teacup.

"I was planning on stopping by Rena's to see if she wanted any help."

"No!" Em cried, nearly sending the hash to the floor as she whirled to face Lily.

Lily started and her knees hit the table painfully. *What the hell was that?* she wondered, searching Em's face for an explanation.

Em cleared her throat as she positioned the hash back on the burner. "If I recall, Rena was fixin' to send you to town on errands. Selma and Richard will need help loadin' the truck. What with all the wine and materials we ordered for the party."

"But I just drove across the country!" Lily whined, her voice high and childlike. "I don't want to get in the car again."

Silence hung between them. Lily hunched over the table, green eyes glaring irritably, while Em did her best to ignore Lily's gaze by tending the hash.

Then it clicked: Rena was trying to surprise her! She'd arrived half a day early and Rena had probably been counting on the morning to finish the surprise. *I'll bet Rena told Em she needed me out of the commune for a few hours*, Lily thought, leaning back in her chair.

It was no secret she'd been looking forward to having her birthday at home for the first time in two years. Rena probably had something amazing up her sleeve, and here Lily was butting in.

"Maybe Selma would let me pick out a bottle of birthday wine for tomorrow?" Lily flashed her impish grin in hopes of smoothing over her tantrum.

"I'm sure she'll help you pick out a nice one, darlin'," Emily said, relief flooding her lined face.

*I should know better than to confront Em*, Lily thought, chastising herself as guilt settled in the pit of her stomach. After escaping the confines of a hard life in Louisiana, Em preferred to avoid conflict. She was good at it, too. Lily had yet to see Em raise her voice or lash out at anyone, and here Lily was picking a fight her first day back. An apology was forming on Lily's tongue when Em laid a plate before her and joined her at the table with an understanding smile. She'd already been forgiven.

They ate in comfortable silence, both savoring the time to be with their thoughts before the start of the day. It was a morning ritual Lily had missed during her overstimulating college years.

Their plates lay newly bare when a perfunctory knock shattered the calm. The front door flung open and the intruder barreled through the living room at astonishing speed, making a direct beeline for Lily.

"Ay, mi corazón! You're home!" Selma de Avila cried, engulfing Lily in a hug so tight she had trouble breathing.

A deep, familiar laugh pierced the air, reminding Lily, as it always did, of a large gong she'd seen at a Buddhist temple. Richard threw Em a sheepish smile as he stepped through the door after Selma.

"Sorry, ladies, it was impossible to hold her back a second longer." His words were apologetic even if his eyes weren't; they were full of nothing but love for the petite Spanish tornado wrapped around Lily's torso. "Welcome home, sweetheart," he added, squeezing Lily's shoulder with a gentleness his work-worn hands did not imply.

"Hola mamacita and Rich! It's great to be home."

Selma slackened her hold and took a half step back to look Lily over.

*I swear she hasn't aged a day*, Lily thought, studying Selma's dewy, olive complexion and perfect white smile as Selma's eyes raked over her. *If I didn't know better I wouldn't put her a day over thirty-two.*

"Sooo—I hear you're here to whisk me off and get me drunk?" Lily teased, excited to start her day, despite the semi-forceful eviction and hours on the road.

"Nah. We just need all that youthful muscle to haul in wine. Old muscles atrophy something awful. Didn't they teach you that at that fancy college of yours?" Richard said, his own muscles standing at attention as he poked Lily's small bicep. "Franco said he'd open early so we can pick up the cases of sangiovese and dolcetto Rena ordered. Then we were thinking Double Mountain for lunch?"

They had her. Lily's breakfast wasn't even settled in her stomach and already her mouth was watering at the thought of pizza.

"I'll get my bag," Lily said, dashing out of the kitchen. She returned seconds later, a tiny crossbody slung over her shoulder, ready to take on the culinary delights of Hood River.

"Y'all have fun now. Sel, could you pick me up a bottle of that Marchesi barbera I like? I can never remember which year," Emily said, wiping her hands on a dish towel before bestowing a quick hug on Lily.

Cramming three people in Margo, Richard's old truck, was

uncomfortable under the best conditions. Considering the number of items stuffed in the cab with them, Lily hailed it as half a miracle when the doors clicked shut. Three bags brimming with berries and jams to be delivered to various restaurants, shops, and wineries sat at Lily's feet. Two bags rested in her lap, while two others perched precariously atop the headrest behind Lily and Selma. Selma sat in the middle, a bag full of Hazel's fragrant soaps and lotions in her lap and another anchored between her feet. Nestled in the truck bed, wrapped in many blankets, lay one of Rena's paintings commissioned by a local gallery owner.

*This is going to take hours*, Lily thought, amused by all they had orchestrated to keep her busy.

As they neared the highway Selma leaned across Lily to point out the latest glass ornaments to adorn the bedazzled fir tree.

"See right there, the red one between the green one that looks like a watermelon and the rust brown one? Si, si, that one's Richard's." Selma rolled her eyes as she pointed out the brown blob.

Lily stifled a giggle. "Red, yellow, and orange?" she asked as an ornament resembling a ball of flame caught her eye.

"Si—holy shit!"

A bag of berries pushed into the back of Lily's head as Richard hit the breaks. Catching the bag before it toppled, Lily righted it and scanned the road for the animal that must have jumped out in front of them.

Instead, she saw a small, black sports car, sideways in the drive, mere inches from Richard's bumper. A long trail of skid marks followed the car, a testament to the speed at which it had turned off the highway onto Terramar's gravel drive. A woman with a dramatic A-line bob, bright red lips, and huge black sunglasses perched atop her head sat behind the wheel. She'd covered her eyes with her hands and her mouth was hanging open in a cartoonish "O" shape.

Lily watched the woman peek between her fingers and sigh with relief. Lifting her hands in the universal sign of apology, she mouthed, "I'm sorry," her eyes begging forgiveness.

Lily started as the woman's eyes met her own. *Where do I know her from? Bryn Mawr? In town? A cross-country mom? No, she's far too glamorous to be from around here. She looks like a celebrity.*

Inexplicably, the woman began to laugh. A small chuckle that grew into peals of hilarity so intense the woman rolled down her window to fan herself.

"Someone's got a case of the nerves," Richard said, his eyes darting from Lily to the dark haired stranger as he leaned back in his seat.

Lily barely heard him.

*Is she laughing at me? s*he wondered, before realizing how ridiculous the question was. It wasn't like the woman could read her mind or anything. *Rich is right, she's probably one of those people who laugh when they're nervous. Or she's unhinged. Either way I wish she'd stop, she's making* me *nervous.*

The transformation happened as if Lily had commanded it.

The woman stopped laughing, wiped away a few stray tears, waggled her fingers in their direction, and threw the car into gear.

Lily peered in the side mirror to see tail lights and bits of rock flying through the air as the woman disappeared down the gravel drive.

***

They returned hours later, laden with wine, complimentary treats from one of the specialty shops Hazel supplied, and a considerable amount of cash.

Lily spent the day laughing and reuniting with people she hadn't seen in years. No one that saw her would have guessed that her attention was split, half on them and half on the bob-haired stranger.

*Will she be there when we get back?* Lily wondered. *Or was she just an emotional woman who took a wrong turn?* As much as Lily would have liked to believe the latter, the niggling feeling that she knew the woman had not disappeared.

As they jostled down the commune's circular thoroughfare, Lily craned her neck, hoping to spot the sleek car in someone's driveway. It wasn't until they pulled up to Rena's cabin that she caught a glimpse of black paint and polished chrome tucked behind Annika's large diesel truck.

The woman hadn't taken a wrong turn, and even more intriguing, she was still at Terramar hours later. Lily wondered if Rena would bring up Annika's visitor or if she would have to ask. There was no question that Rena knew about the visitor. Rena knew everything that happened at the commune. Whether she felt the news was appropriate to gossip about was a different matter. But it wouldn't be the first time Lily had tried to wheedle information from Rena. She'd had an entire lifetime of practice with that.

After all, Rena had been the one to find Lily when she was an infant. Abandoned in a baby carrier on the side of a road, with only a half dozen bottles of warm milk and a note indicating her date of birth tucked into her soft blankets, Lily had been fingering the petals of a wild leopard lily and looking perfectly content with her situation. Rena brought her home and inquired about adoption. She was granted temporary custody until what the state saw as a more suitable family unit came along. None ever did, and Lily became Rena's adoptive daughter a year after Rena found her.

Lily had taken Rena Whiplark's last name, though Rena always joked they should have added at least twenty hyphenations over the years, as she was the definition of a child raised by a village. It was true. The women of Terramar gave love and knowledge in spades, and while each held a special place in Lily's heart, none could compare to Rena. Even during Lily's moodiest teenage years, both recognized their bond was special. So special it was best celebrated with copious amounts of personal space to avoid the sour feelings that often arose between their different personalities. It had been Rena who suggested Lily move in with Em. It was a move that saved not only their relationship but the sanity of other commune residents during those tumultuous years. It was during those same years that Lily, who Rena had homeschooled her entire life, demanded to be enrolled in public school. She wanted to make friends, meet boys, and most of all compete in athletics. For weeks Rena refused, insisting Lily would be too advanced to feel comfortable at a public school.

In the end, it was Annika who won the battle for Lily. "Do you want her to waste all her talent running the river trails? Think of the scholarships Lily could get if she competed!"

Lily enrolled in public school the following week.

Though she stuck by her decision, Lily had to admit Rena had been right about the quality of schooling. She'd spent exactly two weeks in general classes before skipping a grade and advancing into the honors curriculum. Even there Lily was an oddity. Normal teenagers, even super smart ones, knew next to nothing about ancient Egyptology, botany, symbology, mysticism, or Rena's favorite subject, feminist history.

As it turned out, it was the education Rena provided that inspired Lily's undergraduate work. A double major in political science, emphasis on women's rights, and botany. While she had been unsure of her double major, Rena had been all for it. Lily remembered that call home like it was yesterday.

"I don't know what to do. I feel as if a part of me will die if I choose the other," Lily had cried into the receiver, practically begging Rena to decide her major for her. Lily's career, her whole future could depend on this choice. She didn't want to be responsible for something so huge.

"I don't know why you're even bothering to worry!" Rena said, her dismissive tone startling Lily out of self pity. "Do both, of course! Be bold! I assume they'll give you two degrees at once at that fancy school of yours?"

"But it's impractical. I'll have to take summer courses to graduate on time, not to mention the added expenses," Lily stammered. She'd called for sound, level-headed advice, not pipe dreams.

"Vegas is the definition of impractical, but it's there, isn't it? This! Coming from a girl who grew up in a commune of all places. You surprise me, Lily Whiplark! And here I was thinking I raised an open-minded go-getter!" Rena exclaimed with a finality that closed the subject.

Lily enrolled in both programs the next day. Her scholarships, she was shocked to discover, covered the extra credits. If she was fine with subsisting on ramen for a couple of years, taking summer courses, and working in the summer months when her course load was lighter, she could do as she wished.

"Here, chica," Selma said, as a case of wine slammed into Lily's chest.

"Ooopph! Thanks for the heads up Sel."

"Chica! We don't have time for daydreaming! We've got a party to prepare for! Expectations to live up to! Take those and go say hello to your mother." Selma gestured to the door where Rena stood, dark eyes crinkled, and full lips stretched wide into a smile.

"Hey, mom!" Lily beamed, setting the wine at the bottom of the steps before bounding up the stairs.

"My Lil. I'm so glad you're home," Rena said, her wild, curly hair brushing against Lily's cheeks as they hugged. "Let's get all this inside. Then I'll make us tea."

Lily was reminded, as she always was at Terramar, that many hands made light work. The unloading that would have taken one person half an hour was done in minutes.

"I'll have to start charging you and Hazel a courier fee if you keep bringing in this kind of money." Richard set the last case of wine in Rena's entryway and handed over the sum Rena's painting had fetched.

"What do you say I buy you a new truck instead?" Rena suggested, only half joking. She was convinced Richard's truck was going to fall to pieces on the road any day now.

"Aww, come on now, Rena, Margo's got a few thousand miles left in her old wheels. Don't cha, girl?" Richard said, winking out the window at Margo and eliciting eye rolls from the women.

"Well, we best be moving on. We still have to drop off Em's wine and Hazel's cash. Stop by our place later, won't ya', Lil?" Richard said, swinging an arm around Selma.

Lily nodded, waving the pair out the door.

"Green tea alright?" Rena asked as a kettle began to whistle in the kitchen. "I haven't cooked anything in days. You know how it is around solstice, but Ann and I picked strawberries yesterday. I could wash those up for you?"

"Sounds great," Lily said, following her mother to the kitchen, relieved not to be subjected to Rena's cooking.

"How was the drive? You got in earlier than we anticipated."

"Knew you'd bring that up," Lily threw her hands up in defeat. "I admit, I skipped a couple of scheduled stops, but I *swear* I wasn't tired. To be honest, I felt like I was running on rocket fuel. You know I would have stopped if I felt a single eyelid droop." Over the years Lily had learned Rena responded best to a quick and full confession. At any rate, it was her only hope to avoid her millionth lecture on road trip safety.

Rena's lips twitched upward.

"You are a full grown woman, Lil, able to take care of yourself. Though, I am happy you haven't forgotten the virtues of rest stops," Rena handed over a cup of green tea and bowl of strawberries. The familiar smell of the coconut oil Rena used on her skin slid over Lily, mixing with the tea and strawberries comfortingly.

Lily smiled, bemused but unwilling to question how she had gotten off so easy.

"So how was graduation? I know you didn't want to walk, but did you and your girlfriends have one final hurrah?"

Lily cringed. "No party. I packed and left pretty fast." She stared down at the tea, and the temperature in the room seemed to increase as Rena waited for her to elaborate.

"Hmm. Well, there's still much to do so we could use you. And did I mention we have a visitor?" Rena said flatly, setting her untouched cup by the sink.

Lily shook her head and took a compulsive sip of the scalding tea. That was it? No probing questions? And why did *Rena* look tense?

"She's at Annika's becoming reacquainted. An old . . . friend of the commune, though she hasn't visited in years. Would you like to meet her?"

"Is this visitor the classy brunette I saw earlier? The one driving a little black car down the drive like she was street racing?" Lily asked, hoping to come off like she hadn't been wondering about the woman all day.

"That'd be her," Rena said, her full lips flattening. "I'll have to have a word with Nora regarding the commune speed regulations. Did you speak with her?"

"No, we saw each other by the highway turn off. She almost flew past and turned in at the last second by the looks of it. She missed Margo by an inch. I think we startled her. She got kind of hysterical."

Rena's frown deepened, emphasizing the dark lines in her skin.

"So she's been here before? I felt funny seeing her, like I'd met her but couldn't place her." Lily paused, unsure how or if she wanted to articulate the strange feelings she'd felt.

"She hasn't been around since you were small."

Lily gulped down half the hot tea, unreasonably eager to see the woman again. "Well, I'm ready whenever you are."

***

The walk to Annika's cabin was a short one. Rena and Annika had worn a narrow path through the thick trees over their decades as partners. The path had given them the privacy they craved in the early stages of their relationship. Many years later, the path continued to be worn deeper into the dirt. A symbol of their connection and need for personal space all at once.

The door swung open before the second knock, as if Annika had been waiting on the other side.

"Come in, come in! It's wonderful to see you, Lil. Can I get you anything? Coffee? Tea? Juice?" Annika said, her ice blue eyes shining as she folded Lily into a hug and kissed her cheeks. She switched her attentions to Rena and Lily was struck, as she always was, by the stark contrast the pair made. Pale and dark, willowy and strong, pin straight hair and wild afro, they were perfectly opposite as well as perfectly suited for one another.

"She's obsessed with her damn juicer," Rena commented, kicking off her shoes.

"It's healthy! You'd like it, Rena, if you only gave it a chance."

"It's preposterous! You lose all the fiber and waste the produce. Do you realize how much produce grown here is worth in town?"

"Water's good, Ann," Lily cut in.

"Alright, but if you want to try some later let me know. It does wonders for your skin, and I've learned a few combinations I think you'd love. It's all about the cucumber," Annika said looking resigned. "Nora's waiting in the sun room. I'll meet you two in there."

"Hmph," Rena grumbled.

"Thanks, Ann," Lily said, grabbing Rena's arm and pulling her down the hall.

They found Nora examining Annika's Nataraja statue and looking distinctly out of place amid Annika's collection of wellness books and yoga gear.

Nora smiled as they entered and extended her manicured hand to Lily.

A faint, arousing tingle ran up Lily's arm as their skin touched. *What is it about this woman?*

"I'm Nora McFadden," Nora announced, her voice brimming with confidence and panache.

Her accent had an ambiguous origin and lovely musical quality. *Irish?* Lily guessed as she met Nora's piercing blue eyes.

"Lily Whiplark. It's a pleasure to meet you, Ms. McFadden."

"Nora, please." Nora waved her hand. "I can't stand being reminded that I'm becoming old. Particularly by a beautiful young thing such as yourself."

Lily nodded, unsure what else to say.

"Welcome back, Nora. You're looking well. I heard you may have had some trouble finding us again?" Rena raised an eyebrow over her tight-lipped smile.

"Ah! So you heard about our near collision, did you? You should consider a sign. At the very least pave the fecking road. I'd wager my car has as many holes as your bloody drive now. Good thing it's a rental." Nora turned to face Lily. "I am sorry if I startled you, Lily, though I must say you weren't the only one crapping her knickers."

"Yes. Well, as you know, our need for privacy has been paramount these past years," Rena said, her chocolate brown eyes narrowing.

*Their need for privacy? What did that mean?* Rena was meticulous with words, a trait she'd tried to drill into Lily with marginal success.

Annika bustled into the room a wide grin on her face. "I know no one requested anything but I thought a few munchies might be in order." She shot a look at Lily as she set a tray of lemon waters and trail mix on a spindle-legged table and began handing out waters, oblivious to her partner's stiff posture and stern gaze.

"Annika, my dear, you are such a breath of fresh air," Nora said, taking a sip of her water and placing it in the exact middle of a coaster. "Now, then, where were we?"

"You were explaining why you're visiting," Lily said, taking the chance to redirect the conversation.

"Ah, yes! Now, Lily, I doubt you've ever heard of me, but I've actually known you for quite some time. Your entire life in fact, isn't that right, Rena?"

Rena's head twitched in what could have been a nod.

"You see, Lily," Nora said charging along with the story. "Almost twenty-one years ago I took on your adoption case. I've visited a couple of times since then to ensure your well-being. Other than that I've left your upbringing to Rena and the rest of the . . . commune," she said, spitting out "commune" with a distinct air of distaste.

"Alright," Lily said, bristling at the implied slight on her home. "You're right. I don't remember you, and to be honest I'd like to know why you're here, creating all this tension? I'm twenty-one, a legal adult. Rena no longer has jurisdiction over my life, and neither do you."

"You sure can read a room!" Nora exclaimed with a laugh that reminded Lily of wind chimes, the loud, obnoxious kind.

"Well, as you seem to have inferred, your mother and I have rarely seen eye-to-eye. Truth be told, I was holding out hope for a more traditional family to adopt you." Nora's large eyes grazed over Lily. "Though, I must admit, by the look of you Rena has done a fine job, as she said she would." She nodded in a small concession to Rena and raised her glass to her lips.

Lily wished she'd get to the point and leave.

Nora set down her glass with a hard clink. "I'm here to inform you that we've found your biological parents. Would you like to meet them?" She delivered the words casually, as if she were asking if Lily wanted fries with her burger.

Lily's head spun.

It had never been a secret she was adopted. How could it have been? Lily had been raised in the most unique environment she had ever heard of. She didn't look at all like anyone who lived at the commune, so the daydream that one of them was secretly her parent had never even crossed her mind. Yet, searching for her biological family never had either. Everything she needed was here. Why would she spend time and energy searching for someone who had abandoned her? But that wasn't to say she hadn't dreamed of what her biological family would be like.

A dream she hadn't had in years resurfaced. The beautiful mother, the strapping father whom she resembled most. Except for her eyes, Lily had her mother's eyes. Behind them a small boy and girl threw a ball back and forth. They were younger than Lily, but not by much. In the dream Lily sat on her father's knee, reading to him in the halting, high-pitched way of children. Her mother sat next to them, knitting a baby hat.

It was, Lily realized, the most idyllic of scenarios. Her mother and father were probably separated as most were nowadays. They could have been poor, teenagers or addicts of some sort. *Why would they have left me otherwise? Don't most people try their best for their children no matter the circumstances? In their young, drug-addled minds did they think abandoning a child on the side of a road was the best option? Who does that?* She had to know.

She became aware of Rena and Annika holding her up, their hands soft and steady on her back. *Would they be mad? No—they'd be happy she had this chance. Right?* Lily glanced covertly at Rena and her heart sank. She'd take anger any day over the resignation she saw in Rena's face. *Has Rena been waiting for this to happen? Was it common for parents who abandoned their kids to want to reunite? Has Rena been looking over her shoulder for the one person who could have a better claim on her daughter?*

A surge of protectiveness swelled in Lily's chest. Rena had gone through a lot to raise her. Lily doubted her biological parents could have done better, and she wanted them to know that. To know that no one could replace her family here, the people who had given her all they had. *I'll have to practice what I want to say . . . oh my God! What if?*

"Are they here, too?"

"Here? Heavens no, girl! I'm afraid you're in for a much longer journey than a walk down the hall." Nora reached into a black leather bag and pulled out an envelope. She held it out to Lily, who took it unflinchingly.

Lily ripped it open and found plane tickets. Three stiff, paper, old-school tickets, with stops in Seattle, New York and—"Ireland! I'm going to Ireland?" She had never even been out of the United States. She was suddenly thankful Rena had insisted she apply for a passport a couple years back.

"That's right. You'll be flying into Shannon. It's on the west side. A receiving agent will collect you, then you have a bit of a drive to your final destination. Your family lives in the countryside. That's where you'll be meeting."

"I—I can't believe I'm Irish," Lily trailed off. It was strange to be able to identify herself as part anything.

"Full Irish by blood, but we, that is to say those from the Emerald Isle, put a lot of stock in knowing your culture. So I'd say you have a ways to go before you can lay full claim to your Irish roots," Nora smiled, her voice warming a touch.

"You're Irish, too? Why is your accent so strange?"

"I was wondering if you'd catch that." Nora laughed.

Lily found it more charming now, a subtle tinkle in a breeze.

"I've been a sort of diplomat all my life. Spent a fair amount of time here and there because of my job. I suppose my accent's dimmed because of it, though I'll be working my arse off to get it back. You, my dear, were my last assignment for a long while." Nora looked pleased with the thought.

"If you look at your ticket you'll see you depart in two days' time. Rena and the rest of your family here requested to spend your birthday with you. Does that suit you? Or do you wish to leave sooner?"

Lily glanced up at Rena and Annika, and read the worry that she would want to leave sooner etched in their eyes.

"The original date works. I'd like to celebrate with my family."

# *The Emerald Isle*

Odd words and foreign accents flew through the air as Lily exited the security gate of Shannon International Airport. She veered to the side and pivoted on tiptoes as travelers flowed past her. The crowd thinned as the minutes passed, and still she saw no sign bearing her name. *I must look pathetic*, she thought. A warm sensation crept up her neck as another stranger glanced at her curiously and her utter aloneness seeped in. *Did they get the time right? Why didn't I ask for a photo of the adoption agency's receiving agent? Nora said the agent would carry a sign.* Lily scanned the meeting area again and this time an elderly woman standing inches outside the security gate caught her eye. The woman looked as frantic as Lily felt and was waving a tiny card above her head in ever expanding circles.

*Seriously*, Lily thought, walking back toward the gate.

"Ah! You must be Lily," the woman sighed and broke into a well-lined smile at Lily's approach.

"That's me. Sorry I didn't see your . . . sign," Lily replied, forcing her face to remain neutral as she stared at the index card with Whiplark scrawled across the front in pencil.

"Well, it's a wee bit busy in here, so I can see why. I'm Morgane Murphy. I'll be taking you to the agency, along with two others. Let's get out of the way, shall we?" Morgane gestured to a small alcove where a curvy blonde dressed in a chic black pantsuit stood. "It's hard for me to hear in crowded places."

Lily followed Morgane. Her stomach loosening as the knowledge that she wasn't stranded settled in.

The blonde glanced up from her iPhone as they approached. Her large eyes were dark blue and irritated as they flitted past Morgane to latch onto Lily. "Finally. We've been waiting for hours. If I'd have known the adoption agency would set up carpools, I'd have hired my own driver. I've wasted so much time," she said, reaching for one of the two designer suitcases at her feet.

"Evelyn Locksley, meet Lily Whiplark," Morgane said as if the irate blonde hadn't spoken.

"Hi," Lily said, waving in Evelyn's direction.

"Charmed," Evelyn replied, her lips pursed, before turning back to Morgane.

"Can we go now? I'd like some time to decompress before meeting my birth family."

"Of course, dear," Morgane said. "But where has Sara gotten off to?"

"Like I know? She said something about grabbing food. Can't she find us at baggage claim?"

"Hmm, perhaps I should wait here for her? Why don't you show Lily to baggage claim? We'll meet you there."

"Let's go," Evelyn commanded, launching into a power walk.

The leggy blonde was already halfway down the hallway by the time Lily caught up. "I didn't realize we'd be picked up in groups either. You're meeting your birth parents too?"

Evelyn glanced back, an unnatural smile on her face, and nodded tightly.

"Soooo, where are you from?" Lily said, trying another stab at conversation.

"Manhattan," Evelyn's tone was matter-of-fact. "I'm sure forcing us to carpool was some ridiculous attempt at saving a few Euros. I swear, small companies can be so damned inefficient."

"I road-tripped to Manhattan once in college. We saw all the sights. I can't imagine living there. Having all that history and hustle bustle right outside my door." Lily followed as Evelyn wove her way in and out the crowd.

Evelyn shot Lily a withering look over her shoulder. "Real New Yorkers don't do the touristy stuff much. Let me guess, you're from some small town in the Midwest?"

"Oregon."

"Portland?" Evelyn asked, a slight degree of interest creeping into her voice. "I hear it's all the rage now on the west coast."

"About an hour away. I grew up in a commune. It's not on the map. We call it Terramar."

Evelyn rounded on Lily, her eyes circular as saucers. "A commune? Are you *serious*? Like with hippies?"

"I guess so."

"Huh. I thought all the hippies were dead. Come to find out they moved to the west coast. Makes sense. I've heard people out there are lazy. Slow workers. Always out surfing or hiking, no work ethic."

*What the hell?* Lily felt roots of dislike sprouting in her as Evelyn's back turned and retreated once more. *What is this girl's deal?*

"I take it you've never been to a commune before?" Lily asked when she'd caught up at the carousel.

"I don't travel anywhere that doesn't have a five-star hotel." Evelyn paused. "I'm making an exception in this case of course. My parents thought it would be good for me to know my roots. I'm doing this for them."

*Ahhhhh, a rich bitch,* Lily thought, the clouds parting. The type that thought New York was the be-all and end-all in the world. She'd heard stories about this particular breed of New Yorker at Bryn Mawr.

"What does your family do?" Lily asked, unable to keep her curiosity in check despite Evelyn's aloof manner.

"Business. My father founded Locksley Enterprises."

"Cool, my mothers are entrepreneurs, too," Lily said, trying to keep her voice level but failing. Locksley Enterprises was *huge*. Near the single digits on the Fortune 100 list. Their finances influenced the American economy tremendously, and some would say their influence on politics and culture was even larger. Evelyn, Lily realized, had to be the wealthiest person she had ever met.

"Your *mothers*? Don't tell me your family is gay, too?"

"Kind of. Well, Rena and Annika are, but that's it. I was raised by a lot of women, all of them a type of mother, and a couple men who decided to stick around."

Evelyn gaped. "That has got to be the strangest familial arrangement I've ever heard of."

"It was a wonderful way to grow up. Raised by a village, as they say. My family is the best I could have asked for."

"I suppose that's why you're here meeting your biological family, then?" Evelyn raised an eyebrow. "There must be a part of you that wanted a normal family and childhood if you're here. Unless of course, your family forced you, which I doubt. Hippies are free thinkers, right? Free to do whatever you like. Floaters."

Her words carried an acidic tinge that made Lily realize Evelyn's nastiness came from a deep-seated place. This was more about her own family drama than Lily's.

"There's my bag," Lily said, slipping away to retrieve her backpack. She exhaled, glad to be rid of Evelyn, if only for a few moments.

By the time she returned, the group had grown. Morgane and an elfin redhead wearing voluminous harem pants and holding two large, greasy bags of food were chatting away while Evelyn scowled down at her phone.

"Are you sure you don't want any? It's good," the girl said.

"I ate on the jet," Evelyn replied, glaring at the grease spots on the paper bag.

"What is it?" Lily asked, hitching up her enormous backpack as she rejoined the circle.

"Sausage sandwiches. It's all they had left for breakfast." The girl shrugged, holding the bags out to Lily.

The girl, while not traditionally beautiful, was striking in an odd sort of way. She was pale to the point of being translucent, with a dark smattering of freckles across the bridge of her nose. Her lips were plump and small, like a tiny rosebud set above a small, square chin. She had American straight, white teeth that were set askew by her crooked grin. Her eyes were not the typical blue or green Lily had seen on most redheads, but a blazing, burnished copper that engulfed the finer features of her face and provided a gravitas not usually attributed to such a petite woman.

Reaching into the bag, Lily grabbed a sandwich roll. She was, as always, starving. "Thanks. I'm Lily Whiplark. You must be Sara?"

"Sara McKinney," a dimple flashed in Sara's left cheek. "Morgane said you were the last one. One quick bathroom stop and we'll be on our way to meet our families." Her tone, though merely informative, sounded ecstatic after talking to Evelyn.

***

Thirty minutes later Lily found herself careening down a winding country road at breakneck speed. Evelyn, to Lily's relief, had placed headphones over her ears the moment they got into the car. Judging by the set of her shoulders, Evelyn was still annoyed. While Lily considered sitting in the cozy backseat of Morgane's Mini Cooper with Evelyn better than being covered in the vomit Sara claimed would materialize if she was stuck in the back seat for hours, Evelyn as the tallest did not agree. Once or twice, Evelyn had made her displeasure clear by kicking her long legs against the back of Morgane's seat and apologizing half-heartedly. Ambient tension aside, the ride was exactly what Lily needed: a brief period to decompress after the discomfort and long hours of air travel. While Sara and Morgane chatted animatedly in the front—both, it turned out, were historians of the occult—Lily was free to stare at the scenery and think. Between the solstice party, packing to meet her biological family and flying across the world, the last two days had been a whirlwind of epic proportions.

Lily's mind drifted back to the solstice party. To the many toasts to her return home, and the news of her traveling to meet her birth family. Everyone had seemed so happy for her and unsurprised by this new adventure. *But then, maybe that's just my memory?* Lily wondered. She hadn't thought she'd overindulged in Hazel's mead but there was no denying the night was blurry. Scenes she placed vaguely as being in the infamous adult tent were filled only with vivid color, loud music, and bodies dancing, each memory indistinguishable from the next. The one thing she thought she could remember was too preposterous to be true: Selma, belly-dancing on a stage before a crowd of men, twirling and spinning as if to captivate them. *But that can't be real, Selma doesn't know how to belly dance.* Lily shook her head. *Next year I'll have to lay off the mead.*

Unable to tease anymore from the past, Lily spun to thinking of the future. Familiar questions continued to wear tracks in her mind. *Do I look like my mother or father? Do I have siblings? What if I can't understand them? Understanding Morgane is a little difficult.* The rolling green hills outside her window calmed her and energized her all at once. *This is really happening,* Lily thought.

***

"Here we are," Morgane announced hours later as they pulled to the side of a narrow, tree-lined lane.

Lily swiveled her head right, then left. Dirt road, hedges, and grassy hills filled the landscape as far as her eyes could see. She checked again. Nope, definitely no buildings. *Is she joking?* Lily thought uneasily.

"And where exactly is here?" Evelyn asked, voice sharp and eyes narrowed, as she pulled off her headphones and rested them around her long neck. "I've seen nothing but shrubs for the last half hour."

"Aye! But of course! I could find the cottage with me eyes closed. But then, I've been coming here for near on sixty years. You'd never find it without knowing where to look." The old woman grinned sheepishly back at them. "It'll be right through there. See that wee nook in the hedge?"

Three pairs of eyes followed Morgane's finger toward a wall of tall, dense box trees.

The opening, just visible if Lily squinted, peeked through a few rogue branches that seemed to have escaped the pruning shears for years. *I may have to leave my bag on the road*, Lily thought, mentally sizing up the overstuffed 60 liter backpack she'd borrowed from Annika against the tiny gap in the greenery.

"God, it feels good to be out of there," Lily said, stretching her arms wide as she exited the car. "You know, this kind of reminds me of home, quiet and hidden." A sharp sensation cut through the flutter of excitement in her belly as she said the words. Guilt, subtle yet insistent, had been her constant travel companion. Here, in the middle of nowhere Ireland, was where her life would change. Once she disappeared through the overgrown hedge, the commune could never again be her only home. Even if the meeting was awful, Lily knew a part of her would always remain here.

"Lovely," Evelyn muttered, looking as though her worst nightmare had come true.

"Grab your things, girls. I'll lead the way but I'm not staying long once introductions have taken place," Morgane said, already at the hedge.

"Wait! Is anyone coming to help with our bags?" Evelyn asked, her voice high with disbelief as Morgane disappeared through the gap in the hedge. "You'd think we'd get a little help after traveling halfway across the world," she grumbled, heaving the first of her large suitcases out of the trunk.

Lily refrained from rolling her eyes as she grabbed her own backpack. Slinging it on with ease, she waited for Sara to grab the remaining duffle crammed up against the trunk's corner before slamming it shut.

"That's all you brought?" Evelyn asked, eyeing Sara's small duffle bag.

"I'm studying in Ireland for the summer. I only packed for a weekend," Sara said with a shrug.

Lily choked back a laugh at the look of incredulity on Evelyn's face. *Oh, how the other half lives*, she thought, leaving Evelyn to wrangle her two high-end roller bags as she turned to follow Morgane.

"Morgane?" Lily called into the hedge.

Silence. Morgane, it seemed, had left them in her octogenarian dust to find their own way.

*Why am I not surprised,* Lily thought, recalling the tiny index card with her name on it as she stuck her hand in the hedge and began groping for a doorknob. Her hand caught only air. *The door must be farther back*, she thought, walking with her arms extended in front of her, into the foliage.

***

Inside the hedge, a new world emerged. Here, darkness and stifling humidity ruled. Lily coughed as thick, stale air invaded her lungs. She waited for her eyes to adjust to the absence of light, which took longer than she expected. A tunnel two feet wide and unknowably long crawled into the darkness. Huge roots, smaller offshoots of tunnels large enough for a child to crawl through, and multiple sets of glinting eyes stared back at her, daring her to move forward. Lily tried to imagine how wide the hedges must be to create such an illusion. It would be a miracle if anyone ever managed to find this place alone.

"Creepy," Evelyn whispered, her bags clanging over roots as she entered the tunnel.

*No argument there*, Lily thought, batting away an overgrown branch as she inched forward.

"I think I see a door," Lily said, squinting into the darkness at a rounded outline some twenty feet ahead.

"How the hell did the old biddy make it through this tunnel so fast? And without breaking a hip?" Evelyn muttered, as her foot sank into a cavernous hole.

Lily watched Sara assist Evelyn in extracting her foot from the mire. *It is pretty treacherous in here and certainly gives off a "get out" vibe. How had Morgane flitted through here so quickly?*

After what seemed like years, they made it to the tunnel's end. The door was a formidable barrier with Celtic iron detailing overlaying cracks and holes gnawed into the wood by the vermin living in the hedge. Long ago the door had been green, though only flecks of paint remained as evidence to this. An iron knob hung from the wood, loose and wobbly. Lily tensed as her hand closed around the cold iron. *This knob could fall out at any moment and then we'll be stuck in here until Morgane realizes we're not right behind her. Who knows how long that will take*, she thought as she turned the knob gently. It stilled at the end of its rotation. She pushed twice, then pulled. The door didn't budge. Glancing down at the rusted hinges, Lily tried both motions again, adding as much strength as she dared.

*What's the secret? Twist the knob a quarter inch to the left, jiggle, knock three times, and yell the password*, Lily thought, trying to ignore her frustration with Morgane at being left to figure it out herself.

Twenty minutes later the stalwart sentinel had endured so many jiggles, shakes, pushes, pulls, and kicks Lily was shocked it was still standing, let alone closed. The tunnel, unpleasant to begin with, had grown hotter and mustier the longer they stood there. Lily felt her options dwindle as claustrophobia set in. The way she saw it, they had two options: turn around before she died from overheating and wait for Morgane or someone else from the agency to collect their left behind asses in the lane or . . . she sighed.

"Can you guys move back? I need room," she said nudging Sara and Evelyn back the way they came.

*That should be enough*, she thought as they reached the tunnel's halfway point.

"What are you going to do?" Evelyn grumbled, lowering herself onto her dirt-covered bag, sweat glistening on her forehead.

But Lily was already in motion, her legs carrying her down the tunnel in an awkward combination of high knees and sprints, intent on their target. With only two feet left and rudimentary knowledge born from watching hockey games with Rich, Lily flung her body into the door. Her bony hip hit the hard iron with a sickening thwack.

"Shit," she cried crumpling to the ground in pain. *That's definitely going to leave a mark,* she thought gripping her side.

"That was awesome!" Sara exclaimed, rushing to Lily's aid.

"Too bad it didn't work," Evelyn called from down the tunnel.

"Maybe we should knock really loudly? We've been out here almost a half an hour. I'm sure someone will realize Morgane's left us to find our own way soon," Sara suggested, bending down to inspect Lily's side.

Lily pulled herself up to sit with her back to the door, defeated. *Who knows how far away the adoption agency is once we get through the hedge? It could be down a winding forest trail and across a river for all we know. If it isn't, why hasn't someone already come to collect us?*

"We could take turns in here," Sara suggested, wiping sweat from her forehead with her shirt sleeve. "I'll go first. You can wait on the road where it's cooler. I'll come get you two when someone arrives."

Lily moaned and threw her head back against the iron inlay, too exhausted to move. A strange tingle rushed over her as skin met iron, and the air inside the tunnel thinned. Just as Lily was about to ask Evelyn and Sara if they had felt it, too, a squeal of rusty hinges echoed through the tunnel and the door inched open. The hedge seemed to pulse and Lily could have sworn the air shimmered as a cool breeze rushed over her face.

Lily's mouth fell open.

"Finally," Evelyn's whisper echoed through the hedge.

"Thanks for all your help," Lily muttered, grabbing her backpack and turning toward the light, ready for her next chapter.

***

Bright sunlight shone on Lily's cheeks and her lungs filled with fresh air. She gasped. She had walked into a dream. Standing here, on the edge of a garden teeming with heavy blooms and heavenly aromas, Lily felt like she'd been transported hundreds of miles in three short steps. A grove of fruit trees ran the perimeter of the garden, all the way to a charming stone cottage on the other side. A small lake and forest sat behind the cottage perfecting the scene.

"It's an Irish wonderland," Sara said, her lips parted in awe as she emerged from the hedge.

"I'm quite happy to hear you think so."

A slender woman with long auburn hair stepped from the shadows of the orchard.

"It seems Morgane left you to find your own way in? She forgets that our entrance is quite unique. Many have trouble navigating through the tunnel. I'm pleased you managed." She smiled knowingly as Lily brushed dirt from her pants. "That door can be a right bugger. It takes a special type of person to open it. I figured I'd come check that you hadn't passed out in the hedge. My name's Brigit McKay-Clery, and I'll be making your introductions today. Welcome to Fern Cottage."

Lily, Evelyn, and Sara stuck out their hands in turn, a smile plastered on each of their faces. Lily caught the scents of cinnamon and lavender wafting off Brigit as their hands clasped.

"We'd best be moving on. Everyone's waiting," Brigit said, gesturing at the fairytale cottage with the air of someone who wanted to get down to business.

Lily followed, slack-jawed as she took in the lush vegetation. Trees heavy with a wide array of fruit lined one side of the stone path they walked upon. To her left, every inch of earth was flourishing with fruits, vegetables, herbs, and flowers. Even the gardens of Terramar couldn't compete. Smaller stone pathways split off the main one to create attractive and functional partitions in the garden. Familiar scents of basil, lemongrass, and lavender perfumed the air and eased Lily's nerves. She stooped to study a large shrub with purple flowers and black, circular berries. *I'll have to ask someone its name*, she thought, analyzing the bush. *It's pretty; I bet Annika would like it.*

"You'll be having plenty of time to explore after the meeting," said Brigit. She was already at the front door of the cottage with Evelyn, who looked displeased to be waiting on Lily again.

Lily's cheeks flushed.

"Sorry, I . . ."

"You too, Sara," Brigit said, a tease of a smile playing at her lips.

Lily turned to see Sara rising from a stone bench. *At least I'm not the only one who gets easily distracted. Sara looks like she just woke up*, she thought, stifling a laugh.

"Sorry! I stopped to meditate for a second. I needed to calm down," Sara said, her harem pants flapping as she jogged down the path to meet them.

"Understandable," Brigit said warmly. "Lily, I noticed you inspecting our belladonna? If you're interested in plants, we can provide a tour of the gardens after your meeting. There are many exotic plants here."

"I'd love that," Lily said, a wide grin spreading over her face.

"Right, then," Brigit said, placing her hand over the doorknob. It hovered there for a moment and she turned back to face them, her lips parted. For a second it looked like she was about to say something but stopped herself and opened the door.

A welcome trickle of lavender and chamomile flew out on the warm cottage air to meet them. Stepping over the threshold, Lily heard the crackling of logs in the fire and cups being set onto saucers as conversations inside ceased.

They weren't the only ones with a case of the nerves.

Following Brigit's lead, Lily, Evelyn, and Sara kicked off their shoes and set them on a robust wood stand along with dozens of other pairs next to their bags. The slamming of a side door rang through the cottage and Morgane's gray head appeared out the windows framing the front door. They were on their own now.

"The sitting room is this way," Brigit said, waving them in.

*Weird decoration for an office. We can't all be meeting in here . . . they must have separate back rooms for the reunions,* Lily thought, her eyes sweeping the room. It looked like a space designed for deep conversation, like Em's kitchen back home. An enormous hearth was positioned in the center of the cottage, dividing the kitchen and living area while still accessible to both. A large green sofa and two overstuffed armchairs sat opposite the hearth around an oak coffee table. The oak's chipped and scarred surface hinted at the many stories and histories shared there. At the edge of the room a green love seat sat below the window overlooking the garden and orchard they'd walked through. While tones of blue and green dominated the room, it was also peppered with glass Celtic knots and candles in various shades of red that provided warmth and a pop of color. A peculiar cross hung above the fire. Its stark crimson rushes warming the cool gray of the stones it rested against.

"Would anyone fancy tea? Water? I haven't anything stronger, I'm afraid. Though some say circumstances such as these certainly call for it," Brigit said. She hovered by the armchair nearest the door, her fingers tapping its back.

"I'm ready to start," Lily said, holding up her Nalgene and taking a seat next to Evelyn on the couch.

Evelyn and Sara nodded in agreement.

"Of course. You've come such a long way. We should be getting on with it." Brigit lowered herself slowly into the chair and cleared her throat. "It's my understanding that you haven't been told much of anything. Only that each of you are to meet your biological family today. Am I correct?"

Lily stared perplexed. *What else would we have been told? And why is Brigit acting so nervous? Is this her first time introducing birth families to their long-lost children?*

"As you look like intelligent young ladies, you've likely already guessed the people on the other side of the hearth to be your families." Brigit jerked her head toward the fire, where a table, chairs, and three pairs of legs were discernible through the flames and smoke.

Sara laughed nervously.

"Aye," Brigit said. She inhaled deeply and tears popped suddenly into her brown eyes. "Well, you were close to the mark. Those ladies are in fact your kin, though not in the same sense you're probably thinking." Her voice cracked as she averted her gaze and stared into the fire.

A minute that felt like an eternity passed while Brigit composed herself.

Lily caught Sara's questioning gaze and shrugged her shoulders in agreement.

"What I'm trying to say is, they are your aunts, my sisters. I am your mother." The words cascaded from Brigit, quiet as a whisper yet unstoppable and deafening in magnitude. She closed her eyes and exhaled.

Lily's mouth fell open. Unsure what to think, she looked down the length of the couch to gauge the other girls' reactions.

Evelyn frowned. "You must be mistaken. We can't be more than a year apart in age," she said, shaking her head in disbelief.

Tears were flowing down Brigit's face now. It seemed she could no longer control her emotions. As if she had used up all her composure in the act of showing them to the cottage.

"No more than a few minutes apart, actually. You're triplets."

# *Brigit's Tale*

Brigit didn't begrudge their skepticism as her daughters examined each other, their eyes narrowed, brows knitted together in disbelief. After all, it was difficult to believe.

She wiped the tears off her face. *I may as well deliver all the news in one swoop.* She cleared her throat and three pairs of eyes swung back to her, each brimming with questions. Or waiting perhaps, for Brigit to jump up and yell "Gotcha!"

"I mean not to unload too much at once, but you must know there's more."

Evelyn grunted, and a practiced mask of neutrality slid over her face.

Brigit felt fear radiating off the girl. It pained her to see a person, her daughter, so guarded. She could only hope she'd have a chance to see past those walls, though she suspected her next words would not help. She cleared her throat again.

"There are critical aspects of your biology that have been contained, hidden from you, if you will, but will soon become apparent."

Lily's mouth opened a half inch more. It was beginning to remind Brigit of a cave.

"Not only are you sisters. You are also witches by birth. Born of a long line of witches and believed to possess power not seen for generations." Brigit sighed. Finally, the reunion she had longed for could begin. She waited for her words to sink in, for their relationships as mother, daughters, and sisters to begin.

A shriek cut through the room, shattering Brigit's hopes of a quiet reconciliation in one high-pitched note.

"You! This lady is batshit crazy! There is no way *we* are related, much less sisters!" Evelyn screeched, her words amplifying off the cottage stones. "And don't even get me started on this . . . witches bullshit." Her tone had the air of one accustomed to mocking others. "Let's get out of here," Evelyn finished, fixing Brigit with a hard stare as she rose from the couch.

"*Actually*," Sara piped in, "I'd like to hear more. While it sounds far-fetched, I've come all this way and see no harm in listening." She chanced a small smile at Evelyn before continuing. "As unrealistic as it sounds, I can't disregard Brigit as crazy. She appears very sane, don't you think? Definitely not normal, but then I wouldn't call the two of you normal-looking either."

Brigit's body loosened as she witnessed understanding settle in Lily's bright green eyes. *Two are open to this, at least for now*, she thought, inwardly urging Sara on.

"I got this feeling when you said we were sisters. Did you guys?" Sara's tone was measured, exploratory. "I swear, I was vibrating right . . . right here. Like my body recognized the truth when it heard it." Her hand rested on her ribs below her heart.

Lily nodded slowly. "I agree with Sara. Being here feels natural. I didn't realize it when we met at the airport because I was preoccupied, but I wasn't crazy anxious like I usually am when I meet new people." She looked down the couch at Sara and smiled. "And, for the record, you don't seem altogether normal yourself."

Evelyn rolled her eyes. "You're saying you recognized us as family the moment we met?"

"That's not what I said. There's no way I would have thought any of us were related. We look, not to mention *act,* nothing alike," Lily retorted, her eyes boring straight into Evelyn's narrowed blue ones.

Evelyn's face flooded crimson, and a new wave of tension swept the room.

"What I would like to know," Lily continued, turning to Brigit with hardened eyes, "is if you are our mother, why did you let us go? I have to know why a parent wouldn't want their child. You look capable enough, not at all the druggie I had imagined."

Brigit winced. She knew this was just the first of many difficult questions to come, though she wished they could have started smaller.

"It's a long story, longer perhaps than you can imagine, and I hope you will allow me to explain it."

Lily and Sara nodded, and Brigit's gaze turned to Evelyn.

There was tension embedded in every nook and cranny of the girl's body, vibrating like a taut string over the length of her. In a way, Brigit was grateful for Evelyn's willful disbelief. It told her that her daughter had known the love of family and would not allow it to be swept aside.

"You may as well explain yourself. I've traveled this far already," Evelyn said finally, her lips pulled tight as she flung herself back onto the couch.

"Thank you," Brigit said, her heart flooding with relief. "I promise, I'll not waste your time. Let me start at the beginning."

She took a giant breath and exhaled out the story she'd been practicing for years.

"Your father and I met in town at the Beltane celebration a year before you were born. His name was Aengus Clery, and he was tall and strong, with red hair that glinted like fire in the summer sun. He had a smile that could melt glaciers and hands that were strong and worn but gentle, as a man's hands should be. It was a whimsical day to begin a courtship. A day of fertility and new beginnings in old tales. May Day has always been an auspicious day for witches." Her face broke into a sad smile as it often did when she thought of Aengus.

"Aengus and I became inseparable and after a few short months, I noticed the disappearance of my cycle. I still remember the moment, clear as day, when my best friend asked me for a pad. I fell to the floor, struck by the revelation that I hadn't needed to carry one for months. I lied, claimed a migraine had come over me, and begged off. I took a pregnancy test, which only confirmed what I already knew deep down to be true. The test was positive."

"You didn't use protection? And then you ditched us? Sounds irresponsible," Evelyn scoffed.

"In fact, your father and I did use protection, and still, there you were, a truth growing within me. Small and fragile, but a truth nonetheless. Who was I to deny the goddess?" The girls' puzzled gazes followed her own to cross of the goddess Brigid in its place of honor above the hearth.

"I recall being elated but also sick with fear. To know a person, *love* a person, only a few short months and find yourself irrevocably bound is a terrifying and thrilling prospect. Still, that idea was not as frightening as admitting what Aengus didn't yet know about me: that I was a witch." She paused, sucking in a breath to push down the tension she associated with memories of that brief, unsettling period in her life.

"In those days the internet was new and information was harder to come by. People's knowledge came from books, sermons, and stories. Lore in this part of the world runs deep. You'd be hard-pressed to find a more superstitious lot than the people on this island. In the days when the old religions of our blood died for Christ on the Cross, my Great-Gran and those before her had a hard time of it. It's true, witch hunts were few in Ireland, but that didn't stop people from feeling the fever. I'd grown up with these tales and heeded them. Over the years I'd told only a few non-magic folk the truth about myself.

"I knew nothing of Aengus's stance on magic. It was one of the most nerve-wracking days of me life, the day I had to admit to him two truths that would rock anyone's world: That he was to be a father, and that I was a witch. The poor man was so shocked he couldn't talk! Walked me home without a word and left me at my doorstep. I took it as a good sign that he at least walked me home. I was right. Aengus came calling the very next day with questions, most of which pertained to my witchy nature. He accepted his role as a father without hesitation. I suspect he was a man who wanted children sooner rather than later in life. Though we'd never spoken of such things before the time came."

She paused, allowing the girls to take in the fact that despite whatever they thought of her, their father had been good man. She wanted no blame placed on Aengus if she could help it.

"I knew my pregnancy was early enough for me to put off seeing a physician for a few weeks. At the time, the closest doctor with a functional ultrasound was a two-hour journey to Galway. I did not fancy making the trip more times than I needed to. Instead, I sought the advice of my sisters, all of who had experience working with pregnant women.

"As it turns out, I ended up needing the extra time. Your father proposed a mere week after my confessions. I expect he would have proposed the minute I told him I was with child, but my claiming to be a witch threw him off. That and Aengus was a traditionalist. He needed time to buy a Claddagh."

"A Claddagh?" Lily asked, strangling the word.

"It's like an engagement ring. It's traditional in Ireland and represents love, loyalty, and friendship," Sara said as if reciting from a textbook.

Brigit presented her hand to Lily, who stared down at the gold ring, its large center heart topped by an elaborate king's crown and encircled by two hands.

"We used mine as engagement and wedding band. Now couples are more likely to go with a diamond, but this suited me."

"I always thought the Claddagh was more romantic and less materialistic than the rings men save six months for," Sara admitted, admiring the ring.

"I agree," Brigit said. *This one respects the old ways*, she thought, her heart leaping.

"I was relieved by the proposal. In small-town Ireland, even in such recent times, there was an unsavory stigma associated to being pregnant without a promise. Some girls' families turned on them. I knew of many girls left to fend for themselves, disowned, or cut out of wills. I was sure my family would never have deserted me, but I was also sure I wanted Aengus at my side. We wed a week later in an intimate riverside ceremony at dusk. I wore a simple blue gown of Irish lace and a crown of wildflowers—"

"You didn't wear white because you were ashamed to be pregnant?" Evelyn interrupted, her red lips pursed and brows furrowed.

"I was not the slightest bit ashamed by my condition, although I had hoped to keep it quiet for a wee bit. It was a pleasurable secret to keep. I told only my sisters and your father, wanting to savor every bit of quiet I could. A pregnancy is a very private matter between a woman, her body, and, if she is lucky, the man she loves."

Evelyn shrugged, a gesture Brigit took to mean "move along."

"I wore blue because it is a traditional color for an Irish bride to wear on her wedding day. I wore the same frock my mother and eldest sister Gwenn wore on their wedding days. Possibly one of you will wish to wear it one day. It is quite nice, after all," she trailed off as memories of the day threatened to overtake her story.

"After it was official, I came to live with your father here. We christened it Fern Cottage, and we were quite happy with our simple lives." Brigit paused and extended her hand to touch the heavy stone walls. She could still feel Aengus in them. It broke her heart.

"As the holidays approached, your father, a skilled woodworker and carpenter, was in high demand. No matter how much I wanted to see you, I refused to see a doctor without Aengus. I wanted to share that first glimpse of our child on an ultrasound with him. Besides I knew you were inside me, felt you moving and growing as you should. Knew it to be true as I was doing nothing but growing meself! We had our first ultrasound at twenty-two weeks."

"*How* did you wait so long?!" Evelyn exclaimed, unable to maintain her facade of poised indifference. "What about the nursery? The registries? The showers? My cousin bullied her OB into guessing the sex at fifteen weeks so she could start planning."

"It was a different time. Slower and less convenient than what you're used to. Ireland and her people, especially in these parts, were not well off back then." Brigit's eyes met Evelyn's and the girl blushed. Brigit felt the words had landed more harshly than intended and smiled to soften the blow.

"More than anything I wanted to see physical evidence of the life we had created. But was it an absolute necessity? Not really. Women had gone without for thousands of years. A few more weeks were nothing as long as I felt healthy and grew rounder than a whale. I had planned to use my sisters for the birth since the beginning. A visit to the doctor was pure vanity."

"I think it's nice. It brings back a bit of mystery into birth. We know so much now," Sara chimed in.

"Well, that's debatable," Evelyn sighed.

"Aye, I liked the mystery, too," Brigit agreed, brushing off Evelyn's dramatic airs. "So we went to the doctor a bit late. It was all very exciting! The doctor found a girl right away, and then became quiet, a reaction your father and I took no notice of at the time. We were too busy gushing over the news. The doctor corrected us when we stopped for breath. Twins he said! Both girls! We couldn't believe our fortune."

"Hold up!" Evelyn exclaimed, raising both hands in the air, fingers splayed wide. "You said we're triplets. That doctor missed an entire baby? No wonder you don't bother going to doctors here."

"Babes can hide behind their siblings and be missed in such a small space. I'm sure that was the case during our viewing. It's not unheard of with twins, and even more common with triplets. Of course, in our case, there were other factors at play to take into account."

"Like?" Evelyn crossed her arms over her chest.

"Magic," Brigit said simply. She understood Evelyn's misgivings. She'd come close to driving herself mad asking the same question day after day, year after year. In the end, magic was the only answer that allowed her to forgive.

"Rest assured we did not return to his care," Brigit said. "I saw a doctor only once during pregnancy."

Simultaneous looks of horror slid across the girl's faces.

*They have no clue of life here,* Brigit thought, swallowing a chuckle.

"Your Aunt Mary and I were trained midwives by then. My older sister Gwenn is a business woman now, but back then she assisted in many of our births. Aoife, my youngest sister, monitored power flows and mixed potions for my every ache and pain. Drinking her vile concoctions every day was not something I enjoyed, but Aoife swore they were good for you. Who was I to argue with the family potions master? Aoife runs an apothecary and tea shop in town now, but makes most of her living off reading and regulating energy imbalances, just as back then.

"As a matter of fact," Brigit said, rising from her chair, "I think it's time my sisters join us. I'll be needing them to fill in a few gray areas soon."

As if on cue, there was a rough grinding of wood chairs on wood planks and her sisters materialized. Their eyes devoured Lily, Evelyn, and Sara as they hovered on the edge of the room.

"May I present your Aunts Gwenn Dolan, Aoife McKay, and Mary O'Byrne" Brigit said, doing her best to hide her amusement.

Silence and looks of awe that mirrored Brigit's own amazement upon seeing the girls emerge from the hedge filled the stone cottage.

Lily and Gwenn with their wavy espresso hair, olive complexions, bright green eyes, and thin build would be mistaken for mother and daughter for years to come.

Despite the differences in Evelyn's sleek suit and Mary's eccentric pink dress, the pair were twins with blonde hair, blue eyes, and curvaceous figures. Evelyn even carried herself exactly as Mary had at her age. With the confidence and charisma only those sure of their appeal to the opposite sex could pull off.

And then there were Sara and Aoife. Both a bit odd looking, their faces slightly out of proportion, their flaming hair and copper eyes a bit too bright. They even had the same crooked grin.

Brigit watched her daughters' faces morph from astonishment at being introduced to their doppelgangers to something bordering on acceptance. The room's vibrations shifted, tingling with the sensation of like recognizing like.

"If it's alright with everyone, I think we should be moving on now," Brigit said, reclaiming her seat. Her sisters followed suit, positioning themselves across from their nieces on the rough hearthstones.

"My pregnancy was remarkably easy, with only a few hiccups of errant power in the third trimester. The hardest part was quelling your father's anxiety. The idea of having two witchy daughters had him ecstatic and concerned all in the same minute. Daughters always feel like more of a stretch for men. Imagine being told yours were likely to be witches as well! I swear he read every parenting book printed in preparation, the darling man."

Brigit laughed weakly, a coping mechanism she had long employed to bury strong emotional responses.

"Though I had been expecting my first contraction, it still took me by surprise when it came. It was so powerful! I rang up my sisters and all three arrived within the hour." Brigit nodded at her sisters, begging their inclusion. Continuing the story without their assistance was impossible. The hours of pain and near blackouts left her with muddled memories. Her sisters however, witnessed it all right beside her, without the combination of hormones and pain that often cloud the head of a woman in labor.

Lily interjected, her voice cutting. "Why didn't you call our father? He had a right to be there, too."

Brigit studied the hard set lines of Lily's face. *Aengus has his daddy's girl after all,* she thought with a sentimental sniff.

"Your ma knew she might have hours until anything came of her contractions. And your da worried enough over her as it was," Aoife spoke up, her petite frame stiff and protective.

The words ma and da rang through the room like a gunshot. The girls shifted in their seats as Aoife, oblivious to their unease, continued.

"Aengus would have rushed home all a tizzy, anxious as can be. We couldn't have that! Brigit needed a calm environment for as long as possible. We managed to clear her channels, feed her potions, and arrange a proper birthing area before your da arrived with hours to spare." As Aoife spoke, a bemused look came over her face.

"Now that I come to think it, the man was quite more malleable after the few rounds of whiskey Nora served him. Is that a ritual for all the fathers-to-be?" Her question was met with giggles from the other McKay women.

"It's not something we usually encourage as much as we did with Aengus," Mary said, her cherubic cheeks pink.

"A fair number of stout-hearted Irish men head for the bottle once the ma starts yelling. Your da indulged early, and it's true, we pushed it on him a wee bit, but at least we made sure he was well supervised," Gwenn said. "It was apparent this was no normal birth from the start. The power radiating from Brigit was clear as day. It was best Aengus loosen up to deal with that."

"What do you mean by the power radiating off her?" Lily asked, leaning forward.

"I've seen nothing like it before or since, not even from other powerful witches in labor. It was a terrible sight. Magic, *your* magic, clawing its way out of her," Mary said, her voice low and blue eyes wide. "It all started with the water, rivers of it rushing from your ma."

"At least the water found its way out. It was the fire boiling in her veins that terrified me most," Aoife said, running a hand through her bobbed red hair.

"Too true. The fire was the worst of it. And the grass and trees sprouting about the birthing bed weren't much fun either. Obstructed our view of the birthing canal in a bad way," Mary added.

"But start at the beginning, that part I can remember," Brigit said hastily, taking in her daughters' pallor. She didn't know what she would do if they walked out in the middle of the tale, though right now she couldn't say she would blame them. *They probably think us a bunch of crazy old bats.*

"Too right," Mary caught Brigit's eye apologetically. "Your mother's contractions and dilation were normal, or at the very least not alarming, for many hours. We had plenty of time to ensure her comfort and brew fortifying draughts for strength. Twinning births are quite taxing, after all. With the help of Fiona and Nora we were able to keep Aengus occupied and brew additional potions we hadn't foreseen needing. We were quite ahead of schedule," Mary said, sounding far more technical than her vixen appearance would let on.

"The same Nora I met at Terramar?" Lily asked.

"The same," Brigit said, giving Lily a knowing smile. "My oldest and best friend, besides my sisters. I'm terribly sorry if she drew it out. She likes a bit of drama, our Nora."

"How does she know Rena?" Lily asked.

"They only met when Nora brought you over as an infant. Gwenn met Rena at a music festival in the States way back when we did those sorts of things. Hit it off right away, had a bit of a fling, and stayed in touch. When Gwenn couldn't take you to Oregon, Nora volunteered. I can't say she and Rena ever warmed to each other."

"Definitely not," Lily said.

"And Fiona Fallon? My mother's college roommate?" Evelyn asked, her eyes wide.

"Aye, Fiona's your second cousin. It was a gift for her and your mother to be so close. The moment it became clear I had to give you three up Fiona said she knew a kind couple who were unable to have children. They desperately wanted a wee girl and had substantial means to provide for her. I trusted her judgment, and it looks as if she was right."

Evelyn's face softened.

"And your adoptive parents were dear friends of Morgane," Brigit continued, sensing Sara's question. "Morgane knew my own parents long before they died. She was a mentor for my sisters and me growing up. I trusted her when she claimed to know the perfect couple. I only wish she had kept in better touch when—"

Sara cut her off, her face reddening. "So, the birth was bad, but what happened next?"

The witches looked uncomfortable, each glancing from one to the other.

"Gwenn? Please . . ." Aoife trailed off and closed her eyes like an athlete preparing for their event.

"Right," Gwenn sighed, looking as if she'd rather ram her head against the wall than answer Sara's question.

"You see, girls, it's near impossible to describe what happened that day. At best you'd think us a few eggs short of a dozen. At worst you'd run straight out of here and book us spots in the asylum on your way to the airport," Gwenn said in the tone she used to seal deals in business negotiations.

"It would be easy enough for me to cast a persuasion spell. You'd have no doubt what we said was true and we could become one happy family. But seeing as your ma is too noble to do so, and made us all swear not to, we'll have to show you."

"There's a video?" Sara asked eagerly.

"Let's hope so. At this point I need irrefutable proof that I'm not surrounded by crazy," Evelyn muttered.

"Not quite a video. Your aunt Aoife has the ability to project any event she has witnessed into another person's mind. She can also do it with someone else's memory if they don't mind a bit of prodding in their head. It's a rare gift. Much like being present in a movie. If you're open to it, we'd like to propose you view your birth in this manner."

Gwenn paused to allow for questions, though none came.

"As you may be aware, some people know when they're dreaming and have the ability to alter their dreams. If you are among those with this ability, it will not help you here. Aoife alone will be in control of what you see and hear. It's possible you may still physically feel the world you inhabit in the present. However, you will not be able to visualize it, even if you open your eyes. It should be painless for you, though the same cannot be said for your auntie. It's a draining talent and this will be the first time she's shared a memory with more than one other person at a time. Every division puts Aoife at risk for losing a piece of herself. That said, I don't want you to take this decision lightly. Consider: Is this an experience you could accept as evidence that what we say is true? Or will you write it off as a bit of hocus pocus? I do not wish to cause my sister harm if you are not open to believing in what you do not understand."

"We'll give you time to decide," Brigit said, rising from her chair. "As Gwenn said, it's likely you'll be putting Aoife through pain to see things you may wish you hadn't. We'll be in the garden when you've made your decision."

***

The door clicked shut softly and Lily, Evelyn, and Sara stiffened. Each keenly aware that they were alone for the first time as sisters. Several minutes passed as each avoided the other's eyes to study the familiarities of their hands, the fire, the couch fabric, or the floor.

Evelyn shot up from the couch.

"I'm out. Not that I believe a word of what they're saying, but the thought of that woman entering my mind, or me going into hers, or whatever she's going to do, gives me the creeps."

Lily refrained from rolling her eyes. "What do you think?" She turned to Sara.

"I don't know. I can't argue with you, Evelyn. I don't like the idea of someone in my head either."

Evelyn uncrossed her arms, a victorious smirk on her lips.

"*But*, then again, I don't see any other way to find out the truth. If they are witches, which, by the looks of this place, I don't doubt . . ." Sara trailed off and began to circle the room, pausing to examine objects at random. "I mean aren't you two at all curious? A show of magic, *real magic*, could be pretty convincing."

"I've spent years dreaming about my biological family in secret. Now I have a group of women claiming I'm a witch? How could I not be curious? Even with the mind thing it's a fair trade." Lily said the words before she realized she believed them.

"What do you mean by the looks of this place? What's so special about an old stone cottage?" Evelyn asked, her eyes following Sara's path around the room. "Other than its questionable taste in decor."

"The garden, the positioning of the hearth in the middle of the home, the cross of the goddess Brigid, and the color palette representing three of the four elements. They all scream 'a witch lives here.'"

Lily tilted her head in question.

"I'm working toward my Ph.D. in history. My area of expertise is the contribution of women throughout history, specifically women who would have been called witches," Sara explained with a shrug.

"Your doctorate? If we're all twenty-one, how is that possible? And what sort of crock college would award a degree for something like that?" Evelyn asked, unable to keep the tone of judgment from her voice.

"I didn't have many friends as a kid. I spent most my time studying and ended up skipping a couple grades. I started my program last fall at Princeton."

Evelyn's mouth fell open, and Sara resumed her assessment of the cottage.

"Did you notice there are no pictures? I don't see a single family photo anywhere."

"That is odd. They seem so close," Lily mused, looking around for some sign that a person with a family or even friends lived in the cottage. "It's as if she didn't want to be reminded of them."

"Or of us," Sara said, her eyes closing briefly before opening them wide to lock with Lily's.

"I'm in, too. I could never forgive myself if I passed this up."

"I'll get them," Lily said, her heart leaping. "I'm sure they can arrange for Morgane to come back for you Evelyn."

***

"You've made your decisions, then?" Brigit asked, settling back into the blue chair.

"I'm in," Lily said.

"Me, too," Sara nodded.

"I'll do it."

"I see this was a spur-of-the-moment decision?" Brigit asked, taking in Lily and Sara's expressions of shock at Evelyn's answer.

"It was either I go insane by someone messing with my head or by riding back to Shannon with Morgane. I'll take my chances with her," Evelyn said pointing at Aoife.

"Right, then," Aoife said. "Let me explain how this will go."

The flames danced enthusiastically behind Aoife as she rose to stand before the hearth. An aroma of pepper and ginger intensified, spicing the air as the flames grew. The effect of fire on Aoife's face was mesmerizing. In a matter of seconds her cheeks softened, loosening lines of tension as pink roses bloomed, and her eyes began to glow warm and bright.

"I *never* share memories with those unversed in magic. There's always the chance that part of my consciousness will be lost, taken by those I inhabit, or trapped. The risk becomes greater if you are scared or unwilling. That being said, I cannot emphasize enough the importance of this memory. It is because of that importance that I will take you at your word that you are a willing participant. You must *relax* as best you can. Please don't fight what you are feeling in the memory. You risk breaking my mind, possibly your own, or even your sisters' if you do. Let me take over. If all that that is clear, please lie on the ground," Aoife instructed.

"*Now*?" Evelyn squawked.

"You'll never be better prepared for something of this nature, and you're here now," Aoife said, nodding at the plush rugs in the middle of the room.

She waited for the girls to reposition themselves on the floor.

"I'll be starting from right before things went wrong. It *will* be messy. If you're weak at the thought of blood, speak up. We'll get you a bowl for when you wake."

No one spoke.

"Right, then," Aoife said, looking pleased that none of them admitted to such weakness. "I'll count back from ten. Remember to relax your mind; it helps the takeover process. If you meditate, this feeling may be familiar to you."

Sara nodded, closed her eyes, and fell into a relaxed savasana pose.

"When the moment comes for me to take control, you'll feel a faint nudge or click. It differs from person to person. That is the moment to let me in."

"How?" Evelyn asked propping herself up on her elbows, her muscles rigid.

"It's individual but you'll know. Not having let anyone into my mind I can't be sure how it feels, but everyone manages it sooner or later. I am able to force myself in, but I like to be a gracious guest." Aoife winked at her sisters, her first unwilling targets in the early years of exploring her talent.

Evelyn settled back onto the rug with a sigh.

Aoife surveyed the scene, taking in Sara's even, slow breaths. Her gaze moved to Lily's clenched hands and finally Evelyn's rigid shoulders and jaw. She pointed to Evelyn and Lily.

"I'll begin counting down from ten. Ten, nine . . ."

The room filled with the haze of Gwenn's calming spell as it floated to hover above Evelyn and Lily. The girls' bodies slackened and their short, shallow breaths deepened.

"Three, two . . . one."

"*Inruo ego*," Aoife whispered.

And then, Aoife was flying, her mind fractionated and free past the confines of its bony cage. *So far, so good*, she thought with the quarter of herself still residing in her own head. Within seconds Aoife was sitting in the watery spaces between three separate skulls and the minds they guarded. She knocked and waited. The part where her unstable consciousness sought refuge was always the most difficult for her body. It necessitated vast quantities of energy to stay in place until she was allowed inside. A half minute passed before Aoife felt her knees begin to buckle and her body give way to gravity. She gasped and closed her eyes, blocking out any outside stimuli. *This has never happened so soon in a session*, she thought, a wave of adrenaline rising in her. Two pairs of hands lowered her onto a cushion in front of the hearth. Aoife could feel the concentrated heat and energy of fire pouring into her, providing her with the strength she needed to wait it out. She knocked again.

A door flung open and Aoife flew inside, seeking the stability that a mind craved and only another living being could provide. It felt like home. Sara, she knew, grateful that the girl was quick to catch on.

With a renewed sense of strength that stemmed from stabilization, Aoife knocked a third time, steeling herself for the undesirable reality that Lily and Evelyn might not figure it out, that she might have to break into their minds.

To her great relief two channels opened simultaneously, allowing the unclaimed quarters of her mind to rush inside.

"I can see you," Lily said, her eyes sliding from Sara to Evelyn and finally landing on the hideous mustard-colored couch on which they sat.

While arguably the same room she had walked into earlier that day, Lily found the contrasts too stark to be sure. That room had been spacious, color coordinated, cozy, and clean, while this room was . . . well, there was no other way to describe it but *cluttered.* Photos of family and friends lined the walls. The color scheme included shades ranging from sea foam green to rusty orange. The amount of stuff—blankets tossed over furniture, books turned over the arms of chairs, and numerous pairs of muddy shoes by the door—indicated dozens of people could be living here.

"Can you hear me?" Lily asked, turning back to Evelyn and Sara, who looked as shocked as she felt.

Sara reached out to tap Lily on the shoulder.

Lily started at the airy yet still firm sensation.

"Sorry," Sara mumbled. "I assumed we'd see the memory alone, from our own minds. But it seems like we're all sharing Aoife's."

"I thought so, too. She didn't mention we'd be together," Lily said.

"Who cares? We're here now. We may as well go see what all the fuss is about. I see legs on the other side of the fireplace," Evelyn said, rising and striding out of the room.

"Holy hell! She is *huge*!" Evelyn exclaimed seconds later from the other side of the hearth.

Sara and Lily exchanged amused glances and rushed after her.

"How did she not know?" Evelyn said, as Sara and Lily caught up and joined her in staring at twenty-somethings Aoife, Mary, and Gwenn all huddled around a very pregnant Brigit.

"Shhhhh!" Lily admonished, nudging Evelyn toward the tiny kitchen, which had a better view and was out of the way. "Sorry, we'll get out of the way, we. . ." she trailed off as Mary walked through her left arm and into the living room.

"We're ghosts," Sara whispered. "I thought since we could see each other . . . but maybe us being here would change something? Do you think it would alter Aoife's memory?"

"All I know is I've never seen such a huge belly. Do you guys think there may be a fourth in there? Maybe she's saving that meeting for later?" Evelyn joked.

"Keep moving. I don't want to be walked through again," Lily said, rubbing the goosebumps on her arm.

They gave the furniture a wide berth as they wove through a maze of displaced tables and chairs, unsure if their touch could move solid objects and give away their presence.

"Someone's coming," Sara announced, perching herself on the kitchen countertop and peering out the window.

Not a second later the front door flung open. Nora ran into the house, arms laden with a bottle of whiskey and grocery bags. Another woman with chestnut brown hair followed close behind carrying a large box of herbs.

"That feels heavenly," Brigit moaned relaxing into the table as a cool breeze flowed into the room. "Can't we dim the flames a wee bit? Or leave the door open? I'm near about to burst into flames meself."

"Good, they're all there," Aoife said, running her hands through the greenery. "Shut the door, Fiona?"

"Sorry, Brig. You know how finicky some of these potions can be," the dark-haired woman said.

"Indeed." Aoife placed a second cauldron in the hearth. "The palliative potion will be ready right quick. Thanks to Fiona, we have what we need."

*Thank the goddess our Fiona always keeps a proper witches garden. Wish they could have sat a few hours, but fresh-plucked herbs will have to do. If we're lucky the birthing hormones will counteract the strength of greenery straight from the earth.*

Sara gasped. "Did Aoife say that out loud?"

Lily sat up straighter as the realization that she hadn't seen Aoife's mouth move sank in.

"We can hear her thoughts," Sara mused, cocking her head to the side to listen. "Although, I don't hear anything right now. Maybe we can only hear what she wants us to hear? How interesting!"

"Thank God! Otherwise I'd have no clue what they're talking about. What's a palliative potion anyways?" Evelyn asked.

"Painkiller," Lily said, recalling Rena's homeschool course on the classification of plants. "A witchy epidural?"

"Whatever it is, I hope it works. My stomach is starting to hurt just watching her contractions," Evelyn said resting a hand on her flat belly.

"There ya' are, Brig," Aoife said, holding out a chipped mug filled with a steaming green liquid. "Drink this. The herbs are fresh as rain, so you may not be able to feel your fingers and toes after, but it'll ease the contractions."

Brigit tossed back the contents in one gulp.

"Goddess be! That is repulsive!" Brigit said, her hands dropping limply to her side as her body melted into the table.

"I did say the herbs were fresh," Aoife responded, arms crossed over her torso. "It seems to be working though, eh?"

"Yes. At least I can think again. Even if I can't feel me own hands," Brigit said, relief flooding her face.

Gwenn joined Aoife at the head of the table. "What would you like us to do with Aengus? He'll be home any minute."

"Say hello then get him settled in the sitting room," Brigit said, her face brightening at the mention of Aengus. "He needn't see this too closely. The man seems to think a witching birth will somehow be prettier than a normal one. No idea where he came up with that."

"I'll get him settled with a dram to keep him out of the way. I made sure to buy the good stuff. It's a day to celebrate, after all!" Nora said, bending down to kiss Brigit on the forehead, "Don't worry, love, we'll set you aside a wee nightcap for after you've fed the babes."

"I'll get the sitting room in order," Fiona agreed. She strode into the kitchen, and plucked three ornate glasses from the cabinet. "Can't have Aengus drinking alone, can we?" she said, waving off Gwenn's raised eyebrows. "I'll set him up with a cozy spot by the fire." And with that, she grabbed Nora by the wrist and pulled her into the living room, mischievous grins on both their faces.

"Ha! They'll be having a right party over there while we—mostly you, of course, Brig—do all the work! Some healer you'll be, Fiona," Gwenn scoffed, watching the pair retreat.

"Go easy on her, Gwenn. She's still training and knows nothing about births anyhow. They're both best out of the way," Mary said.

"We're going to see him," Lily whispered, her spine tingling with excitement. Evelyn and Sara's faces mirrored her surprise. That Aengus Clery, their biological father, was going to be present somehow hadn't occurred to Lily before now.

"I should tidy up a bit," Brigit said, propping herself up on wobbly elbows and patting down her hair.

"If that man says anything about your looks right now, he's either right brave or right stupid," Mary said, positioning a wayward lock behind Brigit's ear before easing her sister back into a reclined position.

"There isn't time anyhow. He—" Gwenn said.

A man burst through the door before Gwenn could finish her sentence. His broad chest heaved with exertion and his handsome face was as red as a tomato.

"Are—?" Aengus sucked in a breath, "Are they here? Am I late?" His eyes darted past Mary, Gwenn, and Aoife to land firmly on Brigit, her belly still protruding. "Thank God you're alright!"

He pulled Brigit's hands protectively to his mouth, kissing each of her swollen fingertips. "I wish you'd have called sooner."

Brigit reclaimed her hands and clutched Aengus's shirt to pull him in for a kiss.

Lily averted her gaze as the kiss deepened to near indecency.

"Aye, my love," Brigit said coming up for air. She caressed Aengus from the tip of his red sideburn all the way down to the hard mound of his biceps. "There's still time yet. Gwenn tells me I'm at 4 centimeters, so you needn't worry. Why don't you pour yourself a dram and get comfortable? We may be in for a long night."

"Brig! Your water broke!" Mary said, as a gush of liquid cascaded to the floor.

Aengus's eyes lifted from Brigit's face, raced down her torso, and landed on the puddle amassing on the floor. "I think I'll be getting that dram if you don't mind, love."

"Go on then," Brigit turned up her cheek for a parting kiss. "The girls will let you know when it's safe to return," she teased.

"I'm always pleased when the water breaks on its own. I hate using the poker," Mary said, lifting the sheet that covered Brigit's knees to peer under.

"What's wrong?" Brigit demanded as Mary's head shot up seconds later, her mouth gaping.

"That wasn't your water," Mary spoke as if she didn't believe her own words. "The amniotic sac is still intact. It's coming from somewhere else, but I can't see the source."

"Are you sure? There's not a tiny hole?"

"You know that's impossible, Brig," Gwenn interjected, scooting Mary off the stool to inspect the situation herself.

"Goddess be, Mary's right. It's full as a balloon down there."

Aoife placed her hands on Brigit's shoulders as Brigit tried to lift herself from the table.

"Let's not be getting ahead of ourselves. If I remember correctly, Brig, you should remain as calm as possible. Perhaps you tinkled a wee bit? Didn't you three tell me it happens from time to time?" Aoife shifted her hands up and pulled back the sweat-soaked auburn hair that framed Brigit's face to massage her skull. She smiled when Brigit's heavy skull relaxed into her hands. *Brig never could resist a good massage,* Aoife thought, as her fingers tended to each hill and bony indentation of Brigit's skull. Tracing behind the ears, Aoife pulled down firmly along Brigit's mandible, a trick she had learned that eased even her most stressed-out clients. Her fingers froze.

"Mary? Gwenn? Could you come here?" Aoife stuttered, peering down at a small river of water running over her fingers.

Brigit's head craned backward.

"Is something wrong?" Her expression, full of bliss moments before, morphed to one of confusion as she touched her hair. "Am I sweating that much?"

"I'm not sure it's sweat," Aoife said, switching out Brigit's damp pillow for a towel while Gwenn and Mary smelled, touched, and tasted the substance leaking from Brigit's ear.

"It seems we may have a wee water witch on our hands soon," Gwenn announced.

"Water?" Brigit looked relieved. "You had me worried Aoi—"

"Goddess be!" Mary exclaimed jumping aside as a rush of water shot from Brigit's open mouth. "We'll be needing water. Lots of it. Aoife, could you see to keeping her cup filled and at the ready? If that's not enough we may need to send someone for an IV."

"The wee one must be pulling water straight from your blood to produce that large a flow. Unless this stops soon, our first priority becomes keeping you hydrated," Mary said pulling a syringe from a medical bag. "One quick test will let us know if I'm right," she added, plunging the syringe into her sister's abdomen.

***

Lily watched in horror as the syringe filled with thick brownish-red blood.

"What the hell," Evelyn muttered. "It's like molasses."

"If this is real, then one of us caused that," Sara said with a wince.

"Is that grass?" Lily asked, pointing to a spot under the birthing table where a patch of green was sprouting from the hardwood floors.

They watched as the grass grew at a cancerous rate, covering the floor of the dining room within seconds.

Lily lunged forward as a small tree sprouted from between two stones in the wall. "We should warn them!"

"Chill out. We're not here, remember? Besides, Mary's already spotted it," Evelyn said, catching Lily's shoulder and pointing at Mary, who was watching slack-jawed as a root pushed through the hardwood floors.

Suddenly, another tree shot out of the floor and past Brigit's head.

Brigit screamed and threw her arms over her face.

"What's happening? Are you alright, Brig?" Aengus asked, rushing into the room on unsteady legs. He swayed when he caught sight of the six-foot-tall tree inches from his wife's head.

Nora and Fiona followed close behind looking apologetic and a little tipsy.

"Is that an oak tree? Why is it so wet in here? Did a pipe burst? But it's summer . . ."

"It would appear, Aengus, that you and Brig have daughters gifted in the ways of water and earth," Gwenn said.

"But they're not even born yet!"

"It's possible the earth bit is from Brigit. The water, I'm afraid, is all your daughter."

"*That* is *not* from me," Brigit panted, pointing to the oak, now nudging up against the rafters.

"Can't you stop it? What if it falls on her? Or blows straight through the roof?" Aengus said, his eyes swinging between his wife and the ceiling.

"I think it unwise. Besides the fact that they are clearly prodigious, we have little knowledge of your daughters' powers or what could happen to them if we cut them off. Many babes with magic can be temperamental during labor. At this rate, the best we can hope for is that they make a quick appearance and wear themselves out in the process," Mary said.

"I'm not totally in control at this point, darling. And I could never forgive myself if we harmed them." Brigit said.

"You are the bravest, most beautiful, most amazing ma ever," Aengus said, bending to kiss her.

Brigit gasped, her eyes squeezing shut as a contraction shot through her. "We're not there yet, darling! These wee buggers have yet to see the light of day, after all."

"You've been a ma for months already. Now it's time for me to help, to be a da. Should I stay here?"

"No, my love, I'm afraid my sisters will need even more space than anticipated with all the new flora about. They'll make sure you know what's happening." Brigit's voice, though kind, left no room for bargaining.

"Aye, let's be getting you some food to go with that whiskey, Aengus. You can't be meeting your wee darlings with only a half bottle in yer belly!" Nora exclaimed, grabbing bags of chips and cookies from the kitchen and skipping back to the sitting room.

"We'll shout when it's time for the main event." Gwenn waved

Aengus, Nora, and Fiona out.

"I think they'll be able to figure that out on their own. I haven't presided over any births, but I hear there's a fair bit of screaming to be heard when babies make their appearance," Aoife said.

Aengus's laughter transformed his face, and for a brief second, he looked like a man that worry had no hold over. "You may be right there, Aoife," he said kissing Brigit before returning to the sitting room.

A trail of multicolored pansies followed in his wake.

"How will we get rid of all this?" Aoife mused, surveying the meadow now threatening to take over the kitchen.

"I'm more concerned with getting these babies born at the mo'," Mary muttered, wiping Brigit's face with a cool cloth and lifting a cup to her lips. "Drink up, Brig. Your wee one still seems to be pushing water out of you. Would you fancy a snack? Some crackers? I bet you're low on salt, too."

Brigit wrinkled her nose, "Too dry. Do we have any popsicles? Or ice cream? Something cold, I'm so fecking hot."

"At your command. You'll need more water, too," Mary said, throwing Aoife a look that clearly said, *Well what are you waiting for?!*

Lily chuckled as Aoife poked her tongue out at Mary before turning on her heel to fetch supplies.

"She's coming our way," Sara said nervously.

The air around them stilled as they held their breath. Lily knew they were all thinking the same thing. Of anyone here, Aoife would be able to feel their presence. Lily tried to clear her head. What if Aoife could hear their thoughts like they could hers? She exhaled as Aoife passed by.

"It must be a one-way—," Lily began.

"Look!" Sara whispered, pointing behind them to where Aoife stood still in the middle of the kitchen, her nose upturned to sniff the air.

*Jasmine and smoke?* "Gwenn? Could you stir the large cauldron?" Aoife called over her shoulder.

Evelyn's muscles loosened as Aoife resumed her mission and opened the freezer. "I thought for a second she smelled *us*. Did you see her sniffing?"

"She smelled *you*. It's that damned jasmine loaded perfume you put on in the car. It was so strong then, I'm not surprised it followed you here." Lily whispered fiercely. "What if she tried to use magic on us? She

—"

"Shhhh, you guys!" Sara whispered, waving her arms and glancing back at Aoife, clearly still worried the witch might hear them. "It doesn't matter, we're still here, there was no magical attack. Can we please be nice and watch?"

Lily's cheeks grew hot. What had gotten into her? Normally, she would never say things like that to a person, especially one she met only hours before.

"I'm sorry, it's . . ."

The words died in her mouth as the sound of metal crashing at their backs rang through the room. Lily turned to see Aoife, one arm held comically aloft as a scooper filled with chocolate ice cream spun on the floor. Every muscle in her arm stuck out as Aoife stood paralyzed, sniffing the air with greater urgency this time.

*Fire!*

"Fire?" Evelyn asked, her eyes following Aoife's dash from the kitchen. "Oh my God! What happened?"

Brigit's condition had deteriorated in the time they had been distracted by Aoife. Sweat streamed like rivers down her beet red face. Her hands had lost all color from gripping the soaked sheet beneath her so tightly. Soft whimpers sailed across the room as Brigit's chest moved shallowly up and down, fighting for breath.

"The fire's inside her! It's what's making her so hot," Aoife explained, pulling Gwenn from the cauldrons to Brigit's bedside.

"You mean, Brig has been literally burning from the inside out this whole time?" Lily barely heard Mary's horrified whisper.

"I've been smelling it for hours, but thought it was from the hearth fire," Aoife scowled. "I could have had time to stop it or at least slow it! Now I'm not so sure. I'm sorry, Brig. I should have—"

"We'll have plenty of time for regret later," Gwenn interrupted. "The question now is how best to proceed?"

They stared down at Brigit, the oak mere inches from her head and the puddle at her feet dripping steadily to water the grass beneath the table.

"Brig, can you tell where it's coming from?" Gwenn asked, raising her hands to hover over her sister's abdomen.

Brigit's eyes popped open, hard and full of defiance.

"Don't do anything. You might hurt her . . . she doesn't know any better." She placed a trembling hand on her belly to shield it.

"Brig, I would never," Gwenn said, hurt creeping into her voice. "I thought a wee calming spell in the area—"

"*No spells*. I can make it. I have to. Give me water. And ice. Lots of ice."

Mary handed her a glass and Brigit brought it to her lips, took a sip, and promptly spit the water across the room.

"It burns! Oh, it burns!" Brigit sobbed as she hurled the water glass to the floor where it shattered.

Then, many things happened at once. A stream of water gushed from Brigit's nether regions, marking the spot for a rhododendron bush to sprout in the space between her legs, while a half dozen bamboo stalks shot up to erect a tall cage-like barrier around her.

"Goddess be!" Mary cried. "Don't worry, Brig! We'll clear this mess up."

"Could we focus on clearing down here first? Unless of course we want the twins born in a bush," Gwenn said. She squeezed herself through the bamboo stalks and tore a branch off the bush. A crack of wood sounded from across the room and Gwenn looked up as another tree shoot from the floorboards. She ripped a second branch from the rhododendron's trunk, and felt a new bush rub against her backside. "That's how it is, then?" She sighed and began patting the rhododendron down as flat as possible. Creating just enough room for a pair of hands and a newborn to land without harm.

"Has her water broken yet?" Mary asked, reaching through the bamboo stalks to pat Brigit's cheeks with a cold cloth.

Gwenn shook her head. "From what I can see the amniotic sac is still intact. I'm thinking we should perforate it soon. She looks fully dilated, though it's difficult to tell with all this fecking greenery in the way. It can't be much longer before the twins come on their own."

Mary strode to the hearth and selected a long metal rod with a handle on one end and a small hook on the other from a tray of instruments.

Lily's stomach turned. "Please tell me she's not going to do what I think she is with that."

Before anyone could respond, Mary strode over and handed the rod to Gwenn, who stuck it inside Brigit. Water dripped to the floor, adding to the considerable puddle at Gwenn's feet.

Aengus barreled back into the room. His face fell when he saw Brigit trapped behind a wall of tall bamboo.

"I'm coming, Brig!" he said, tearing a chunk of bamboo from the floor with his bare hands.

Two more stalks popped up on the other side of Brigit.

"Stop, Aengus!" Gwenn cried, rushing to her brother-in-law's side and pulling him from the table. "It's a damn bamboo hydra. Who knows where the next one will crop up? What if it's right underneath her? We have to be careful."

"I need to be with her. I heard her crying," he said, tears streaming down his weathered face.

Aoife swooped in. "Aye, Brig's in a terrible pain, but she'll battle through. What she needs most right now is for you to be calm and for us to work on getting these babes out. For that we need access to her, a feat becoming more difficult with every sprouted tree. This is no normal birth, brother. The best we can hope is that it's over quickly," Aoife said, guiding him from the birthing table.

"Let Mary and Gwenn do their work. I'm going to go check on the expulsion potion. If you'd like, you can stay over here. You'll be able to see everything," Aoife said, pulling out a stool two feet from where Lily sat.

Lily watched, mesmerized, as their father sat down next to them. *I have his fingers*, she thought, marveling at the small parts of herself she found in the man. Evelyn, the tallest of the three sisters, appeared to have inherited Aengus's height. Sara had inherited his deep dimples. *I wonder who . . . ?*

Sara hopped off the counter, shattering Lily's musings as she positioned herself in front of Aengus. Lily watched Sara's eyes rake over the man. Then Sara did the unthinkable: She touched him.

Aengus gasped and swung his head from side to side.

Lily shot a glance at the birthing table. Thankfully they all seemed too preoccupied to notice Aengus's strange behavior.

"Sara, maybe you should—"

"It'll be alright, Aengus," Sara said, her voice calm and soothing. "Brigit will survive this, and your girls will be here soon."

Aengus's head dropped to rest on the back of the chair, his face open to the ceiling and eyes glistening.

"Thank you," he whispered, as two tears plummeted down his freckled cheeks.

"That was freaking wild! It's like you were God," Evelyn whispered, her eyes wide as Sara scurried back to the counter.

"I can't believe you spoke to him," Lily said, unable to tamp down her rising jealousy. *Why didn't I think to make contact with him? Why hadn't—?*

*It all depends on who's born first. If the wee one with fire is left in there, alone, with no sister for comfort, things could go badly. Merciful goddess Brighid, please, I'm begging you: Don't let anything happen to my sister, your namesake. I'll do anything you ask.*

Aoife's voice floated through Lily's head. She glanced at Evelyn and Sara and knew they'd heard it, too.

"I see a head! Our first lass is coming!" Gwenn said, waving Mary over.

"I. Want. Them. Out. NOW!" Brigit screamed between breaths.

"Only a few pushes and she's out, Brig. You can do this!" Gwenn reassured her, placing her hands palms up over the rhododendron.

Brigit gripped the bamboo at her side and with a monstrous grunt pushed.

Lily watched awed as Brigit's torso lifted a foot in the air before collapsing back down to the table. She sure as hell had never seen anything like that in the birthing videos Rena had made her watch.

Five blood-chilling screams later, a small girl slipped into Gwenn's waiting hands, which were supported by the rhododendron bush as it sprang up to catch the babe, its leaves swaying in greeting.

***

She was flawless, with ten fingers, ten toes, a headful of brown hair, and a perfect pair of working lungs.

"Is she out? How is she? What does she look like?" Brigit asked, trying and failing to see over the protruding belly between her and her first born.

"She's the most perfect wee thing I've ever seen. Though I expect you'll be having to share that honor with your sister soon, little darling,"

Gwenn said, smiling down at her new niece while Mary cut the cord. Turning to a table beside her, Gwenn wiped the babe off and swaddled her in a soft yellow wrap laying in wait beside a green one. The girl's cries quieted the moment the cloth tightened around her. Finally, Gwenn presented the babe to Brigit, slipping her tiny body through the bamboo.

"Goddess be. Look at those eyes. They're so very green," Brigit whispered, as she took her daughter.

Lily's stomach flipped and she sat up straighter.

"That they are," Gwenn agreed. "I'm thinking this may be our earth witch. The bushes about caught her before I could."

"You are so perfect," Brigit murmured in the way of mothers and babes.

The child let out a hearty cry.

"Aye, I'll be betting you're hungry, but you'll have to wait. Your sister feels to be not far behind," Brigit admitted with a cringe.

"I'll let Aengus meet her, then?" Gwenn asked, reaching her hands back through the bamboo to take the girl.

Brigit nodded, clenching her jaw tight as another contraction bore down.

Lily watched Aengus hungrily as Gwenn brought her over and deposited her in her father's arms. Her heart broke as Aengus's face split into a smile so large Lily thought it might crack his face in half. The man looked ready to burst into song. His large hands cradled her with a gentleness no one would guess them capable of.

*I'm glad I came here and let someone break into my mind, if only to see this*, Lily thought, hugging her arms tight around herself.

A choked sob at her side broke the moment of peace. Lily turned to find Sara sobbing as Evelyn wrapped an arm around her awkwardly.

"I never had a father. No man came into my life until I was ten. Rich loved me, and filled that role when he could, but it was never like that. I never thought I'd have that. It turns out I already did," Lily said the words without knowing why she felt like she had to explain.

Sara's lips tightened into a watery smile, and Lily realized she might not be the only one with daddy issues.

"Not to be insensitive or anything you guys, but look at all that water," Evelyn said, clearly relieved to have a reason to evade the emotional conversation.

Water, startling volumes of it, was surging from Brigit's mouth, ears, and nether regions, wetting everything and everyone within a six-foot radius. Small tributaries were shooting off from the main geysers to form puddles and creeks in the split hardwood floors. Bamboo, bushes, trees, and flowers rustled their foliage with pleasure as they soaked up the life-giving liquid.

"This is it, Brigit. I can see her head. She's performing her finale. Let's be happy it's not the fire she's using," Mary said, wiping her face as the water eased up.

"That is disgusting," Evelyn said, "I mean, that came from . . . Eww! She should go wash."

"A little water is the least of her worries," Lily retorted, unable to hide her exasperation. *Good god, a baby's about to be born! Does she really think now's the time to take a nice hot shower?*

Time traveled at warp speed, and less than ten minutes after Lily's birth Mary welcomed a larger and completely bald baby girl into the world. She cleaned the girl and wrapped her expertly in a green swaddle.

"They're so different! This one's eyes are as blue as her sister's are green. Goddess be, we are in trouble. Aengus is going to have a task in beating the boys off you, isn't he, little one?" Brigit cooed, holding her newest daughter tight to her chest. Aengus sidled up next to her, his face glowing with joy.

"That baby looks like *my* baby photos. She even has the exact same birthmark *I have* on my neck," Evelyn stuttered. "That's—oh my god, that's me."

Lily watched the shifting of Evelyn's emotions as they darted across her face. Disbelief, hurt, and sadness all took a turn before finally settling on acceptance.

"Want to hold them both?" Aengus asked, beaming down at baby Evelyn and Brigit.

"For a mo'. The afterbirth hasn't come yet, but I am desperate to see them side by side," Brigit said, stretching her arms through a narrow slit in the bamboo stalks for Lily. She gasped. The stalks were moving on their own accord, leaning to the side to accommodate the passing of the girl. "It seems she wants to meet her baby sister, too," Brigit said breaking into a smile.

***

Aoife grinned at the contented murmurs of the new mother and father. *I'll take me time*, she thought, filling one lidded cup—or secure sippy, as Mary liked to call it—to the brim with the placenta expulsion potion and another with the revival elixir. *I wouldn't like to be the one that spoiled that sweet scene.* She set the secure sippy within Brigit's reach before beginning to clean up. She heard a loud clank of metal coming from the kitchen and turned to see Gwenn throwing instruments in the sink as Mary, Nora, and Fiona began the arduous task of mopping up water. They'd had the same idea. There would be time for everyone to bond soon enough, and goddess help them, Brig and Aengus wouldn't be rid of her once she got hold of the wee ones.

Aoife rounded the hearth to pull the iron cauldrons off their hooks and placed them on the stone ledge to cool. The last thing they needed was for someone to trip and fall into the cauldron with a babe in their arms.

She sighed when she noticed the fire burning in the hearth, on the verge of death. Reluctantly, Aoife extinguished what remained, an act that always made her feel as if she was smothering a piece of her soul. *Even I'm feeling a touch uncomfortable, though*, she thought, wiping the sweat from her forehead. Smoke slithered up from the blackened logs, and Aoife walked across the room. *This smoke can't be good for the babes*, she thought, throwing the window open wide and wafting the smoke outside.

Darkness had fallen upon the quiet Irish countryside. Aoife hoped Gwenn had remembered to check the time for the official birth records. A full moon dominated the star-spangled sky, illuminating Brigit's small garden and lake with an ethereal glow. *The eve of summer solstice and a full moon—what an auspicious day for witches to be born*, Aoife thought, delightedly. *These girls are sure to be full of surprises. I best be heading back if I'm to get my hands on one while Brig finishes up*, she thought, reluctant to leave the fresh air despite the greater reward. She leaned out the window and inhaled, savoring the cool air as it dipped in and swirled around her lungs.

*Fire?*

Aoife's head whipped to face the fireplace. Gray tendrils of dying smoke swirled low in the pit, but no flame.

Her stomach clenched as the only other possibility hit her. *One of the twins is trying to use magic!*

Aoife made it three steps from the window before Brigit's terrified voice rose over the sounds of chat and cleaning.

"Take them, Aengus, take the girls. Something's happening. Gwenn, Mary, Aoife! Something's wrong!"

Aoife rounded the fireplace in time to see Brigit pushing the twins into Aengus's arms.

"Which one is it?" Aoife said, rushing to Aengus's side, searching for a sign of fire magic. Power born of fire was often dangerous and unpredictable when used by trained witches. An infant with undisciplined power was always a terrifying prospect for a family. Still, Aoife hadn't expected problems this early. To hear Gwenn and Mary tell it, the birth usually wore babies out.

"I—I don't know," Aengus said, his thick arms trembling as he held the girls out to Aoife for inspection.

It took Aoife less than five seconds to determine neither was using magic at all, let alone fire magic.

"Aoife, it's in me," Brigit squeaked, her back arching into an unnatural bend. "There's another."

"Another?" Aoife asked, knitting her brows together.

"Baby," Brigit grunted, "I felt it move after the second girl was born but hoped they were phantom kicks. But I can feel it moving more strongly now, and I'm still so hot. She . . . or he is fire."

"Goddess be! Another baby!" Mary cried dropping her rag.

"Stand over there, as far as you can," Aoife hissed at Aengus, who complied without question.

"Are you sure it's not the placenta, Brig? Birthing twins can make a ma feel a bit off," Mary said, looking at her sister with concern as she situated herself on the stool.

"Positive," Brigit shot back irritably. She closed her eyes, and took a deep breath as if begging for the patience to explain something unexplainable. "The fire—I thought it would pass but the sensation only grew stronger. I feel so stupid. This whole time I've been so hot that I've been using what power I could to dampen the heat. I don't think I'll be able to keep it up anymore once I have to push again. I haven't much energy left." She opened her eyes and Aoife saw they were full of tears. "Do you think you can control the babe, Aoife? Fight fire with fire? You'll understand it best."

Aoife considered the matter. *At the very least I can absorb whatever heat the babe emits and channel it out of Brigit's body.*

"I'll be right here," Aoife said, reaching through the bamboo. She knew Brigit was right the second she touched her boiling hot belly. There was power there. Power that was not Brigit's. *She's been pulling from far too deep*, Aoife thought, watching her sister's arms and legs tremble.

"What was two will soon be three," Aoife said, nodding at Mary to be ready. "Hold tight, Brig, this one's ready to make an entrance. I can feel it."

Brigit nodded, her eyes screwed shut as she bore down under the force of mounting contractions.

"Goddess be . . . yes! They're coming faster now, Brig, I should be seeing a head any minute," Mary said. Her lips began to move silently, counting seconds.

"Every time one's about to hit, my blood burns. Can you dissipate it?" Brigit asked Aoife, her eyes pleading.

Aoife focused on pulling any wayward magic from Brigit's body. It was easy enough to tell the babe's power from her sister's. The babe's magic ran free, flowing out of the womb and through Brigit at the babe's will. Brigit's power simmered weakly near the womb, acting as gatekeeper to cut the fire off at the source. *There you are, you wee bugger*, Aoife thought shifting her hands to a congregated mass of fire over Brigit's heart. She jumped as a jolt of red hot energy ran through her open channels. It hurt, but it was better she absorb it than Brigit.

"Ahh," Brigit sighed, her lips easing from white to pink.

"Push now, Brig," Mary coached, arms at the ready.

Fire sprang up in the hearth. Brigit yelped and ground her body into the table to push.

Aoife put out the flames with a flick of her wrist, as her other hand pulled magic from her sister's blood.

"Couldn't let your sisters have all the fun, isn't that right?" Aoife said, careful to keep her tone playful despite the terror pulsing through her. *What else would the babe set ablaze?* She moved her hand to the left and her stomach sank as another energy store burned hot. *It's like it's got an eternal supply in there.*

Brigit pushed again, and insidious gray tendrils floated out of her ears to frame her face.

Aoife's heart raced as the smoke traveled down Brigit's body toward Mary, as if marking a path for the babe to follow.

"One more big push and you're done, Brig. I see the crown now," Mary urged.

Brigit complied, and a third girl, much smaller than her sisters, slid into Mary's hands.

Her misshapen head was topped with a mop of bright red hair. Matching large red spots dotted her milky skin. Her discontent at being left alone was plain upon first breath. Aoife thought she sounded outraged, as if she'd known all along that no one realized she existed.

Mary cleaned the girl, wrapping her in a plain white towel Gwenn procured from the bath. She was about to hand her over to Brigit when Aoife plucked the furious babe from her arms.

"Brig needs a rest. I'll calm this one for her first," she said, nodding at Brigit, who lay panting on the table. *Cradling a babe never feels quite as natural as others make it seem*, Aoife thought. She stared down at the girl, her hands shifting, unable to find a natural hold on the girl's tiny body. *If it were any other I'd have let Mary keep her, but Mary won't understand her as I do.*

Aoife sat on the hearth stones. A fire sprang up at her bidding and she began to rock the girl, humming in low tones. Before she knew it, her tuneless hum morphed into an ancient Irish ballad of unrequited love, a lonesome life, and death by the flames. *Not the most child-appropriate song*, she thought, *but this little one doesn't seem to mind.*

"This right here is your destiny," Aoife whispered to the girl, nodding at the flames.

With each rock of the baby's body, Aoife felt a bit of the raging heat and temper radiate off her. The baby's florid skin calmed to leave stretches of unblemished flesh as the fire soothed her nerves.

"Now you're ready to meet your mammy, aren't you?" Aoife asked when the last red ring dissolved to white.

"Thank you, Aoife. I'm not sure I would have pulled through without your help," Brigit said, her face glowing with happiness as Aoife handed over her youngest daughter.

"Nonsense, you'd have been fine. Might have taken a bit longer is all," Aoife said, hoping the lie wasn't too obvious. No part of her thought Brigit would have been fine. In fact, without her siphoning off the fire magic, the exertion of keeping it at bay might have killed Brigit. And that was without factoring in the immense effort it took to birth three babies in less than an hour.

"Looks to me as if you and Aengus have a little bonding to do." She glanced up at her brother-in-law, who was beaming like an idiot, a baby crooked in each of his muscular arms. "I'll be reminding you of that goofy grin when you're going on and on about changing dirty nappies all night, Aengus," Aoife teased, leaving the new parents alone with their babies.

***

"What are we going to name them now?" Aengus asked gazing down at the green, yellow, and white bundles.

"I was thinking that, too. After all that happened, Elizabeth and Claire don't seem quite right anymore, do they? And then there's this wee one who doesn't have a name at all," Brigit said gazing down at the tiny redhead.

"Seeing as it took us months to come up those names, we may have to use temporary ones. How about one, two, and three? We can use our hands to signal each other."

Brigit smacked him on the shoulder, earning herself a mischievous grin.

"It won't take us months! It can't. And we'll call them by their eye color until we decide, Green, Blue, and Amber." Brigit said.

"Sounds grand, love," Aengus said, seeking her lips through a slit of mangled bamboo. They lingered happily, five faces side by side, as their scents mingled for the first time.

"Looks like I'll be getting to know the fairer sex even better than we thought, won't I?" Aengus said, his jubilant smile morphing into a thin line. "Good God, think of all the lads I'll have to scare off."

Brigit's bark of laughter woke Green and Amber.

"They'll be wanting milk." Brigit motioned for Aengus to hand over Green, as the babies' cries saturated the room. "To think I was worried at feeding two at once. I've no idea how I'm to manage three."

"We'll figure out a way," Aengus reassured her. "I'll take Blue for a quick stroll about the room. She doesn't seem hungry yet and we don't need her—or any of them, really—getting jealous, do we?" He grinned, snuggled a sleeping Blue close to his chest, and began to stroll the room's perimeter.

The aunts converged on Brigit.

"How are they?" Gwenn cooed.

"Perfect," Brigit replied, beaming up at them.

"Milk come in alright then?" Mary asked, bending down to get a closer look at the babies.

"For now, though I'm more worried than I ever was about not producing enough with an extra mouth to feed."

"Don't fret, Brig, your body will compensate. I can't believe there was one hiding in there all along! I'll bet the doctor didn't spot the youngest. She's so small." Mary drew her finger over Amber's smooth cheeks.

"Her name's Amber, the other two are Green and Blue, after their eyes, at least until we get proper names sorted. The old ones didn't seem to be . . . enough for them anymore."

"You'll be wanting powerful names for these girls. All three are forces to be reckoned with," Aoife inclined her head at Amber. "And we'll need to keep a close watch on her so she doesn't burn the house down, at least until she can control herself."

"Lucky for us she has her very own fire auntie," Brigit said. "Between your mind magic—sorry, *ceremens*—and fire magic, I doubt Amber will be getting away with anything with you around, Aoife."

"We'll all do our share," Gwenn added, clearly not wanting to be left out of auntie duty so early on.

"'Course you will. I think knowing you three are around is the only reason Aengus hasn't faked his death by now."

"I reckon he hasn't ruled it out," Aoife chortled. "He's a smart man. Probably keeping it in his back pocket for when times get really tough. Like when they start dating."

The room erupted with laughter.

***

"That was freaking wild!" Lily exclaimed. Watching the births and keeping track of the conversations going on inside and outside Aoife's head had been like being a novice in a professional doubles tennis match.

Sara nodded, mesmerized. "I'm pretty sure Aoife can manipulate what thoughts we're privy to. And when we knew to follow Aoife to the living room when she opened the window! Total mind control!"

"I wish she'd pull us out of here. We've seen what they wanted us to see and I for one would like to go home. Or at least to the present,"

Evelyn said, shifting uncomfortably on the tiled counter. "The last part was nice and all, but I'm still feeling queasy from all those contractions."

"There must be something else," Sara said.

"It's still so hard to believe, isn't it? That she had no idea there were three babies?" Evelyn asked, following her own train of thought.

"Maybe witch pregnancies are a little different from what we are used to. They're certainly unpredictable. Makes me wonder how I would deal with any pregnancies if we never came here," Lily said, her eyes glued to Brigit and her sisters fawning over her.

"That's been bugging me. Why did they even bring us here? My parents forced me. Said the meeting had been arranged years ago, as a stipulation of the adoption."

"Why wouldn't she want to meet her daughters?" Sara asked, a puzzled look on her elfin face.

"I mean, I can see why she wanted to meet us and have us meet each other, but it seems so . . . coordinated. Why now? Why the secrecy? And why did my parents know about it years ago? I doubt most adoption reunions are this big a production."

"Most adoptions don't involve witches or triplets either," Sara shrugged.

"I think we're about to find out why we're still here," Lily said, her eyes widening. "Something's up with Mary."

Mary stood rigidly next to Aengus. Her arms hovered at awkward angles by her sides, and her mouth hung wide open. Her skin had lost all color, creating an unpleasant, possessed quality that made Lily shiver.

"Alright, Mary?" Aengus asked, assessing her stance and taking a step back.

Mary's eyes bulged at the sound of his voice, and Lily saw they'd changed color, from bright blue to black.

"Stand back Aengus! Mary's not with us," Aoife said, taking a protective stance in front of Aengus and Blue.

Brigit and Gwenn's heads swiveled to face their sister, their arms tightening around their charges.

"Is she having a stroke?" Aengus asked, his voice shaking.

"I've only ever heard of such signs, but I believe our Mary is about to deliver a prophecy—" A booming voice, so unlike Mary's sweet soprano, shot out of her overstretched mouth, cutting Aoife off.

"Three, three, three, shall it be,
The ones to save humanity.
Desperate to expand his throne,
He seeks to conquer all Earth grown.
Though abandoned years ago,
His time is nearing,
The fata king will soon know.
Hecate's daughters are born anew,
Chimeric spawn from him they flew.

"The Earth's power in fair Lilith's hands,
Is given to you to sow your plans.
Eve with beauty, wit, and spite,
Offers all oceans as your birthright.
Fire, power born of this soil,
Is Seraphina's weapon for all who toil.
'Twas the magic of the three,
As they were, so will you be.

"But know this, long-awaited star,
Use only magic and you will be par,
Only a life, a family all your own,
Love, and knowledge can thwart the throne.

"You must be canny,
remain unseen.
Hidden, until the time is right.
Or all human life,
Shall endure a timeless night.

"Unearth Seraphina's tome."

Mary's mouth began to pulsate as her body contracted and relaxed in spastic intervals. Her eyes, once again their original bright blue, flew around the room in terror. It seemed the spasms would go on forever when all of a sudden Mary's body stiffened and she collapsed to the floor.

# *Chance and Choice*

"What the hell was that about?"

Lily's eyes cracked open.

"What did it mean? Were you possessed? *Are* you possessed? Who the fuck is Seraphina?" Evelyn screeched, her pitch escalating with each word.

*God, I wish she'd shut up*, Lily thought, her head throbbing.

"We'll answer what we can, as soon as the other two wake up," Brigit said.

"I'm awake," Lily pushed herself up and swayed where she sat, small spots clouding her vision.

"Me, too," Sara said, rising to rest on her elbows.

"Why don't you girls have a seat on the couch? Does anyone need food or water? Your first magical experience can be quite draining," Brigit said, her eyes raking over them.

*I must look as bad as I feel*, Lily thought as Brigit rushed past Sara and Evelyn to help her up, eyes wide with concern.

"Thanks," she said, doing her best to sound grateful when all she wanted to do was curl into a ball and cry.

Lily's legs shook as she shuffled to the couch, where the others were waiting. Neither Sara nor Evelyn had needed help to hobble around like an eighty-year-old woman. Lily pretended not to see Sara extend her hand as she collapsed onto the couch, cheeks burning. *Why am I the only one who looks like they've been hit by a truck?* Even Aoife seemed better off than her, though not by much. Lily watched as Gwenn brought Aoife a blanket, wrapped it around her trembling shoulders, and stoked the fire at her sister's back.

"Some people have a bad reaction to mind magic. It's not natural to have someone rooting around in your head. I made these before you came. They're my own recipe. Full of fortifying herbs and plenty of chocolate to hide the taste," Mary said, handing Lily a plate of cookies.

Lily ignored her nausea and shoved a cookie in her mouth.

"Well, I must say you all did quite well. Most vomit or pass out their first time. Now that we're all stable, we'll *try* to explain what you saw. We won't have all the answers. To be honest, we're hoping you can help us find them. Where would you like to start?" Brigit asked.

"Evelyn seemed to have a few questions," Mary said with a small smile. "You were curious about what I said at the end? Is that right?"

Evelyn nodded, her red lips taut.

"It was a prophecy that we believe is based off an ancient, little-known tale. We suspect the prophecy is old and was created under duress —else I'd like to think the creator would have been a wee bit more detailed. It's a warning from a witch who knew more than us of the evil in this universe. It was destined to reveal itself under a specific set of circumstances. Your births set it free."

Lily massaged her temples. She knew Brigit was speaking English, but it may as well have been Arabic, for all she understood.

"And Seraphina?" The odd name tripped off Evelyn's tongue.

"We don't want to get in too deep right off. It would overload you, and we haven't all the proper materials to back up the story with us. Let's just say Seraphina wrote a very important book. The prophecy is the first we'd heard of it, but Mary's been searching for Seraphina's book ever since," Brigit said.

"There's mention of three in the prophecy, and we're three. I assume that's not an error. So how does the prophecy affect us?" Sara asked, leaning forward and resting her forearms on her knees.

"It means someone has been waiting a very long time for you three to be born. And if you're willing to accept it, you have one hell of a job to take on." Mary jumped into action, producing a whiteboard from a crevice on the far side of the fireplace. "Aoife wrote down the prophecy in case you needed to study it further."

Lily squinted at the blurry, blue writing scrawled across the board.

There they were, the same troubling words Mary had spoken moments (years?) before. The triplets eyes raced over curves and angles, craving sense out of the senseless.

"A timeless night," Sara mused out loud, as Lily wondered dimly whether the name Lilith or Hecate intensified her headache more. "The three of us are destined to save the earth from someone. A king of some sort? And we are Hecate's daughters? She's a goddess right? And what does chimeric spawn mean?"

Lily had to hand it to her. The degree of academic detachment in Sara's voice was downright impressive. *She's probably considering every goddess in history, and here I am proud I haven't broken out in tears yet.*

Aoife, who until that point had been breathing deeply with her eyes closed, opened her eyes. She, too, looked impressed. "Taking into account the spell work performed, there's room for debate on translation. We believe the caster used one of two methods to ensure the prophecy would be understood. The first would have been weaving a translation spell in with the prophecy. This is problematic as languages change every day. Therefore, the caster's translation could change with time and information could be lost. All signs point to this being sensitive material. I'd put money down that our caster knew better than to use a translation spell. The second method would ensure the prophecy could be understood by all magical creatures no matter the year or culture." Aoife paused and lifted a steaming cup of tea to her lips. "It's called lingua primum, the first language of magic. It's said that as witches, we know it when we hear it, though the talent to speak lingua primum died with the druids."

"You're telling me we actually understood another language, one we've never even heard of, without knowing it?" Lily asked, her throat burning as the words rushed out of her.

"Not quite. The first language is a magical entity in itself. It can, as it did in Mary's prophecy, translate itself into the native language of the listener. You would know if you heard raw lingua primum. Not with your head, but with your intuition. It's said that to hear it spoken is an alien experience."

"Can we get back to Sara's questions, please?" Evelyn asked, looking frustrated. "What about the chimeric spawn?"

"Ahh yes, sorry—got a wee bit distracted. The lingua primum is a passion of mine. Anyhow, for people in antiquity, a chimera meant a creature composed of more than one animal. A mix of species, if you will. There are many legends that claim witches are chimeras. Some say it's the other, the non-human in us that gives us power. It makes sense in a way, don't you think?" Aoife tented her fingers together.

"How should I know?" Evelyn's voice rose in anger with each word. "You are the first people in my life to accuse me of being a witch. How am I supposed to know where magic comes from? Until today I didn't even believe magic existed!"

"I don't believe that for a second," Mary whispered. "You've never been accused of getting everything you wanted, even though you didn't deserve it? No man has ever accused you of putting a spell on him?"

"*Of course* people have said those things! People suck up to me all the time, hoping to get in my parents' good graces!" Evelyn roared, throwing her hands to the ceiling.

"Mary's right, dear," Brigit said apologetically. "No doubt you have led a charmed life, but I'd wager to guess that your power seeped through a bit here and there to help you along. No matter how well our binding took, magic was sure to find a way out. We only hoped it would be gradual to draw less attention. I'm guessing you may have gotten more attention than you deserved at times."

"And what exactly do you mean by that?" Evelyn said, leaning forward, her eyes narrowed into slits.

"Your binding? What is that?" Sara interrupted, placing her hand on Evelyn's chest and pushing her back into the couch.

"This one takes after you in more than looks, Aoife. She's quick to get to the heart of the matter," Gwenn said, nodding with approval.

Sara blushed, though her gaze never left Brigit.

"I couldn't very well send three powerful infant witchlings out into the world. Even in a proper magical home it would have been years before you had any control over your magic. You'd have been a danger to everyone around you in the normal world. We couldn't have that. There was only one solution as far as I could tell. I bound your power to my own, to my own life, before hiding you—as the prophecy instructed—in the normal world. I hoped no one would think to look for you there. Then we waited until the time was right, until you were full grown women as the prophecy specified," Brigit said.

"So that's what we're here for?" Sara asked, a look of understanding coming over her. "You're hoping we'll consent to be unbound, whatever that entails?"

"That is a large part of why you're here, though it's a bit more complex than that," Brigit said hesitantly.

"It's so much to take in," Lily said, her voice ragged. The mere thought of more magic was making her feel worse.

"We don't expect you to decide right this minute," Brigit said. "We have extra rooms you can take to rest in and think, though I'm afraid two of you will have to share." She eyed Lily with concern.

"I'd like that," Lily replied. At any rate, it saved her a trip into town to find a hotel room. She wasn't even sure how she'd get there or if she could manage the trip with her pounding headache.

"Me, too," Sara said.

"I call the solo room," Evelyn said. "Do you get WiFi or phone service out here?" She pulled a sleek new iPhone from her purse and scowled. "My phone's been acting strange since we hit that dirt road. I'd like to discuss this with my parents."

"We've set a temporary charm around the property to interfere with phone signals," Aoife said. "We'd prefer that you not tell anyone of your circumstances at this time. There's much more to tell you, and we need time to ensure that those around your families are trustworthy. Of course we trust your families. We would not have left you with them otherwise. But what if your disappearance didn't go unnoticed? People have been watching our family for years. It's possible they were watching yours, too. They may even have seen you arrive here. Once you're unbound, if you choose to do so, all sorts of creatures will come out of the woodwork. It's impossible to release the kind of power we believe you three control and have it go unnoticed. You wouldn't want to put your parents in danger by giving them information they won't understand. What if they confided in the wrong person? It could threaten their safety."

"Is that a threat?" Evelyn said, slipping the phone back into her bag.

"Not at all," Brigit jumped in, her tone soothing after Aoife's gravelly voice. "Sometimes being yourself is enough to bring about danger. I'm sorry for it, too. We owe each of your families more than they know."

"I'll show you to the rooms," Mary said, rising before the conversation could escalate further.

Lily and Sara rose, but Evelyn remained seated, her back rigid as she glared at Aoife. Finally, she stood, her mouth set in a scowl, and joined them.

"This here's the double. Make yourselves at home," Mary said, presenting the room to them with a flourish of her arms. She smelled of grapefruit and rain, and the shiny pink sleeves of her dress reminded Lily of something Vanna White would wear.

Lily sighed with relief as Sara shut the bedroom door behind them. It was a large room, reminiscent of a college dorm but cozier, with two twin beds, two desks, two velvet wingback chairs, and a large closet. Faint afternoon light seeped through curtains. The wall farthest from the beds was covered with photos. Lily collapsed face first on the bed closest to the door. Her mouth opened as a loud groan escaped her lips. *At last, a moment of peace to sort all this out. Or try to,* she thought.

Springs squeaked as Sara eased herself onto the other bed. Lily considered talking to the petite redhead but found she simply didn't have the energy. *No, it'll be best if I go over everything first, that way I can't be swayed. I'll meditate on it,* she thought, allowing her eyes to close. *That's what Annika always says to do when faced with a tough decision.*

***

A whisper of rustling fabric filtered through her dream. Someone was in her room. Lily's eyes shot open. *Where the hell am I?* she thought, her heart pounding as she gripped the unfamiliar gingham bedspread. Slowly, she lifted her head to see Sara seated in a wingback chair by the window. She sighed. How odd it was to wake up in the strangest house she had ever set foot in and feel relief at seeing a near total stranger in the room. The bones in her back popped as she sat up and stretched her arms overhead. Sara had pulled back the curtains to reveal a large stained glass Celtic knot in the middle of the window. It's deep red color stood out proudly against the luminous, star-filled sky. The scene made Lily's heart ache for home—her own, steady, star-filled sky half a world away.

Sara turned from the window, a serene smile so unlike how Lily felt on her elfin face. "How was your nap? I'm sorry if I woke you."

"Needed," Lily said, chancing a grin. "At least now my headache is gone. What does that symbol mean? It's seems to be everywhere in this house," Lily said, recalling the symbols prominence in the sitting room.

Sara followed her finger and smiled. "The triquetra has a lot of meanings depending on the culture. In this instance, I would guess it symbolizes one of the Celtic triple goddesses, but I'd have to ask Brigit to be sure. Christianity picked it up from the pagans, so it could be Christian. Though from what I've seen of this house that seems less likely."

Lily nodded. She would have to brush up on her Celtic

mythology. "Did you manage to get any rest?"

"No. I meditated for a while. Did a little yoga. And thought, of course."

"Of course . . . So, what do you make of this whole scenario?" Lily asked. "Sisters, triplets, and witches—it's a lot to take in. Don't even get me started on Aoife's little magic trick. I hope I never have to go through that again."

"It was a definitely an experience," Sara said, fingering a tassel hanging from the green mala bead necklace around her neck. "One I'm not dying to repeat either, but as far as I can tell everything rings true." She paused to stare down at her hands. A protracted silence followed in which Sara appeared to be weighing her words.

Lily didn't mind. Rena, too, was partial to long pauses before she spoke.

"Morgane was the one to find me at university. She told me she had a hell of a time tracking me down. You see, the first couple they entrusted me to, the ones I thought were my biological parents, died when I was four. Brigit didn't find out for a couple of months, and by then I had disappeared into the U.S. foster care system. That's where they lost track of me. I got adopted quickly by a couple. My adoptive father was a highly ranked military officer. He worked with sensitive information, which meant our location was confidential. We moved a lot, sometimes every six months. I never understood how kids felt when they said they'd had the same best friend for years. I was always starting anew, by myself."

"Sara, I can't even imagine . . ." Lily let the sentence hang. What was she going to say anyways? She'd always had a family and a home to count on.

Sara shrugged.

"You want to know the worst part? My first parents, the ones Morgane knew, died in a car crash. It was stupid. My dad was fiddling around, doing huge curves and stuff on a country road. Then a drunk driver came out of a field and rammed them from the side. Dad was killed instantly. Mom was unconscious but alive. I had a couple of scrapes but was fine otherwise. I remember sitting in my car seat screaming my head off as my parents sat unresponsive in the front. It's one of my first vivid memories."

"They couldn't save her?" Lily asked, hugging her blanket.

Sara's eyes flew back to her hands, and she sucked in a long breath.

"They could have—if the car hadn't caught fire."

*Holy crap.*

"When the paramedics arrived, I was wiggling out of the vehicle. The car was engulfed in flames, but I didn't have a single burn. I used to have nightmares about flames parting before me while everyone around me died. Brigit's story explains so much about my life. It's impossible for me not to believe her."

"You think it was magic that saved you?" Lily asked, tiptoeing around the question of why the fire had started in the first place.

Sara smiled gratefully, sensing the omission. "I know so. I don't know about you or Evelyn, but I'm doing the unbinding. I need to know how I'm meant to feel. I've felt like a part of me has been missing for so long. Now I think it's possible it's still there, and all I have to do is set it free." Her words hung in the air between them, resonating, then floating away.

*Have I come this far, learned this much, and gone through all that shit with mind magic to leave with my tail between my legs?* Lily wondered. The pain of her first official magical experience was still fresh, but she couldn't deny the truth in Sara's words. Aside from when she was home, surrounded by the love of her family at the commune, she'd never felt like she fit in either.

Slowly Lily rose and set her feet on the ground. She wobbled as she leaned into her base, allowing the floorboards to take her weight. *I hope all magic doesn't affect me this way*, she thought, shaking her head. More than anything it rankled Lily that she seemed to be the only one affected.

"I can do it," Lily said when Sara stood to help.

Sara sat down, though she didn't look convinced. She relaxed only when Lily's hands were resting on the back of the armchair.

"You know, I'm usually very athlet—"

A small, faded photo of three baby girls encircled by a dozen other framed photos caught her eye. The babies were staring back at the camera, their green, blue, and penny colored eyes all wide open.

"Is that—us?" Lily asked, her gaze shifting to take in the photos surrounding the baby picture. Brigit, Aoife, Mary, Gwenn, even one of Aengus and Brigit all smiled back at her. *It's like they're protecting us.*

"I've never seen a happier baby picture of myself," Sara replied. "I always look sullen, angry even, in the few I was able to obtain after my adoption. I wonder if I remembered what I lost."

Lily sighed and studied the photos. "I'm so conflicted. I want to be upset. To rage and storm that Brigit gave us up. To make Brigit *work for my love*. But at the same time, I can't deny I had a great life up until now. I have family that loves me, and it's obvious the witches out there do, too, even if they barely know me. I guess what I'm trying to say is . . . what's the point? I'm convinced magic is real. That they're my blood. Shit watching Gwenn in that memory was like staring at myself in a few years. Why waste more time?" She touched the photo of Brigit and Aengus and wondered where their father was, before turning back to Sara. "I'm going to do it."

"I thought you would," Sara said with a warm smile, "though I'm not so sure about Evelyn. She's not taking this well at all, is she?"

"I can't say I've been much better. It's strange . . . not only do I disagree with most of what Evelyn says, it's like I want to make sure she knows I disagree with her. I swear I'm not usually so hard to get along with," Lily said, shaking her head at her own behavior.

"You haven't clicked yet. This was a pretty stressful day to be meeting new people. Don't judge yourself, or Evelyn, too harshly."

Lily nodded. "You're right. Maybe we should go see what she's thinking?"

***

"I think they put her there," Sara said, pointing to a door at the end of the hallway.

"You'd know better than me," Lily shrugged.

The faint sound of pots clanking together in the kitchen, masked their footsteps on the creaky wood floor.

Sara raised her hand to knock, let it drop, and spun around to face Lily, a conflicted look on her face. "What if she's asleep? It is pretty late."

"Did you see her? I doubt she sleeps for a week after what we learned," Lily said, reaching around Sara to rap lightly on the door.

No answer.

Sara turned to retreat, but Lily blocked her. Her arm shot out under Sara's elbow to grasp the door knob. The door opened without a sound.

Evelyn's room was like theirs, sparse but comfortable, with a set of drawers, a nightstand, and a single bed. They found Evelyn lying face down on the bed, sobbing into her pillow, unaware of their intrusion.

"Um, Evelyn? Are you alright?" Sara squeaked from the doorway.

"Christ!" Evelyn exclaimed, her head whirling around to face them. "Don't you two have any manners?"

"We came to check on you," Sara said, letting herself in and easing onto the bottom corner of the bed.

Evelyn's sneer grew the tiniest bit smaller.

"We were wondering if you've made a decision about the unbinding? Sara and I are planning on doing it."

"Like I didn't already know that. What have you two got to lose anyways?

"Uhh . . . A chance at a normal life? Just like you," Lily replied.

"A normal life!" Evelyn wailed, rubbing her temples. "I've never been normal. Even in utero. Didn't you see what I did to that woman?" Evelyn jabbed her finger in the direction of the living room. "Don't you two have any idea who I am?"

Lily rolled her eyes. Her patience had already run out. *I am so over this diva bullshit.* "What does it matter? Do you really think that you can go back to being who you were before? Do you even want to? Don't you want to see what could happen?" The words flew from Lily's mouth, completely unplanned, but also completely honest.

"No," Evelyn's head dropped and she sighed. "I was happy being who I was. I have a family that loves me. A family with money, power, and a good reputation. I have friends and people who wanted to be me. I bet you wouldn't want to trade being a Locksley for a bit of magic either."

"Wait a minute," Sara said, her copper eyes bulging from their sockets, "Locksley? As in Locksley Enterprises?"

Evelyn nodded.

"Oh my God! My friend at Princeton would kill to have a job there!" Sara paused, before adding, "You're possibly the richest person I've ever met."

"Most wealthy heiress in the U.S. according to a recent Forbes poll. Not that it matters much now," Evelyn muttered.

"Why's that?" Lily asked, stitching her brows together.

"Isn't it obvious? Even if I go back to my normal life like nothing ever happened, no one would do business with me. Who in their right mind would do business with a witch? Somehow word would get out. It always does." She threw Lily a thinly veiled accusatory glance.

"Are you insinuating that I would sell you to the media? Because let me tell you, Miss Locksley, if you were to leave and go back to your hoity-toity life I'd never so much as . . ."

"So does that mean you're staying? You'll do the unbinding?" Sara interrupted, her face radiating a hopefulness that Lily found difficult to comprehend.

The question hung in the air, wafting through the room before Evelyn finally claimed it.

"I feel like I have no choice. Knowing I've never been the person I thought I was—it changes everything. I always envisioned myself powering through the board room. That seems like such a mundane aspiration compared to what I could have if I'm unbound. I mean, did you see what I did, what *we did*, before we were even born?"

Lily felt her frustration wane. No matter how often Evelyn insulted her, she couldn't deny the truth in her words. In the things that mattered, they were more alike than different.

"I feel the same way, you know. Sara, too. I didn't have all the finery you had, but none of us can deny what we saw. I'm scared as hell but ready to feel how I'm meant to feel," Lily said, shooting an apologetic glance at Sara for poaching her line.

Sara rose from the bed and extended a hand to each of them.

***

For the first time, Lily, Evelyn, and Sara were an united front. Lily had no idea how long the camaraderie would last, but she felt better knowing that for now, they were all on the same page.

Brigit looked up the moment Lily turned the corner into the kitchen.

"Please have a seat. I was about to make a cuppa before bed. Would you care for any?" She pointed to the table laid for four.

"We'd love some," Sara answered, taking a seat.

Brigit joined them seconds later with a kettle full of steaming, fragrant tea.

"Magic has its practical uses," she said with a wink as she poured hot tea into their mugs. The room filled with the calming scent of lemon balm. Setting the kettle on a knit square in the center of the table, Brigit took the remaining seat between Lily and Evelyn. She raised her eyebrows in question.

Sara, their self-appointed triplet spokeswoman, took the lead. "We've decided to do the unbinding. But we still have many questions. First of all, will it hurt?"

Despite the effects of her first magical experience, Lily hadn't yet wondered if the unbinding would hurt. She was thankful that at least one of them went to the trouble of having "many questions." *I sleep and Sara comes up with a game plan. Way to contribute to the team.*

Brigit beamed at the three of them. The transformation on her face from reserved to joyful was astounding. While pretty before, when lit up from within Brigit looked ethereal.

"You've no idea how happy that makes me. I've prayed to the goddess for years that I'd see you again, that we'd set our relationships to right, and that you'd find your way among our people. Thank you for giving me the chance. I know this was a lot to take in, but you've shown you have open minds and ready hearts by saying yes. Both qualities you will need in the months to come." She paused and wiped her eyes.

"As for your questions, I can only hope I'll be able to answer them. Your binding is the only one I've ever performed. As you were unable to talk, I'm unsure if you felt pain, though I'd prefer to think it was a painless experience."

Brigit's gaze fell on Lily, and she felt her face redden. *I'm the weak one in her eyes*, she thought.

"How does it work? The mechanics, I mean," Sara plowed on.

"Bindings and their inverse, unbindings, take best during full moons. We missed that window but she's still rather on the full side. We'll take advantage of that and do the unbinding tomorrow if you three are amenable. It will look exactly as your binding looked twenty-one years ago. Three circles of three, with myself in the center. As caster and the life to whom your magic is bound, it's imperative that I have equal access to each of you. The first and smallest circle from the center will be composed of you three. My sisters will form the next circle. They'll act as the muscle, and protect us if need be. The final circle will be Nora, Fiona, and Morgane, the very three who were tasked with taking you from this place.

Their primary goal is to create a barrier between us and the outside world. This is quite difficult and important. We have no idea how magic pent up so long will act. It's imperative as little energy as possible be allowed to leave the perimeters we've set for our circle. We must keep your existence a secret for as long as possible and not send up loads of sparks or grow a forest twenty kilometers east."

"Sooo, who exactly are we fighting? The prophecy mentioned a fata king? Is that like a nationality I've never heard of?" Evelyn's eyes were still red, but her voice had regained some of its strength and bluntness.

Brigit's face darkened. "It's late and that tale is too long for tonight. Tomorrow when my sisters are here—Mary has spent years studying, preparing what she could for you. Rest assured you will know everything we know before the unbinding; I only wish it was more. I will tell you that we believe your unbinding will set in motion events millennia in the making."

"Oh, is that all?" Evelyn asked dripping sarcasm.

"I don't understand the secrecy. If we're about to save humanity from a timeless night, which sounds like mass deaths to me, wouldn't people want to know who they are up against? Why leave this to us? It turns out we don't even know ourselves very well, let alone each other," Sara said looking troubled.

"The history of our people is bound to the strongest forces on the planet. Non-magic folk could never believe that; most hardly believe in magic at all nowadays. Magic shows how powerless they are. It frightens them. They'd deny, deny, deny, and then try using bombs, weapons, and war—all useless against the forces we are up against. No, my dears, this a fight for the old powers. The new ones have no place here," Brigit said, looking as if the very thought exhausted her. "I promise you will understand more tomorrow, but for now I must retire. It's been a long, emotional day for all of us. Please make yourselves at home. Eat whatever you like. The bath's next to my room, towels are under the sink. I'll leave the door cracked open so you know which one." Her knees popped as she stood.

"Wait!" Lily cried, knowing she'd be unable to sleep without the answer she needed most. "What happened to our father?"

Brigit shrank in on herself before them. "Your father knew what we did and why we did it. He consented, but couldn't live with the guilt and sorrow of giving you up. After we lost track of Sara he changed. He stopped taking care of himself and thought little of his own life. He contracted pneumonia and did not seek medical help. Refused even our own family's potions and assistance. He told me right before he died that the pain of not knowing you and that he couldn't save you from your fate drove him to it. I blame myself every day for that. Aengus died when you three were six years old. I can tell you with surety that he thought of you every day, until the day he died."

*He's gone. I'll never know him,* Lily thought as sorrow blanketed the room.

"I'm sorry to hear that," Sara said, her voice cracking. "He seemed like such a good man and father."

"The best I've ever known," Brigit croaked.

Evelyn coughed uncomfortably, "So is there anything we can do to prepare for the unbinding?"

Brigit raised her watery gaze, her head tilting as she considered Evelyn's question. "I expect it would be easier if you three took the morning to get to know one another. As you'll soon learn, stronger bonds make for stronger magic. Sleep well."

# *A History of Witches*

The cottage was still, its silence punctuated only by the sound of Sara's heavy breathing. Easing herself from the bed, Lily shed her night clothes, pulled on a shirt and pants, and tiptoed out the door. The living room was empty and serene, bathed in soothing morning light. She walked to the window. Some of the flowers in Brigit's garden were still asleep, closed in on themselves, like the women inside the cottage. A gurgle punctuated the morning calm and Lily cringed. The last thing she wanted to do was wake everyone by clanging about pots and pans, but her stomach had other ideas. She was ravenous. *Maybe I can find bread to tide me over until the others wake up,* she thought hopefully.

Rounding the corner of the stone hearth, Lily jerked to a stop and inhaled sharply. Gwenn and Aoife sat at the table with two steaming cups of tea. Neither noticed Lily's arrival, absorbed as they were with a mess of papers in front of them.

"Morning," Lily said, her voice plugged up with sleep.

"Was wondering when we'd see one of you. Brigit's a late sleeper and we thought it best someone be up to help cook you breakfast," Gwenn said. She looked up from the stacks, a sleepy smile on her heart-shaped face that so resembled Lily's own. "Pity for you Mary isn't the one cooking. So what'll it be? We've got everything you can think."

"Just something to tide me over until the others wake up. Tea and toast?" Lily said trying her best to focus on the women's—*her aunts'*—faces and not the strange manuscripts on the table.

"Tea and toast it is," Gwenn said, bustling into the kitchen.

"You slept well?" Aoife asked. "Generally the more difficult a time someone has with ceremens, mind magic to you, the better they sleep. The brain uses more energy than any other organ, so messing with it can knock a person out for quite a while."

"Out like a light. Even after my nap," Lily said taking a seat next to Aoife, who smelled strongly of pepper and ginger.

Aoife nodded and pulled a handful of papers closer to her.

"What's all this?"

"Old myths, legends, fairy tales, even a couple primary documents. We've been collecting them for years. Most are Mary's finds, though I've done my share of research, too." She plucked out a particularly old-looking scrap of paper. "This one here is my favorite. I found it in a crumbling Albanian church."

Lily held the paper with nimble fingers. It was thin, with a texture unlike anything she'd ever felt. It was also, without a doubt, the oldest thing she'd ever touched. Words lined the paper's frayed edges, as indecipherable to Lily as Chinese—or, she thought, half of what Brigit and her sisters said. She squinted at a drawing in the middle of the document, the one thing she could make sense of. It was faded and almost ludicrously small, but Lily thought she understood why Aoife had shown it to her. The illustration depicted three women standing in a circle, hands clasped together. Two smaller solid circles hovered, protected within the confines of their arms. A stick man stood atop one of the circles, while an undefined blob with a roughly drawn face stood atop the other. Above each woman was a small symbol.

"What do those mean?" Lily pointed at the symbols as a plate of toast smothered with gold butter and a cup of tea were set before her.

Aoife grinned, and Lily realized she had played right into her hands.

"Those are ancient Sumerian symbols for earth, water, and fire. It's one of the few pieces we've found that correlates with the prophecy."

"That's enough, Aoife. We can't be telling her what we know before the other two, and certainly not without Mary. It isn't right," Gwenn said, glaring at her sister.

Aoife looked as if Christmas, or whatever witches celebrated, had been canceled.

Lily shrugged, unfazed. She was sure whatever Aoife was about to tell her would still be insane and unbelievable a few hours from now. She sipped her tea. Her eyes popped opened. A dozen distinct, mouthwatering flavors were rolling over her tongue.

"Oh my God . . . what is this tea?"

"Ah, you like that, eh? That's our Brig's Irish breakfast blend. All your traditional ingredients, but Brig grows everything here. Plus she adds holy basil for a twist," Gwenn said, her eyebrows raised. "I'd sooner climb Mt. Kilimanjaro than blend my own tea. Our Brig has a knack for it, though."

Lily nodded. It was close to being the best tea she'd ever had. *Close, but not quite*, she thought, unwilling to place it above Em's homemade blends. Those would always be the best.

A floorboard creaked, and Lily turned to see Evelyn and Sara hovering at the edge of the dining room.

"Morning?" Sara asked, clearly unsure if she was interrupting something.

"Good morning, my dears!" Gwenn called from the kitchen. "Aoife, let's get those papers out of the way and help me make these girls a proper breakfast." She fluttered her hands and the papers arranged themselves into neat piles before soaring out of the room.

"I suppose we'll be able to do that by next week," Evelyn muttered, pulling a cashmere wrap around herself.

"Feel better?" Sara asked, eyeing Lily with concern.

"I'm fine. What do you two think about going out to the lake today? Brigit mentioned we should bond a bit," Lily said, steering the subject away from her mortifying experience with mind magic.

"I'm in," Sara said, wrapping her hands around a mug of tea Aoife placed in front of her.

Lily looked at Evelyn and was shocked to see something akin to shyness in her eyes. Or maybe she was still half asleep; it was hard to tell.

"Sure," Evelyn said with a shrug.

"Great. How about we head down after breakfast and showers? Does that work with your plans to brief us, Aoife? Gwenn?"

"Sounds grand," Aoife said, her head bobbing to a beat only she could hear as she chopped a scallion into irregularly sized chunks. "Mary's organizing and going over the majority of her papers at home. She did most of the research, and that's quite a large job. She won't be here before three. We'll have our chat, relax, and eat supper. From there it's down to waiting for the moon to show herself."

Conversation slowed to a lull as Aoife and Gwenn set plates of fluffy omelets, buttery hash browns, and beans before them. Despite the strangeness of having beans for breakfast, Lily inhaled it all. *Not quite Em's, but pretty good,* she thought. *I guess when you have magic you can be good at anything you like. Shit, why not abracadabra and take over the world?*

Gwenn chuckled, earning her a pointed glare from Aoife.

"What's funny?" Sara asked.

"Oh, only thinking to meself," Gwenn said glancing sheepishly at Lily.

"Lily, if you're done, why don't you take the first bath? There are a couple hair dryers under the sink. We don't want you three going out with wet heads now. Mornings here tend to have a nip to them," Aoife said, scooping up Lily's empty plate and herding her from the room.

***

"It was like showering in glacier water," Evelyn proclaimed, tying a plush scarf over her damp braid as they left the house.

"You can have the first shower next time," Lily said, hoping to smooth over Evelyn's sour mood.

The trio trudged to the lake armed with a blanket, a huge thermos full of tea, and a heaping basket of food that Gwenn had thrust upon them despite their protestations they couldn't eat another bite. Lily relished being outside after the cramped quarters of Fern Cottage. The air was the perfect temperature, punctuated by cool breezes that took her breath away. The small lake lay a quarter mile from the cottage at the edge of the forest. The stretch of land between the lake and Fern Cottage was a rugged mix of tended garden, unmaintained grasses, and a few bushes.

"You'd think they'd do some landscaping out here. At least cut the grass and get rid of these scraggly looking bushes," Evelyn said, hitting a bush with her hand as she walked by.

"Don't count on it," Sara said, her copper eyes glittering in the bright sun. "I bet they'd cut off a finger before cutting a fairy bush down."

"*Fairy bushes*?" Evelyn asked, her eyes wide. "You are joking, right? Adults don't believe in fairies!"

"Like they don't believe in witches?" Sara said, half her lip curved up in a lopsided smile. "Like Brigit said, the Irish are cautious about their superstitions. A lot of them wouldn't admit it outright, but yeah, they believe in fairies."

"How 'bout here?" Lily asked as they approached a relatively manicured spot near the lake.

They settled in, and within seconds Lily found herself playing with her corner of the blanket, flattening and rolling it in her hands repeatedly. *How do you force yourself to bond with someone you're not sure you even like?* she wondered, stealing a glance at Evelyn, who was staring at the lake. *If it were only Sara and me, this would be so much easier.* Awkward seconds became minutes. Despite being stuffed, Lily debated searching the picnic basket for a snack or at least something different for her hands to play with.

"So, I guess I'll start then?" Sara asked, breaking the ice. "I've already had two families; this is my third. I'm a military brat, so no real home, no real family either, come to think it. My adoptive family, the one I actually thought of as my adoptive family, only chose me for my hair color. Apparently, there was a shortage of ginger orphans at the time. My adoptive mother is a redhead and wanted a child she could pass off as her own at new military posts. Fewer questions that way. They were infertile and quite ashamed of it. My father didn't care what kid they got as long as it made her happy. He had enough connections to secure my adoption quickly and easily. My childhood was spent moving from base to base. At each new base I was told to lie about my family being my biological family, a situation that practically ensured I never felt a true connection to anyone. The first time I felt I belonged was when I attended Princeton. At least there people were into the same stuff I was. Being here is the second time I've felt that way. Though it's weird and more than a little scary, I can't say I wouldn't want to be here. Or be meeting you two."

Lily gawked at Sara's matter-of-factness. She'd never heard anyone describe their life in such a detached, cold way. Lily found it impossible to correlate with the vibrant, caring person before her.

"So, Lily, what about you? I'm curious to hear all about the commune," Sara said.

Lily had been mildly anxious about telling her story since Brigit mentioned they should bond. Despite having a happy childhood, she found she didn't always like talking about it. The dynamics of a commune were unconventional, and Lily had found many people distrusted the unconventional. Unfortunately, those people were usually the same people who had no qualms letting her know what they thought of her home. *Here goes nothing*, Lily thought, launching into the past. Sara and Evelyn turned out to be a good audience, laughing, nodding, and scowling in all the right parts. Lily even found herself telling them about Liam. How he'd seemed so perfect. How his amazing violet flecked eyes had mesmerized her. And how he'd turned on her, growing violent in the span of a night.

"The commune sounds amazing," Sara sighed. "Rena, Em, Annika, and Selma sound so interesting."

"They were my pillars growing up. So many other women came and went, but those four were always there looking out for me."

"And Liam. What an asshole! You did the right thing getting out of there. Even if he hadn't gotten in your face, the way he said it," Sara shivered. "That gives me the creeps!"

Lily shuddered as she remembered his words. *"Rest assured, I'll uncover your secrets." Who the hell says something like that anyhow?*

"So, I guess I'm up," Evelyn sighed. "Though I probably can't tell you anything you haven't already found online."

"We've been busy dealing with our own issues, Evelyn. Plus there's no internet, so how could we have?" Sara said kindly.

Evelyn cocked her head as if considering their lack of preconceived notions.

Lily bit back the sarcastic remark on the tip of her tongue. How strange it would be to be so rich, so searchable. The thought made her cringe.

And suddenly, Evelyn was spilling her guts. It was odd to hear Rockefellers, Kennedys, and Clintons referred to as playmates, classmates, and family friends. Evelyn's parents were loving and encouraging of their daughter's quirks. Yet they made it clear that networking with the right people was paramount to success. And success was the end goal. Lily felt sure they would have been shocked by Evelyn's current means of networking: A scheme that relied on Evelyn using her beauty to get to know promising businessmen. Lily sat enthralled as Evelyn regaled them with the story of her latest conquest, a Russian oil tycoon named Dmitry, who ended up revealing damning secrets to get in her pants.

"Of course I left alone that night. What do I care if he has blue balls?" Evelyn smirked. "I wouldn't want to give him any ammo to fight back with later on."

Lily could only marvel at the confidence Evelyn exuded about her life in New York. *She must be damn good at what she does*, Lily thought wistfully. She had never felt so sure about her own future, especially recently. *If I had even an ounce of that confidence, I could rule the world.*

"It's strange, don't you think? You have more money and privilege than I'll ever see, but you're the one that had the normal childhood, compared to Lily and me." Sara said.

"You know . . . I hadn't thought of it that way, but you're right. I suppose being rich is more normal than growing up in a commune or what happened to you," Evelyn said, an easy smile growing on her face.

"It's almost three," Lily said, glancing at her runners watch and stretching her legs. Hours of talking had felt like minutes. "You guys feel up for a walk around the lake? I'm dying for some exercise. It helps me think."

"I'm going to head in. I'd like to try to call my parents or at least the office if the witches will allow me to do so," Evelyn said.

"I'm going to meditate." Sara motioned to a rock jutting out over the edge of the lake, her hands already running over her mala beads. "Come get me when you're ready to go in, will you?"

Lily nodded. "See you soon."

She hugged the banks of the lake as she walked, breathing in the scent of algae mixed with mud and reveling in the solitude she knew would be short lived. The past twenty-four hours astounded her and something told her the punches weren't going to stop anytime soon. Usually being outside helped Lily forget her worries right away, but not this time. Questions began to swarm her mind. Anxiety bloomed in her chest, shortening her breath and slicking her palms. *What's the big secret? Who's looking for us? What else were are we going to learn?*

All of a sudden, she was running. *Five minutes*, she thought, her eyes on the expansive field before her. *Five minutes to move, to clear my head, and then I'll get Sara. We'll be back in no time.*

She'd worn the wrong shoes, and her jeans were too tight, but it didn't matter. As Lily flew over the uneven ground, she felt like she could handle anything the witches threw at her. A white picket fence that presumably indicated Brigit's property line appeared in front of her. *Maybe I'll hop the fence and go a little further? Who's going to care all the way out here if I run a little on their land?* she thought. She covered the space easily and with the muscle memory instilled in her from high school hurdling leapt.

"Shit!" Lily cried, falling awkwardly short of the fence, one leg bent at a ninety-degree angle against the wood. *What the hell*?

She looked around as if to spot some huge animal that had run in front of her, knocked her leg out of place, and scurried off without her noticing. She was alone.

Then it hit her. *It's enchanted,* she thought. She lifted her leg again and it stopped, having come up against an invisible barrier.

The laugh escaped her before she knew it was there, echoing through the empty countryside. *I guess I'll have to get used to running into walls here*, she thought, turning on her heels and sprinting back to the lake.

***

Lily and Sara could hear the buzz of excitement radiating out of Fern Cottage all the way from the garden.

"There they are! We were wondering when you'd make it back. Saw you running like the wind out there, Lily," Gwenn said, green eyes twinkling, as Lily and Sara opened the front door.

"I'd reached my limit," Lily replied with forced nonchalance as she hung her jacket. The shock of hitting an enchanted fence had faded. Now, Lily found she was unsure how she felt about it, and even more unsure if she wanted to share her concerns. *Is it meant to keep others out or us in?* she wondered.

"It's there to keep out those who have no business being here," Aoife said. "Most will feel a pull in another direction leading them to skirt the property line before they even reach the fence. The fence itself, besides keeping people out, acts as a mirage of sorts. It renders the cottage invisible to those who haven't explicitly been told of its existence. Brigit's property will appear as a dark, foreboding wood. We put most of these spells in place after you three were born and kept them as a precaution. You need not worry, you'll not be held here against your will."

The tightness in Lily's chest lifted.

"Shall we get started?" Mary asked, waiting until Lily situated herself on the couch. "So far you've seen only what we've witnessed with our own eyes. The facts, as it were. But tonight we venture into theory. Aoife and I spent years combing libraries, coven archives, church collections, and the minds of our fellow witches for information pertaining to the prophecy you heard last night and a volume referred to as Seraphina's tome. We didn't have as much as we would like to go on, but we did have a few keywords we could use."

"We began by searching for any mention of fata, Hecate, Lilith, Eve, and Seraphina," Aoife said, taking over seamlessly. "As you may imagine, some of those words yielded more results than others. Eve and Hecate are revered and demonized throughout history and religion. Lilith was a bit more rare but by no means unheard of. Our white whale was fata, and we found no mention of the word in the libraries or archives we searched."

"Any record from a *reputable* archive, that is," Mary corrected, clearly enjoying herself. "It was only when we ventured into the libraries scorned by academia and the larger churches that we got lucky. We found the term fata littered here and there, mostly in long-running coven archives of Eastern Europe and Northern Africa. It even cropped up in a small number of ancient pagan churches. Thanks be to those clergymen who couldn't bear to throw out the heretical material. Well, heretical in their eyes—"

"And then there were the elders," Aoife interrupted, steering Mary off a tangent.

"To be sure," Mary nodded, "The elders were a wealth of knowledge, especially once we knew which covens to seek out."

Mary pulled a thin stack of papers from a bright red laptop bag that matched her tunic and tennis shoes. The smell of old paper wafted up mixing with Mary's scent of grapefruit and rain as she set the stack on the table. "We hit gold with these."

Lily leaned forward. There couldn't be more than ten sheets of paper there, some of which displayed only one illustration. *How much information could they have gotten from that?* she wondered.

"Can we touch them?" Sara asked, her eyes shining with reverence.

"Aye, after we go over them you'll have your fill. They don't look like much, but these few pages pack a wallop. And they're backed by dozens more Mary wasn't able to take." Aoife's tone left Lily with the feeling that the confiscation of these materials had not been sanctioned by their previous owners.

"This one is my favorite," Mary said, plucking a sheet from the stack and holding it up for all to see.

The sheet was filled with Egyptian symbols, its colors still vibrant despite its obvious age and clear lack of proper preservation techniques. Like the paper Aoife had shown Lily that morning, it depicted three women with their arms outstretched to link hand in hand. One wore a cape of blue waves that mirrored the blonde ripple of her hair and startling blue of her eyes. The middle woman was depicted as the smallest and also the most frightening to behold. Fire blazed from the top of her head and out of her eyes as she stared at the viewer, unyielding and fierce. A smile played on the lips of the third woman, whose dark hair cascaded down a green cloak to mix with the flora they stood upon.

"Is that Earth?" Sara asked, pointing behind the women to a blue circle Lily hadn't noticed.

"And they are shielding it? Protecting it from that?" Sara continued, pointing to a smaller red circle on the corner of the page.

Lily had thought it a slip of the artist's hand or even a drop of dried blood. Looking closer she saw it was intricately decorated. Different colors of ink dotted the surface to indicate mountains and crevices. It was a planet.

"Aye," Aoife repeated, grinning.

"It looks so old," Sara whispered, looking as if she wanted to reach out and pluck the page from Mary's fingers.

"We had it dated in a laboratory. It hails from around 45 B.C.," Mary said, blue eyes twinkling.

"That piece of paper is from before the birth of Jesus?! And it's sitting *here*? On this coffee table?" Evelyn's mouth gaped as she looked down at the water-stained and chipped table in horror.

"And the tale it tells is far more ancient," Mary said, pointing to the indecipherable hieroglyphics. "Would you like to hear it? I had it translated by a witch gifted in ancient languages." She pulled a new piece of computer paper from the stack and, taking their silence as confirmation, began to read.

***

*The History of Witches*

*Transcribed from memory by*

*Amenia Trypheana, High Priestess of the Coven of Isis*

*Translated by Bahiti Basara*

*"Many years ago, on the red planet of Hecate, a great king*

*named Dimia ruled what remained of the fata race. Millennia of few fata choosing to die led to a pilfering of Hecate's soul, the very source from which fata obtained their magic. Most of the young began to find the simplest magical feats impossible. The king knew they had sown all they could from Hecate. In an act both brave and rash, he banned the birth of any new fata until he found a solution. The king knew that if fata were to thrive once more, they would need a new home. A home full of power that his kind could harness to become great again, as they had been in the time of the ancients. A new world to call their own.*

*"Dimia looked to his daughters, Lilith, Eve, and Seraphina, as the last hope for their kind. As triplets born full of magic in a time of infertility, their birth was hailed an omen of greatness to come. Dimia ensured they received the best and his daughters became the strongest fata on Hecate since the time of the ancients.*

*"It was only when Dimia received a testament from a seneschal by the name of Noro that the king thought he had found a solution. Noro had but one great skill with which to please his ruler. The midnight blue fata could send his pneuma, an entity much like the human soul, outside his body to explore. It was during a recent journey that he had found a planet much like Hecate. He called this planet Earth, and as Dimia listened to Noro's tale, he realized Earth was the answer.*

*"Dimia hatched a plan. His daughters would travel to Earth, body and pneuma, and bring over the rest of their kind if Earth proved hospitable. If they could not thrive there, he knew no other fata stood a chance. He informed his daughters, who were dutiful and agreed to fulfill their father's wishes.*

*"It is said once they made the journey to Earth they traveled far and wide, accumulating power and seeking a land that called to them. It was only when they came across a tribe of men that they stopped, found mates, and built a life. From these unions the first witches were born. Half human, half fata, the first witches were rumored to resemble fata and humans equally, though most disguised themselves as humans through magic. In time, the human appearance prevailed—though many believe that the fata pneuma, or soul, has remained with us and is the source of a witch's magic.*

*"The sisters died on Earth with their father's wishes unfulfilled. Some say their strength never recovered from their journey. Others postulate Earth could not fulfill their needs for magic as Hecate did. Whatever the case, we witches give thanks to the three: our ancestors and mothers of our magical lineage."*

***

"So putting this together with the prophecy, and the whole timeless night thing which sounds a whole lot like death to me . . . you're basically telling me aliens are looking for us because they think we can do what Lilith, Eve, and Seraphina did? Create a . . . portal between Hecate, a planet . . . not a goddess, and Earth?" Sara asked, her voice cracking as she worked it out.

"Searching for centuries, I'd dare say," Mary agreed, placing the parchment back on the stack. "Since finding this gem, we've come to discover that there is an alternate side to this tale and those willing to support it. They have a small network of spies. Many of them are witches who wish to align with the fata side of their ancestry rather than humans. They believe that if the fata make it to Earth, humans, even witches or other supernaturals, would be relegated to the lowest caste in a new realm. In return for their services, the spies hope to be placed above other humans and supernaturals in social status. Or if humans are killed off, the spies hope to be spared for their loyalty. These spies search for witches possessing extraordinary power, specifically hedgecrossers. For the last two decades, there have been rumors circulating about witches of untold power in hiding. We believe your binding has something to do with this. A magical vacuum of that size and magnitude would have been felt for hundreds of miles. Questions were sure to arise."

"Hedgecrossers?" Sara asked, her brows furrowed.

"You've heard of astral travel? When a person can send their spirit to travel this world?" Aoife asked.

A vague image of an out-of-body experience she had read about online popped into Lily's mind and she nodded.

"Well, a hedgecrosser is a witch whose spirit can cross between worlds in addition to exploring this one. They're rare. Only about one in a million are born with the gift, and even with natural proclivity, it takes years of practice to become adept at hedgecrossing. In the past, some chose to disregard their gift entirely, because it came at a cost. More than one hedgecrosser has lost their soul during travels. Taking into account the power you three demonstrated at birth and the prophecy, it's possible you may be hedgecrossers."

*Holy crap*, Lily thought, her stomach dropping at the terrifying idea of losing her soul.

"You said the binding caused a vacuum. What will happen after the unbinding?" Evelyn asked, her voice shaking.

*They'll come for us. They'll try to force us to open a door . . . a freaking portal between worlds! We'd have to allow aliens—fata—and then a timeless night. Death. The fata king wants to kill off humans so his kind can have the planet*, Lily realized before Evelyn had even finished her question. The idea was ludicrous. She didn't know the first thing about magic! How could anyone expect her to open a portal to another world?

The triplets fidgeted in their seats as Mary revealed a world simmering beneath their own, a world composed of creatures that lived only in fairy tales. Kings, gods, and goddesses from all eras and cultures were intertwined, connected in some way to Lilith, Eve, and Seraphina. Hecate, Eve, and Lilith became popularized and demonized in religions to fit the evolving beliefs of humans. Witches and other supernaturals were hunted by humans for their otherness, though Mary found these witch hunts far less interesting than the ones led by other supernaturals. Those supernatural hunts targeted the strongest witches of an age to suss out the second coming of the three.

"What if we change our mind and remain bound? If we live normal lives, the portal would never open, right? I mean, it's lasted this long." The words flew from Lily's mouth, cutting off Mary's retelling of a bloody Grecian exploit involving Empusa and Amon, infamous, ancient, and powerful vampire twins, in search of a witch rumored to be a hedgecrosser.

No one spoke.

"It doesn't work like that, does it?" Lily asked, her face burning as the fear in her voice grew.

Brigit shook her head, her face grave. "My binding has lasted twenty-one years. That's a long time, but it won't hold for much longer. Already I can feel the binding cracking and fraying along the edges. You may have felt it yourself as unexplainable sensations in your body. Especially if you were under stress—"

"Like pain?" Lily croaked, recalling the mysterious aches and pains that had plagued her last months of college.

Brigit nodded. "Pain is possible. After all, your power yearns to be free. But you're adults now, and I no longer have the same jurisdiction I did when you were babes. The binding may last another five years or another week. It may even last different lengths of time for each of you, no one can know. What is certain is that in time the binding will break and your magic will be free. We didn't tell you this last night so as not to bully or overwhelm you into a decision. It would have been too much pressure after everything else you learned. Above all, I wanted to make sure if you chose to do the unbinding it was *your choice.* That you wanted to do it. The implications of you being the ones to choose are not only practical, but ceremonial. You'll be claiming your own power. Choice and intent play a large role in magic. I would never want to force you into something you don't want to do." Brigit sucked in a large breath and made eye contact with each of them before continuing.

"If you want to change your minds and go back to your lives, we can work around the situation. Your lives will never be quite like before of course, but we can make them as close as possible. We'd put wards up around where you live in hopes that no one finds you. We could monitor your magic and teach you the basics of how to control it so you can live a near normal life. We won't leave you stranded no matter what you decide."

"But we're twenty-one. Are you saying we've been in danger for three years?" Evelyn interrupted.

"The traditional age of adulthood in Ireland is twenty-one. I bound you to the tradition of your homeland's soil, for it's from here that your power stems."

"So you bought us time, gave us a normal life for as long as you could," Sara mused, turning her eyes on Brigit. "But anyone looking for us for centuries wouldn't care if we knew how to use our magic or not. They'd force us to learn what they wanted. Probably teach us their own warped side of things. At least here we can learn to defend ourselves. The alternative, being stuck behind wards, always waiting for someone to pounce . . . It's a half-life."

Brigit nodded, clearly unwilling to defend herself, and the room fell into silence.

*What would Rena want me to do,* Lily wondered. Her answer presented itself as if Rena was sitting there with her. *She'd want me to be bold. Rena's never taken the easy path, the safe life. Sara's right, I can't live with a half-lived life. No matter how scared I am, I couldn't live with myself if all this came true.*

"I need some more information. For starters, we've seen the prophecy, and I don't think anyone could make that shit up, but how do we know these are legit?" Evelyn said, gesturing at the pages. "Anyone in the past could have written anything. Maybe they just wanted to draw?"

Aoife gave her a small grin. "And I thought Sara would be the one to ask how we cross-checked our sources. Aside from the fact that these documents correlate with obscure myths and stories from cultures the world over you mean? I suppose the simplest answer to your question is cults."

Lily's mouth fell open. *We're relying on information provided by cults?*

"Quit trying to shock them, Aoife," Mary said, waving her hand at her sister. "Thousands of years ago a cult meant something different than it does today. Back then it was simply a group dedicated to the worship of a particular god or goddess. Once we found documents containing our keywords, we began to question those who held the documents about past members, specifically if their members had ever worshiped Lilith, Eve, or Seraphina. No one had a clue what we were on about until we came across a very old Alexandrian coven."

"Did they worship Lilith or Eve?" Sara asked, eyes alight once more with curiosity.

"Neither," Mary said smiling. "Naturally, they'd heard the names, but it was the third and most elusive sister their members worshiped: Seraphina, your namesake and maker of the volume mentioned in Mary's prophecy. Even today the Alexandrian coven believes the triplets to be the first witches, though that's about all they know. Local legend has it Seraphina's story died with a witch named Hypatia. She was a librarian for the great Library of Alexandria and a cult member herself. Alexandrian coven rumor claims Hypatia secreted Seraphina's tale into the library for protection. When the building burned, so did the scroll. But Hypatia was a clever witch and knew how important her ward was to humanity's survival. She memorized the original word for word should a tragedy ever befall it. She penned it back into history from memory, then placed it under a spell coupled with a prophecy. A spell that could be broken only when the three with the power of the original three were born. A secret book bound with a prophecy delivered at birth. Sounds a bit like your birth, does it not?"

"I need time to think," Evelyn said, shooting up from the couch, her face set in hard lines. "When is the unbinding?"

"Be ready at dusk," Mary answered, taken aback by Evelyn's abrupt mood swing.

Lily watched her retreat, barely overcoming the urge to follow. She was sure Evelyn wouldn't welcome the intrusion. No matter how chummy they were that morning, they were still little more than strangers.

"I need time, too. I'm going to take a walk," Lily said, before adding, "Want to join, Sara?"

"I'll stay." Sara drew her legs onto the couch, hugging them close to her chest. "That is, if you guys don't mind? I have so many questions."

***

Lily shivered as the wind whipped over her skin, stealing her cocoon of body heat in an instant. She rubbed her hands over her bare arms, wishing she had thought to grab a sweater but unwilling to turn around. Before she knew it, she was back at the lakeside. It looked different now, colder, more mysterious. *Like the world,* Lily thought, stopping at the edge of the forest to gaze in. *Not only do I have a new family, I have an entire magical legacy. And it's up to me to save humanity? How the hell does that happen? Brigit and her sisters look far more capable and witchy. They could take the fata on. I mean, how do people not notice they are different?*

"People think the same of you, I'd wager to guess."

Lily started and turned to see Gwenn, a sweater clenched in her hand.

"So you can read minds?" Lily asked, taking the proffered sweater and pulling it over her head. A scent she could now identify as holy basil clung to her aunt as Gwenn fell into an easy cross-legged position beside Lily.

"A bit. I'm not as gifted as Aoife or Brig, but I hear yours well enough. You're rather open right now. Could be the stress of all you're learning. Mind you, I try not to. Even among witches it's considered rude to eavesdrop. I only wanted to make sure I wasn't interrupting something I ought not to."

"Can you read Sara and Evelyn's, too?" Lily asked, thinking it strange that the idea of Gwenn reading her mind didn't totally freak her out.

"Their minds are closed to me. I suspect you and I share a common core element, which would make it easier for me to connect with you." Her finger twirled in the air, guiding a buttercup below to spin on its stem. "Earth."

Lily nodded, her gaze traveling from the flower back to the

woods. Even in her ghost form she'd felt it: the surge of energy rushing through her when the oak tree broke through the floorboards.

They sat in silence, watching squirrels dart in and out of the trees. It was quieter here than the commune. Lily felt she could hear the minutiae of twitching ravens' wings and dropping leaves. A deer's appearance from the trees didn't even startle her. She'd sensed the crunching of needles under hooves seconds before it emerged from the tree line.

"Am I more sensitive here?" she asked, locking eyes with the graceful creature.

"It's as Brigit said: Your bind is unraveling. Being in the land of your birth may be rushing it along. Magic, and our ancestral ties to it, run deep here."

"It's all so much. Having another family and sisters, I can handle that easy. I can even handle being a witch. I mean, I've always been a little weird anyways, but saving the world from aliens? I'm not sure I can . . . I haven't done anything that daring, that important. I'm not special enough."

"I have to disagree with the last statement. Ask your family back home, they'll tell you. As for not having done much, well, let's say you're about to do more than you ever dreamed possible." Gwenn stood and brushed grass off her faded jeans. "I'm fancying a kip before the unbinding. Be sure to get some rest yourself. You'll be needing it."

# *The Unbinding*

Lily returned as darkness took over the sky to find the inhabitants of Fern Cottage had grown to include Morgane, Fiona, and Nora. She introduced herself to Fiona before making her way toward Sara, who sat removed on the couch beneath the window.

"Evelyn?" Lily whispered.

"In her room all day."

Lily turned and walked down the hall, aware of Sara's light tread following her.

"Ohhh!" Lily breathed, as Evelyn swung her bedroom door open right when Lily was preparing to knock.

Lily's gaze flitted past the tall blonde to take in the bulging suitcases beside the door. Anxiety rose in her chest and she prepared to bargain.

"Don't we have an unbinding to get to?" Evelyn asked, stepping into the hallway with them.

Lily exhaled. For the first time, she allowed herself to acknowledge what she'd expected to see: an empty room and Evelyn's back as it disappeared through the hedge.

The triplets ate a quick dinner of reheated spaghetti and meatballs, sheathed in nervous silence as the women babbled in the next room.

Shortly after their plates were clean, the witches filed out the door, each touching a wrought iron triquetra hanging by the front door as they left. *Hopefully it's for luck,* Lily thought as her hand brushed the cold iron.

She followed the witches as they led her back to the forest and into the trees. A feeling of calm settled over Lily as the wood grew dense. Words flew around her. Fairy tree, hawthorn, Sirius, and shields, but she caught few of them as the rustling of the leaves and scent of damp earth engulfed her.

She knew they were nearing the unbinding site long before they set foot in it. A foreboding residue clung to this part of the forest. The feeling intensified with each step Lily took in Brigit's path. She turned to see Sara's eyes darting from side to side and Evelyn's arms crossed over her body. They felt it, too.

Just when Lily thought the urge to turn around had grown too strong to resist, she stepped into a small paddock and her jitters vanished. It was unnaturally circular, overgrown with grass, and orbited by tall oak trees. Something had happened here. A distinct void of emotion characterized the spot, as if this clearing was waiting to be filled once more. *Just like us,* Lily thought.

Aoife and Mary set to work, laying the wood they had floated in behind them in the center of the clearing. Lily watched a fire spring up to devour the wood as Aoife bid it. Mary followed, swirling her pointer finger in the air to create a narrow trench around the fire pit. She then lifted her hands to fill the trench with water from the ground.

Lily turned to Gwenn, eager for the next bit of magic.

"My part is done for me," Gwenn said, anticipating the question. Her arms swept wide indicating the lush vegetation all around them.

Earth, water, and fire, all accounted for.

"They've been planning this for years," Sara whispered, sidling up next to Lily. "Aoife told me that wood is from the same oak tree you grew from the floorboards. They used it in the binding and saved some, thinking it might help."

Lily's mouth fell open. *They saved a pile of wood for twenty-one years?*

"I've never seen a spot so suited to Irish lore and magic. See all those mushrooms?" Sara pointed down at a circle of vivid red mushrooms surrounding a tree.

Lily nodded but saw nothing special about a group of mushrooms. At least half the trees in the dell looked identical.

"They're perfect fairy circles, which according to Irish lore means there's probably a fairy city in each oak tree. This little clearing is like an entire fairy world! Did you know oaks were the druids' sacred trees? Witches loved them too. They used to dance beneath them when there was a full moon. Oaks were called the witches tree," Sara said dreamily. "And then there's the moon."

*No explanation needed there*, Lily thought, smiling at Sara's need to share her knowledge as she stretched her chin skyward. Despite not being quite full, Lily had never seen the moon so bright.

"Let's be getting you in your places," Aoife said, coming up behind them and guiding them into position.

Lily watched, amazed by the effort Aoife took to space them equidistant from one another. She then formed an identical circle consisting of herself, Mary, and Gwenn. Morgane, Fiona, and Nora circled the clearing's periphery on their own accord. Brigit stood next to the fire at the heart of the circle. It seemed to Lily that all living things in the forest quieted as they assembled, anticipating the witches' next move. She wondered if the animals and trees could feel it, too—the tension, the crackling of what she could only guess to be magic hovering in the air.

"It appears everything is in order," Brigit said, assessing her surroundings with a keen eye. "Girls, I want to thank you for having the audacity to believe me. For giving me, all of us, a second chance. This may not be pleasant. You will leave this circle changed in ways we cannot imagine."

Lily cast about within herself, a hurried, last-ditch effort to find the parts she liked best and cling to them.

"Let's begin," Brigit said, gripping the hem of her sweater. Her hands trembled as they paused on the soft wool, before pulling the sweater over her head to reveal yards of rope coiled around her torso.

Lily stared, mystified. *How did Brigit managed to get all that rope around her? What was it for?*

Evelyn's gasp ripped through the circle.

Lily's eyes shot up from the rope in time to catch a gleam of metal flying toward Brigit's neck. She lunged forward and her heart sped up as an invisible wire tugged between her shoulder blades.

"Stay," Gwenn whispered, easing Lily into position like a fleshy marionette.

Her body trembled with unused adrenaline as Brigit lopped off a hank of her auburn hair. Lily felt her heart race again when Brigit approached her, her face both powerful and vulnerable. She raised the knife to Lily's hair and snipped a small lock before moving on to Sara and Evelyn.

The strands of blonde, brown, red, and auburn clenched in Brigit's fist, caught the fire's light as Brigit moved back into the circle's center. Lily became distracted by a prism of color—rich violets, blues, and greens—flitting over her arm before disappearing altogether into the night.

When she looked up again it was to see Brigit holding the end of the rope to the flames.

*This is madness. What is she doing?* Lily thought, as the rope caught and her palms began to sweat.

In answer, Brigit's voice cut through the night, clear and eerie, as the flames raced up the rope toward her skin.

"Three circles round, bodies bound, it's now time to release.

My spell unwinds, their magic freed, my spirit finds its peace.

Daughters of Hecate asked of me.

Now's the time of three times three.

I give their magic back to thee.

As I will, so mote it be"

As the final word left Brigit's lips, the mass of rope around her torso caught and the flames began their feast upon flesh. Ignoring the inferno encasing her, Brigit thrust out her hand and dropped the strands of blonde, brown, red, and auburn into the fire.

Lily's skin crawled as the flames dancing upon Brigit's body became multicolored, almost cartoonish. The scent of burning skin began to permeate the fresh air of the woods.

"Solvo!" Brigit screamed. Then, the flaming rope became a snake, wiggling and thrashing in the air as Brigit unwound it from her torso.

Lily's heart hummed and her breath shortened, urging Brigit to hurry, as the stench of burnt flesh surrounded her.

Finally, the last coil unwound and Brigit tossed the flailing rope upon the flames.

A silent scream escaped Lily as Brigit slumped to the ground, her raw skin hitting the dirt with a sickening thud.

Then Lily felt it. The twisting of her insides and spinning of her body through space. She closed her eyes. It was happening. Flashbacks of every carnival ride she ever dared go on came flooding back. She flexed her abdomen, hoping to quell the nausea. She chanced a glance around the circle through slitted eyes. Why was it everyone else was standing still, while she felt like a top?

*Oh my god*, she thought, eyes popping open. *I'm not moving, my insides are!*

She stood rooted in place. Her body trembled violently as a double helix of energy unraveled deep in her groin. The helix unzipped its way up her spine, gaining momentum as it ascended. A curious sensation of leaping came over her and beams of blue light shot from the top of her head. The light illuminated the night sky above before falling to shower the trees around them.

"Whoa," Lily whispered, as smaller beams blasted out of the ends of her fingers and the toes of her shoes and rushed into the dark wood after their predecessor. Lily cast a glance at Evelyn and Sara. *Had the same thing happened to them? she wondered.*

Her questions slid down her throat as the sound of hundreds of boulders cascading down a mountain overtook the quiet forest. The ground cracked to form a crevice that cut Morgane, Nora, and Fiona off from the rest of the circle and lifted the others onto a platform two feet above the forest floor. Small rocks pelted Lily's legs, all the way to her hips, as the earth shook beneath her. Chunks of earth ripped themselves from the ground and flew five feet in the air before falling back down with a thud. Dirt and dust whipped around them like a tornado. Tree branches swayed menacingly above and a dozen stout oaks shot up like dandelions next to their kin to climb heavenward.

*Shit, shit, shit*! Lily's legs flexed, primed for flight.

"STOP!" Gwenn bellowed, and Lily's body seized, controlled by a will that was not her own, as a ring of fire sprang up from the ground behind her.

Evelyn screamed and shook out a smoking sleeve, her eyes wide with terror.

*We're trapped*, Lily thought. Her panic grew as the flames circling the triplets rose to block Aoife, Mary, and Gwenn from sight. Sara's voice cut through the commotion and fear, and Lily pivoted to see Sara, her hands flying through the air in a flamboyant manner. Lily watched in awe as the tiny redhead manipulated the fire, allowing them a momentary glimpse of their aunts. Sara was saving them!

A neon glow flashed in her periphery. Lily gasped when she saw the center bonfire transform into an unnatural green hue before her eyes. The green flame acted like a living being, crawling insidiously from the pit toward Brigit. "Uh, Sara, I think you should—"

"Hebeto!" Aoife howled. A beam of light shot past Lily and the green fire *whined* and retreated into the pit.

"Sara! Stop casting!" Aoife demanded.

The circle of flames shot twenty feet high before falling into embers and dying.

"Sorry! I—"

A roar of wind shook the treetops, overwhelming Sara's apology.

"There!" Evelyn shrieked, pointing into the forest.

Lily gasped. Full-grown trees were collapsing beneath a wave of water fifty feet high. A wave on a trajectory straight for them.

"Shield charm together on three. One. Two. Three!" Mary shouted, her high soprano a whisper over the roar of the water.

"Arma!"

A sparkling silver dome rose up to enclose the circle, joining at the center milliseconds before the first wave crashed upon it.

Lily rose from her protective crouch. Relief flooded through her as the last of the great waves cascaded over the dome. A delicate sound of trickling water surrounded them. The witches released their shields, and Lily choked back a sob.

They were alive! She ran her hands over her body, feeling for anything different, anything *other*. Besides the insane amount of adrenaline coursing through her veins, she felt unchanged. For the first time in what felt like hours, Lily cracked a smile. *Nothing too terrible happened. At least nothing that can't be healed with time*, she thought, turning from her aunts to go to Brigit's aid. She froze.

Deep in the forest a bright blue light barreled toward them, shattering the few oaks and bushes still standing after the tidal wave. The hairs on the back of Lily's neck rose, and her muscles tensed. There was only one thing it could be.

The magic penetrated her mercilessly, pushing past her body's protective barriers to the depths of her heart. An ethereal mix of pain and pleasure rose inside her as magic rolled through her skin, fascia, muscles, and bones. She shuddered at the intensity, at the raw, rebellious energy flowing wild in places where she knew no shape, in the liquid and gasses between her tissues. It was home.

She was whole.

Only later would Lily recall the fall. How her limbs convulsed, her muscles seized and released. How she clenched her jaw so hard it threatened to shatter her teeth. And how three screams pierced the quiet Irish countryside.

***

"Thank the Goddess you're here, Fiona," a worried voice sighed into Lily's consciousness as her eyes eased open. Damp dirt, mounds of it, surrounded her, enclosing her in a small trench.

Forcing herself upright, Lily let out a yelp of pain and collapsed. *Holy hell*, she thought, clutching her chest to numb the stabbing sensation radiating from her heart down her limbs.

"Lily's coming round," a voice said. "Where's the potion?"

Mary rushed over from out of nowhere and raised a canteen to Lily's lips. "Drink this. It'll help."

Lily swallowed and gagged.

"It's awful, I know, but it will work wonders. Drain the canteen; we brought one for each of us," Mary urged, tilting the silver container back.

It tasted terrible, but she knew Mary was right. Already the throbbing in her chest had subsided. She chugged the potion, stopping only for breath.

"It's working. Your eyes are clearing already," Mary said, looking pleased as she sat back on her heels. She wiped the dirt from her face using a soaked sleeve with marginal success.

Lily wondered bleakly if she looked as filthy as Mary did.

"It'll be the forest," Aoife's deep voice called from somewhere past the trench walls, "She's strong here. Let's hope the others recover as well."

Tossing the empty canteen beside her, Lily grabbed the sodden ground. She was determined to sit up, to see what had happened. Her fingers trembled with the effort of lifting her torso.

"Easy now, Lil," Mary said, righting Lily as she swayed.

Aided by Mary's strong arms, Lily pulled herself to her knees and leaned over the side of the muddy trench. Downed trees, puddles masquerading as backyard ponds, and chunks of displaced earth the size of small cars littered the clearing. Brigit, Evelyn, and Sara lay amongst the destruction, limbs splayed out at awkward angles. A metallic scent hung in the air, and Lily's heart lurched when she spotted a large puddle of blood by Brigit's head.

"Is Brigit alive?"

"Brig hit her head on a rock on the way down, and her burns are worse than we'd prepared for. But we have Fiona, and she's a fine healer. She hasn't detected any irreparable damage," Mary said.

"Evelyn and Sara?"

"They're fine. Or they will be when they wake up. They've had a bit of a shock to the system . . . Well I suppose we all had a bit of a shock, didn't we?"

"Did our magic do this?" Lily asked, scanning the destruction again.

"We'll have a time keeping this under wraps. Let's hope none of our enemies were within fifty kilometers of this place tonight." Mary pulled her blonde hair up and back with mud-covered hands.

They knelt there in the muck, taking in the destruction, until suddenly Mary hooked her arms beneath Lily's and helped her to her feet. "You should be over there," she said. "Your sisters will want to see your face when they wake."

*I wouldn't be so sure about that,* Lily thought. She took in the fierce scowl on Evelyn's unconscious face and veered toward Sara.

Aoife was wiping Sara's dirt-caked arms with a cloth when Lily lowered herself to the ground next to her. Sara's face was covered in small burns that trickled down her neck, all the way to her hands.

"She's a brave wee thing. Foolish, but brave. Thinking she could help, but fire . . . well, it's difficult to control, even for the strongest of us," Aoife said without a glance up.

"How did she know what to do?" Lily breathed. The sight of Sara battling the flames would be forever etched in her mind.

"She's already used magic once without knowing, as a child. That's how she escaped the car fire that landed her in foster care. Aye, we know about that. It was the only way she'd have survived such an inferno.

Our best guess is that Sara formed a shield around herself and crawled out of the car. There are always loopholes in bindings—danger to one's life is one. The difference between you and Sara is she already knew the feeling of magic. She remembered it and called it to her when she felt threatened."

"But I thought it all left and came back? That's what hit us right?" Lily said recalling the bright blue light.

"Most of it," Aoife said with a nod. "There's another exception for you. Not all your magic could leave you during the unbinding process, though you can bet it wanted to run free for a bit, pent up as it was. As witches, it's impossible for magic to leave us entirely. A small part has to stay behind. It's part of us always, deep within."

Lily nodded, not quite sure she understood, and took Sara's limp hand in her own. She felt both very close and very inadequate compared to her sister. *I can only hope I catch some of her bravery*, she thought, looking down at the angry marks marring Sara's pale skin. She closed her eyes and began to . . . pray? Were witches allowed to pray? Despite her lack of prayer in the past, now seemed as appropriate a time as any to beg the help of a higher power.

"Goddess be! Look at her eyes," Aoife whispered. "Mary! Over here with the tonic! Sara's waking!"

Lily's eyes flew open and locked onto two bright pennies. *Thank God! Goddess? Oh whatever*, she thought, throwing herself at Sara.

"Ooophh!" Sara grunted.

Lily shot back up.

"I'm sorry! I'm just so relieved you're awake."

"What happened?"

Mary thumped to the ground next to Lily, a cup of vile concoction in her hand.

"It appears we have a fledgling healer on our hands, Mary!" Aoife said, patting Lily on the back. "I wasn't expecting Sara would wake for at least half an hour after she tormented the fire like that."

"Healer? No, I was," Lily paused, she could feel her cheeks growing red. "Well, I was praying . . . I guess."

"Be that as it may, I've no doubt it was your touch that woke her. I performed a body scan not two minutes before. Sara was out cold," Aoife said, watching Sara sit up and drink her tonic unaided. "Go to Evelyn and do the same. Let's hope it will work again. The sooner we make it back to the house, the better. All our protective wards around the clearing are gone."

Lily approached Evelyn warily. Though they had made up, verged on friendship even, Lily still recognized Evelyn for the mercurial being she was.

*Please don't be pissed at me if you wake up*, she thought, grabbing Evelyn's ringed hand in her own and closing her eyes. This time Lily felt the faint spasm. The warming of Evelyn's hand when their skin met. The palpable quickening of Evelyn's pulse, and the sharp sip of breath.

She opened her eyes and saw Evelyn's eyelashes flutter before snapping open with the urgency of a person being woken by a bomb.

"What was that?" she screeched, shooting up before collapsing back into the mud.

"The light?" Lily asked, jumping back and feeling stupid for the question. "It was our magic returning to us. It hit us in the chest, and we passed out."

"Up," Evelyn grunted, holding out her arms to Lily, who stared back dubiously.

Aoife materialized to lift Evelyn from the ground with an ease Lily doubted she'd have been able to pull off.

"As long as you three can walk, we should get moving. The rest of us are going to take turns carrying Brigit. We can't float her out of here. Too many trees, she might hit her head again," Aoife said, glancing back at the sagging form held aloft between Gwenn and Nora.

"Should I try—?" Lily began looking at her hands.

"Brigit's lost a lot of blood, not to mention used up a tremendous amount of power. It's going to take the work of a serious healer to fix her up. We've all the materials at the cottage. Fiona can tend to her there," Aoife said, steering Lily onto the path.

***

The walk to the cottage felt like it took twice as long as the walk to the clearing. Lily, normally surefooted from years of trail running, stumbled at least a dozen times on the uneven forest floor. Evelyn and Sara were even worse off, stopping every few feet to catch their breath.

"I thought we'd never make it," Evelyn sighed dramatically,

tripping through the front door of Fern Cottage and sinking into the couch cushions.

"Clear the table," Fiona said, as the caravan carrying Brigit entered behind them.

Curiosity trumped exhaustion and Lily followed the witches to the dining room.

"Aye, this will be good for you to watch," Aoife said, a grim look on her face. "Our Fiona is the best healer in Ireland. It's a true pity you'll have to settle for me as a teacher most of the time."

It was the first time Lily had looked at Brigit up close since the unbinding. Dried rivers of red ran from Brigit's temples over her high cheekbones and down to her lips. Her body sported many small cuts and bruises surrounded by serious burns and raw, oozing skin. The aroma of metal and burned flesh clung to Brigit. Lily winced. *She looks terrible*, she thought, her hand reaching out instinctively.

Fiona's eyes shot up and Lily pulled her hand back.

"Sorry. I didn't mean—" Lily said, a faint flush creeping up her neck.

"Go on, touch her. It can't hurt," Fiona replied, her hands flying in and out of her medicine bag at lighting speed.

Lily hesitated. The thing was, she wasn't sure she wanted to. She had no idea where this sudden compulsion to touch people was coming from. She'd always considered herself an introvert, fully comfortable around only a select few, none of whom were in Fern Cottage. *It does feel natural, though*, she thought, her hands hovering awkwardly in the air before coming to rest on Brigit's shoulder.

She waited for what felt like hours before finally admitting Aoife had been right. It wasn't going to work. The fact that her talent had failed her, even if she didn't yet understand how it worked, left a bitter taste in her mouth.

"It's alright. We'll get Brig sorted out," Gwenn said, patting Lily's shoulder, her dark green eyes understanding.

*God, I'm getting tired of people reading my mind.*

"We'll teach you how to guard against that soon enough. Right now it's impossible for me not to hear you. Must be the stress of the unbinding. I'd wager even Mary can hear what you're thinking loud and clear. Mar?"

Mary smiled sheepishly. "A bit."

"And she's shit at mind magic," Gwenn said, throwing an apologetic glance at Mary.

"Can you hear the others now, too?"

"Sara's locked up tight. Excellent mind-body connection, that one. Evelyn seems to have control over what we hear, though I doubt even she realizes it."

Lily wrapped her arms around her waist.

"Did you see that, Fiona?" Gwenn asked, staring wide-eyed down at Brigit.

"Her arm. But I wasn't sure, it was so small," Fiona paused as if considering. "Goddess be . . . put your hands back!" She guided Lily's hands to Brigit's stomach, and peered under Brigit's eyelids. "Her pupils are nearly back to normal. The damage must have been worse than we thought, possible brain damage or a hemorrhage. Your magic must have been fixing the worst of it first. Don't move," Fiona instructed as she added bits of leaves and bark to a small, smoking vial.

Lily watched, trying her best to identify the plants Fiona was using. *Maybe my botany degree will be useful after all.*

"It will be most useful, I'm sure," a puff of air drifted past Lily's face, and she looked down to see Brigit smiling weakly up at her.

"You're awake! How do you feel?"

"Like hell, but it was worth it. Seeing this makes it worth it."

"It's not like I actually know what I'm doing," Lily said, trying to tamp down the swell of pride blossoming within her.

Brigit lifted her fingers an inch, waving away Lily's modesty.

"This one saved you, Brig," Fiona said, lifting Brigit's head and guiding a small vial to her lips. "I expect she'll crash any minute with the amount of energy she's expended."

"Um, I do feel a bit tired. I'll go sit down," Lily said as an uncomfortable sensation of being scanned came over her. "Feel better, Brigit."

Aoife followed, and while Lily felt she should mind being followed around like a child, she found she didn't have the energy.

"Where are Sara and Evelyn?"

"I sent them to bed," Aoife said as if she were referring to a couple of five years olds. "You should join them. You look like hell."

"Feel like it, too," Lily said, comforted once again by the Renaesque honesty.

"Go on, get some sleep then. Tomorrow's a big day after all."

"Tomorrow?"

"Aye, tomorrow we start magic lessons."

# *Magic Lessons*

Autumn had always been Lily's favorite season. Stocking up on teas, fuzzy socks, and new pencils were rituals she anticipated as the sun set on summer each year. But in Ireland, things were different. The forest around Fern Cottage had long been overtaken by red and orange before Lily even realized summer had slipped away.

Since the unbinding, Lily had spent almost every waking minute learning and practicing magic. She collapsed into bed each night exhausted, positive her body couldn't take another day. While Lily often thought the aching muscles and frequent fainting spells were reason enough to quit her training, she never went through with it. None of it mattered, when there was the rush. The pure elation she felt after a perfectly executed spell had the ability to erase all the bad from her mind. This reaction had Lily questioning her sanity because for her, executing a perfect spell was rare. After all, she was no Sara. Her youngest sister had yet to falter with any spell, charm, jinx, or hex thrown at her. Lily had nicknamed Sara Hermione, though only in her head.

Healing was by far her favorite branch of magic. This was in no small way related to the fact that it was unequivocally her best subject. It also allowed her free reign in Brigit's fabulous garden.

As Brigit was part earth witch, her garden bloomed year round, unaffected by the changing seasons. It reminded Lily of a fairytale garden, overflowing with exotic flowers, healing herbs, spiraling vines, and berry-laden bushes. Lily spent hours there, sniffing the various herbs and flowers to commit their scents at various stages of development to memory. Her hands grew sensitive to the moisture gradient of mosses and the potential vitality of petals from a newly opened bud. Under Fiona's and Aoife's tutelage, Lily learned the art of creating healthful tinctures from arnica and milk thistle, how to brew a calming potion from witch hazel and mountain lovage, and how to coax the slippery healing compounds from the infamous belladonna plant. Aoife had even sold a few of Lily's better tinctures at Aoife's Apothecary in town.

Most mornings the triplets had group lessons—usually charms, spells, and hexes having to do with defense or basic manipulation of elements. Spells Brigit claimed every witch should know, like producing fireballs from their palms to defend against hostile vampires or pulling iron from the earth to ward off rogue fae, neither of which felt basic to Lily. Specialty classes were in the afternoon and consisted of one-on-one lessons with a rotation of experts in their field.

"There's no need for you to take lessons from the strongest fire witch in all the Isles," Aoife explained that morning when Lily expressed interest in attending one of Sara's upcoming special lessons. "You aren't able to perform at the caliber Deirdre Phoenix demands of her students yet. We can reassess in a couple months."

"How do we know how fast we need to progress anyway? What if Deirdre never comes back and we miss out? Or what if she dies? None of these masters have been spring chickens," Evelyn asked, her tone snide.

"It's nearly a sure thing that the other side knows something is up here. We've heard reports of increasing power flows circulating all around the countryside. We can't be certain when they'll make a move, but we can be as efficient as possible until the time comes. Deirdre was my mentor. I know what she expects and I'll not bother my mentor with two pupils whose fireballs still resemble a candle flame," Aoife said slapping labels on brown tincture bottles without so much as a glance up.

"Right. Keep working like little robots," Evelyn replied, slamming her book shut and stalking out of the cottage.

*She's so dramatic*, Lily thought. Their relationship since the unbinding had reached an unprecedented degree of frigidity. It was as if the hours by the lake, laughing and telling stories had never happened. Even Sara, often the bridge between her older sisters, fell victim to Evelyn's bad moods now.

"Brigit did say we could emerge from the unbinding changed," Sara whispered. Her fingers danced through the beads of her mala necklace as she watched Evelyn out the sitting room window.

Lily nodded, though she didn't agree. Sara's eyes, so sensitive to the slightest flick of the hand during casting, seemed blind to the nuances of Evelyn Locksley, a topic Lily considered herself fluent in. Lily had seen the darkening of Evelyn's blue eyes and the stiffening of her shoulders as Aoife spoke. This was not the "change" Brigit spoke of. It was envy, and Lily knew why. Sara's magical excellence was enough to color almost anyone's vision green. Add in the fact Lily and Sara had discovered their specialties, but Evelyn hadn't—well, it didn't take a genius to see why the girl used to having everything her way was pissed off most of the time.

Though it guilted her a little, Lily couldn't deny the perverse pleasure she often felt at Evelyn's irritation. It was hard feeling sorry for a gorgeous blonde raised with a silver spoon in her perfect mouth.

"Can we go over the types of magic again, Aoife?" Lily asked, hoping to distract herself from another round of mental Evelyn bashing.

"Aye. There'll be two types. The one referred to in movies is witchcraft, though they've got the specifics all wrong, as usual. Witchcraft is magic that relies on objects such as a potion, scrying bowl, or crystal. Healing is a good example. Witchcraft is what usually gets non-hereditary witches interested in magic."

"Like tarot cards?"

"Hmm," Aoife bowed her head to hide her disapproval at what she deemed carnival magic.

Lily suppressed a grin. "Then there's elemental, right?"

"Some call it elemental. Others, like myself, call it blood magic. It's the magic hereditary witches are born with. Blood magic thrives off power taken from the elements and gifted by the Goddess. It includes enhancements, ceremens, energy and element manipulation, spirit magic, and astral projection, to name a few. Anything you perform under your own steam or pulled from the surrounding elements. Most of what we are teaching you is blood magic. This is because you can bet fata and their cronies are not going to be cowed by a scrying bowl or a fecking tarot card."

Lily sighed. To her, blood magic was an umbrella term for magical subjects she was terrible at. *Why can't I fight off a fata with a crystal?* She imagined herself battling a menacing blob with a stick of amethyst and chuckled.

"Something funny?" Aoife said, peering up from her labeling.

Lily shook her head, knowing Aoife would be unamused by that plan of attack.

"So, what do fata look like? I always pictured them as some sort of blob," she asked before Aoife sniffed out the hilarious image still running through Lily's leaky mind.

"You're not far off. We've found a few documents claiming a handful of fata made it here after the triplets' disappearance. Those sources indicate they looked a bit like a colorful ghost. That is, until they learned to transform themselves to fit in with humans like Lilith, Eve, and Seraphina," Aoife said.

"What happened to the ones that made it here?" Lily asked, captivated by where her off-the-cuff question had led them.

"They bred, or at least they tried. Even here it seems most fata were weak and infertile. The few pure fata births that came to fruition on Earth produced magical offspring never before seen: daemons, fairies, vampires, shifters, sirens, djinn, all sorts of creatures. I spoke once with a wizard as knowledgeable as one could be on the subject. He thought this was because of the different magics found on Earth and Hecate. He explained that only fata-human unions produced the same type of creature with consistency and hypothesized this was due to the influence of human DNA, which belongs completely to the earth. Children born to fata and humans were always witches."

Lily's head spun. They had learned a little about vampires and fae, but the others were mysteries to her. *There must be different types of magic to consider? What would we use as weapons against them?* Her eye began to twitch.

"How do we fight other creatures?"

"Well, let's see, where to start—"

"Lily. Sara." Brigit strode into the room, the scents of cinnamon and lavender wafted in behind her lazily. She cast a quizzical look at Aoife. "Where's Evelyn? Morgane and Nora have been waiting outside for ages."

Lily brightened. She'd forgotten about their special group lesson that afternoon.

"Mind magic," Gwenn clarified the night before, with a roll of her eyes. "Aoife's quite proud of her speciality, but I doubt you'll hear anyone else call it *ceremens* at a coven gathering."

Mind magic, as Lily understood, indicated phase two of their training. They weren't just standing behind shields as someone threw curses at them, or pulling tiny bits of metal from the ground. This was some real shit. They were going to read someone's mind. Having been on the receiving end of ceremens for weeks, Lily was more than ready to learn how to defend herself.

"I'll go get her. She went to get some sun," Sara lied, and rushed outside to collect Evelyn, her fringed top swaying as she ran.

***

"Alright, ladies," Morgane said, clapping her veiny hands together as they assembled on the lawn. "I've got to be getting back to Trinity by nightfall, so let's get started.

"Ceremens is a slippery branch of magic. Most can manage a bit, especially with those close to them or who share an element—like Gwenn can with Lily, though she's not a great ceremens otherwise. Few are truly powerful. We're hoping you three are in the minority. Our enemies would be foolish not to have a few prodigious ceremens. If you're not a ceremens and they get ahold of you . . . well, that would be what my students call a mind fuck."

Lily giggled. Morgane, she'd learned, had a refreshing disregard for social etiquette.

"Ceremens is used to invade others' thoughts, project your thoughts—or, in Aoife's case, memories—plant falsehoods, read emotions, and most pertinent for our situation, bend others to your will. There's a charm and a technique for each scenario except reading emotions. That's more a natural ability. We shall begin with the first two, which are mirrors of each other."

"Reading emotions would be an empath?" Sara asked.

"Correct," Morgane beamed. "Empaths can be quite nice to have around. Wouldn't you agree, Lily?"

"Excuse me?" Lily cocked her head to the side.

Morgane mirrored the gesture, confusion clouding her eyes.

Nora interjected, a knowing smirk on her face. "They haven't told you yet? What are they dragging their arses about? Well, I suppose someone's got to tell you now. Emily is an empath. Oh, and Selma de Avila is one of the most famous sirens of our time. Sirens possess a specialized, usually genetic, branch of mind magic. Selma's powers have likely gone unused for decades, being around all those women, though rumor has it she practiced quite a bit in her youth."

Lily's mouth fell open at the strange words used to describe two of the people she loved best. She flipped frantically through memories of anything resembling magic at the commune. It didn't take long to hit on one. The adult tent! Selma belly dancing before a captivated group of men, twirling on the stage as if floating on water. Lily had never seen anyone move in quite that way. Her mind raced on, but most of her memories from that night were vague, unplaceable.

"Now she remembers. Rena did mention she obscured some of that night for you. A few other times, too, until you were ready to digest them," Nora said, studying Lily's reaction with a smug smile.

Lily glared at Nora. *Why is she enjoying this so much?*

"Don't worry. Rena is too noble to do it often," Nora said, as if being noble were something too ridiculous to fathom. "Most of the time they were simply careful around you. It wasn't difficult. There aren't many strong witches at Terramar. Rena, Annika, and Selma are the only ones who would register against our lot, and Annika only if she could use her wand. Unlike your mother and aunts, Annika has trouble without a channeling agent. Emily is a moderate empath, but she'd never manipulate anyone."

Lily's shoulders softened. A call to Rena would still be necessary, but for now she could live with the knowledge that she hadn't been toyed with her entire life.

"I didn't show up to learn all about commune drama. Could we move on?" Evelyn interrupted.

For once, Lily was grateful for her intrusion.

"Aye," Aoife nodded, "What do you ladies say we partner up, and we'll break into your heads?"

Evelyn tensed.

Lily made a beeline for Morgane. There was no way she wanted Nora in her head. She already knew too much as it was.

Sara and Aoife, a natural pair, gravitated toward the orchard together without a word.

Evelyn's face fell as she realized what had happened.

Lily smirked. Apparently, Nora hadn't been Evelyn's first choice either.

Morgane claimed one of Lily's favorite patches of garden filled with buttercups as their battleground. She pulled Lily to the far side, under a trestle decorated with a stained glass triquetra and rose bushes crawling up it's wood frame. "I'm so sorry," she whispered. "I thought you knew by now."

Despite the shock she felt, a small part of Lily agreed with Morgane. She *had* known, on an intuitive level, though she'd never taken time to think about it. She found she wasn't even mad at her Terramar family. Despite the enchantments on their cell phones being lifted, service at Fern Cottage was poor. Her calls home had become rare, short, and she always seemed to be the one ending them, claiming mental exhaustion. No wonder they hadn't told her yet.

She inhaled and the scents of thyme, lady's mantle, lemon balm, and roses washed over her as truth seeped in. She felt it distill down into the deepest parts of her, clarifying her memories. Even her grade school years had whispered of magic. Lily recalled her shock the first day of high school when she discovered no one else had studied botany or occult religions. The truth hadn't been hidden so deep after all, she realized. Her chest warmed as lessons with Rena came rushing back in a new light.

"No changing the past," she said, her face softening into a smile. "Now what do you say you have a go at my head?"

***

Three hours later, Lily, Evelyn, and Sara were practiced, though not entirely successful, at keeping their partners' advancements at bay. Having employed crude, inefficient mind barriers for weeks, Lily found the correct way, while still difficult, was far easier than her self-taught method. Never again would she have to envision a large iron gate around her head, or keep it there through sheer willpower, because there was a charm for that. One word and poof! A barrier that would suffice for the day-to-day surrounded her mind. It was only in cases of probing or stress that force of will and mental stamina would be needed for protection. Despite exercising her mental muscles vigorously since arriving at Fern Cottage, Lily still found herself woefully unprepared to fend off Morgane's advanced attacks.

"You'll not be keeping a master ceremens from dipping in until you've built up the strength, though you will be able to protect yourself around most witches," Morgane admitted.

*Cludo, cludo, cludo.* Lily repeated her new favorite charm to herself.

"Alright, ladies, it's near supper time. What do you say we do a few rounds where you three are the intruders for a bit of fun? The charm is *inruo*. You will have to project your mind out as Aoife does, though without the memory attached. Try to empty your mind of extraneous thoughts before searching for another mind. Eye contact helps when first learning, but often develops into a crutch. And don't be too hard on yourself if you don't succeed the first time. Offense is more difficult than defense in this case," Morgane said.

Lily tried to hide her groan of exhaustion beneath a loud cough. She took small solace in seeing that she wasn't the only one feeling the stress. Both Evelyn and Sara looked spent, too.

"New casters often find it easiest to imagine their minds being thrown out, as a fisherman would when casting for salmon. Leave it out there a wee bit, wait for the mind to catch on, and reel it back in if you come up empty." Morgane's voice was oddly encouraging for a person who theoretically was about to have their mind broken into.

*Like a fishing line it is then*, Lily thought, trying to recall if she'd ever handled a fishing pole. Growing up with a bunch of hippie vegetarians had the oddest drawbacks sometimes.

*Empty your mind*, she thought, closing her eyes and breathing deep.

"Inruo," she whispered, and threw. Instinct took over and Lily felt her own sluggish thoughts dissolve into black. Her back arched and face angled toward the sky as a sensation of lightness overcame her. She became aware that a small but strong part of herself was missing. *Is it working?* she wondered, before shoving the question down into oblivion.

"Goddess be!" Morgane screeched.

Lily's tenuous grasp on the charm broke at the sound and her mind snapped back into place. She opened her eyes wide and her limbs tingled as feeling returned. *Did I hurt Morgane? What did I do wrong? What the hell?*

Morgane was no longer in the buttercup patch but jogging toward a lump in the mint patch near a glassy eyed Evelyn. Lily squinted and realized the lump was Nora, her body curled in on itself like a sleeping dog.

"What happened, Nora? Are you alright?" Morgane asked, dropping to the ground.

Nora peeked up.

"Her," she said, locking eyes with Morgane and pointing her finger at Evelyn. "She did it," her voice fell into a low whisper before trailing off into silence.

"Evelyn broke in?" Morgane asked disbelievingly.

Nora's eyes flicked up to see a group gathering around her before resuming staring at the ground.

"Goddess be," Aoife said, whirling to face Evelyn.

Evelyn winced and her eyes cleared a bit.

Lily guessed that Aoife was performing her sophisticated variant of ceremens on Evelyn.

"Nora's right, Morgane," Aoife said, turning back to the old witch.

"Of course I'm right," Nora snapped though she kept her head lowered. "Felt her soaring through my head, didn't I? No regard for niceties or safety either. Think of what I could have lost."

"You know full well Evelyn couldn't have controlled it, Nora. Not her first time. None of us could," Aoife said, cutting Nora's tirade short.

Evelyn had flown through Nora's mind? Already? Lily shot a covert look at Sara, disheveled and panting on the damp ground. Pity rose in her. Somehow Sara looked even worse than five minutes ago, as if broken by her efforts to intrude on Aoife's undoubtedly secure mind. Evelyn was glowing by comparison.

"How'd you do it?" Aoife asked, spinning back to face Evelyn.

"I just *did.* It was easy enough," Evelyn said, putting a hand on her hip and tossing back her mane of gold confidently.

"Well, that much is obvious. You're not on the floor, nor have you lost any of your faculties or sanity."

Alarm flickered over Evelyn's face, and her stance softened. "I'm not sure how. I threw my mind out like Morgane said and then I was flying." She glanced down at Nora, who with Morgane's help, had managed to sit up.

"It was too fast, though. I couldn't tell one memory from the next. It was like seeing a movie through static on fast forward," Evelyn said.

"This isn't the first time you've mind read, is it?" Aoife asked, her eyes probing Evelyn with more intensity.

Evelyn's brows furrowed.

"The other times would not have looked as this did. You'd never have been able to do this even weeks ago. Not against a ceremens of Nora's repute. It would have been small intrusions. Knowing how to get to people, manipulate them and realizing what they wanted from you." She paused before adding slyly, "And if I had to guess, I'd say it worked best on those of the male persuasion."

Evelyn inhaled. "It's not the first time," she admitted.

"Are you thinking a siren, Aoife? One with a greater proclivity for mind magic?" Morgane asked the question as one would ask someone if they preferred cream in their coffee.

"There's only one way to be sure," Aoife said. "We need a man to test her on."

Laughter bubbled around the garden, and Lily realized that she hadn't seen a single man in months. The thought of a man at Fern Cottage seemed absurd.

"Are we sure they won't turn into frogs when they walk through the gate?" Lily asked joining the laughter.

Aoife grinned mischievously. "Perhaps you three would like to earn a few bonus points?"

***

Evelyn's specialties as a potent ceremens and siren were confirmed that night. Under Aoife's watchful eye, Evelyn had been unleashed at the local village pub. The men at Drunken Duck Tavern hadn't known what hit them.

In the weeks that followed the tension between Lily and Evelyn soared. While Lily was tempted to blame it all on Evelyn, she knew she was partially to blame. The more she thought about it, the less she was sure she could trust the mercurial blonde, especially now that Lily knew Evelyn was powerful in an sect of magic Lily was susceptible to. Her first impression of her sister—the arrogance, entitlement, and vanity she'd displayed at Shannon Airport—clung to Lily's memory. It made for one hell of a scary mind reader. Nora had been making herself scarce since their afternoon in the garden, a fact Lily added to her arsenal of reasons not to open herself up too much. She'd begun dedicating her mornings to strengthening her mental barriers. Progress was slow, but Gwenn assured her they were getting stronger.

Lily had long since gotten used to their routine, so much so she'd completely forgotten it was Em's birthday until the notification popped up on her phone. Luckily, it was still early morning in Oregon. Not wanting to be hindered by the cottage's spotty cell service, Lily grabbed Brigit's cordless landline and retreated to her room.

"Happy birthday, Em! What do you have planned?"

"Well thank you, darlin'. So good to hear your voice again. We miss you here, you know. These old bones are laying low this year. Rena's planning a small party on her porch. They meant to surprise me, but you know how things are."

Lily stifled a laugh. Selma, no doubt, had been the one to slip.

"I wish I could be there." Their recent studies had taken on a fervor that had Lily dreaming of lazy days at Terramar. She had a suspicion that the upcoming Halloween holiday, or Samhain as the McKay clan women called it, was to blame.

"I wish you were too, love. But what's happenin' there? What have they taught you? I wish I could see you three cast. I'm sure it's a real treat."

"Yeah, it's great," Lily said, immediately regretting her tone.

"Doesn't sound great. What's eatin' you?"

"Besides the fact that Sara's kicking my ass at pretty much everything?" Lily released a breath she hadn't realized she'd been holding. "I know I'm improving. Brigit says we've had about three years of magical education in three months. I realize it's dramatic but I can't help feel that my greatest talent is almost useless. What good is healing going to be in battle? I doubt I'll have time to whip up potions or cast healing spells during a fight."

"Hmm," Emily hummed knowingly.

Silence rang across an ocean and a continent before Lily felt obliged to confess further.

"And I'm uncomfortable with the fact that Evelyn is a mind-reading prodigy. The exact type of magic I'm most deficient at," she trailed off, feeling ashamed. They were in this together. Every strength the triplets cultivated made it more likely they would succeed. Still, Lily found herself wishing Evelyn had never discovered her ceremens capabilities.

"That's what I was waitin' for," Em said. "Have you spoken with her about it?"

"No. I'm not going to. I'm dealing with it. Or trying to."

"And wearing yourself out in the process."

*Damn Em and her empathic talents*, Lily thought, though she knew it was true. Even with their increased number of lessons, she shouldn't be this exhausted.

"Maybe I'll mention it."

"You will or you won't, but it will sure make your time there and your relationship with your *sister* easier," Em said.

"So how are things going there? I hear you're all free-practicing witches now that I'm finally in on the dirty secret?" Lily asked, careful to keep the accusation she'd heaped onto Rena from her tone.

"Darlin', we've been free practicin' all along! Just less so with you around. When you went to college, we blew the lid off the place. Didn't you ever wonder about that mess of iron surroundin' us? The remoteness? The secrecy?"

*No*, she thought, still a touch bitter. She'd never wondered anything about her life. It had all seemed so normal, despite the obvious fact that it was not.

"The iron gates and posts are to keep out any fae that may be working against us? Probably enchanted to keep out other creatures too. The secrecy is obvious now." Lily sighed. "You all gave up so much because of me."

"We'd do it again, too," Em said, her voice radiating love. "Though I'll admit most of us can't hold a candle to your Irish clan. The McKay women are legendary, Lil. Brigit and Aoife are particularly well known, though Mary and Gwenn are nothin' to sniff at when it comes to water and earth magics. Only Rena, Annika, and Selma even come close in our little group. The rest of us have fun dabbling, though."

Lily envied her lighthearted tone. *What would it be like to have power but not be fated to try and save humanity with it? Add that to the list of things I'll never know.*

"Thanks, Em. Hey! We're starting astral projection and spirit magic tomorrow. Maybe I'll make it over to see you!" Lily said, her spirits lifting at the far-fetched idea.

"Lord have mercy. They are workin' you girls. Be careful with projection, Lil. More than one witch has gotten lost outside her body. It's a terrible fate."

"Thanks for the advice, Em, I'll be sure to pass it on to Sara," Lily said.

"You never know, love. You've only touched the tip of what magic has to offer, and are growin' stronger each day."

Lily's shoulders softened. "I know. Thanks for listening. I called to wish you a happy birthday, and all we talked about was me. Unfortunately, I've got to run, but I wanted you to know I'm thinking about you. I was looking forward to your birthday this year."

"I know, darlin', but what you're doing is much more important than this old lady's birthday. Keep up the good work and know we're all behind you. Love you, Lil."

"Love you, too, Em."

# *A Change of Heart*

"That's it. One petal at a time. Caaaareful now," Brigit whispered, her eyes locked on the iron cauldron Lily hunched over.

"Wanna switch?" Lily wheezed, resisting the overwhelming urge to toss the flowers in all at once and be done with it.

A smirk skipped across Brigit's face, though her concentration remained, as always, maddeningly focused on the task at hand.

"Then how would you ever learn to prepare a proper Samhain flying brew? I wouldn't steal that pleasure from you, Lil. This is your time," she said, patting her daughter's shoulder.

Lily didn't doubt the potion would be awesome. She'd been enamored with the idea of flying through the woods surrounding the cabin ever since Brigit mentioned the potion weeks ago. But three hours in and two aching arms later, she found herself wishing it was Sara or Evelyn who had volunteered to make the potion. *At least I don't have to sit here while it simmers for hours*, she thought. She gazed through the hearth into the living room where her aunts and sisters sat drinking mulled wine and preparing decorations.

For days the group had been hard at work transforming Fern Cottage for Samhain. The pathway to the door had been lined with ancient torches that looked impressively spooky once lit. Enchanted cotton cobwebs and plastic bats were already swaying playfully from every tree in the orchard. Bedsheet ghosts, brought to life by Gwenn, were haunting DIY tombstones honoring Morgan Le Fay, Merlin, Mother Shipton, and other legendary witches and wizards in the garden.

"You can never count on the real things to show up when you

want them. They're flighty buggers," Gwenn had lamented when Lily asked if real ghosts ever attended the party.

The playful ambiance of the grounds morphed inside the confines of Fern Cottage. Within those stone walls the witches blended the history of their people with lore in a way that gave Lily shivers it was so beautiful. Crystal balls, glowing from Sara's candeo charm, cast warm light into dark corners as they circulated the room on currents of air Mary had charmed into existence. Ornamental skulls, ravens, and goddess idols covered every possible surface not set aside for the display of magical books and grimoires. Samhain, Brigit explained, was the only day of the year coven members were urged to dust off their familial books of knowledge and bring them out into the open for all to see. Most families respected the tradition for the night, despite the strong pull to keep their grimoires—books that in another era equated a death sentence—hidden. The cross of Brighid was brought into greater prominence on Samhain by the hanging of tea lights around it. Each crimson rush of the cross glowed against the hearth stones with a pride befitting the goddess it honored. More candles climbed up the doorways and perched on windowsills.

"The candles are said to help spirits find their way over the threshold into our world on Samhain night," Gwenn explained when Sara questioned the safety of so many candles in such a small space.

The pomp and preparation brought back memories of Terramar's solstice gathering, leaving Lily with an uncanny feeling that her life was destined to change as much on Samhain as it had on solstice.

Best of all, Samhain meant a break. A whole day with no lessons. A day to play and learn from whomever they wanted.

"Are you going to fly?" Lily asked Evelyn as they gathered for breakfast the morning of Samhain. It was always easier to talk to her sister in the morning. Sleep helped them forget the tension that plagued their relationship by midday. Whether they'd be on speaking terms by dinner was anyone's guess.

"I suppose so," Evelyn answered, picking at her eggs and bacon, "but I'm more interested in astral travel. If it's ever going to work, tonight would be the night, right?"

Sara nodded, her mouth full of oats and eyes wide with excitement.

They'd had six lessons on astral travel, but none of them had yet to travel. Lily had little doubt it would be Sara who succeeded on Samhain, when the veil between the worlds was at its thinnest.

"Maybe I will, too," Lily mused. It hadn't been at the top of her list, but Evelyn was right. It'd be a shame not to try. "I wonder if it'd be easier after taking the flying potion? Maybe it would help my spirit fly, too?"

"Well, there's an idea. Mary tried it once. Didn't do a damn thing for her," Brigit said, sweeping into the room and beelining it toward the coffee.

Lily's cheeks flushed as a small smirk appeared on Evelyn's face. She wished she hadn't said the last bit out loud. It sounded too desperate.

Brigit turned to face them, a mug of coffee filled to the brim clutched between her hands. "But then, you're not Mary, are you? I say you try it. No one knows what could happen on Samhain."

Evelyn's smirk flattened.

"Now then," Brigit said, easing herself into a chair, "which of you wants to lead a circle tomorrow? It's a big responsibility, but I think any of you would be up for it."

Three pairs of eyes popped open.

"You won't be on your own, of course. Aoife or I will be there, assisting. The combined power of so many people's magic you aren't familiar with would be too much otherwise. Even those who have been practicing witches all their lives often desire assistance when leading Samhain night."

"What's the circle for?" Evelyn asked, leaning forward in her chair.

"Seeing as it's Samhain, we'll be having a few circles. Most are small and for fun. You can do anything you like, but the one I'm thinking you'd enjoy best is the invitation to our ancestors for a visit."

Lily coughed and a small bit of toast landed on her plate.

"You mean ghosts? We're bringing the dead to life?" Sara asked, her eyes in danger of bulging out of their sockets.

"That's the idea." Brigit took a slow sip of coffee, her cinnamon-lavender scent mixing with the early morning brew. "It hasn't happened once in the last hundred years. All the old grimoires say that when it works the ghosts only stay for a mo' or so, just long enough for a chat or to answer a question. Even if it doesn't work, people get a thrill out of watching. It's a wee bit of fun and a good chance to let our power flow. It's not often we get to turn it up full blast."

Lily shrugged. *Sounds cool, but pretty unlikely,* she thought.

"Oh," Sara said, unable to hide her disappointment. "Well, then, what will we be doing that might actually work?"

"We call down the moon every year. That never fails to impress."

"Like it actually comes down?" Evelyn asked skeptically.

"It's more like we feel it more, and sometimes it appears closer. Rest assured, it's beyond anyone's power to pull the moon from orbit, though many have tried."

"What else?" Sara asked, searching for a circle that would reap real benefits.

"Bonfire magic is a huge draw. You'll want to be a part of that, Sara. All the fire witches go mad for it. Air circles are fun too, could be a good way to test your skills, though our coven is light on air witches. Then there's the reflections. It's not magic, per se, but brings a community together in a way that magic lacks."

"Reflections?" Lily asked.

"Aye. You tell the circle how your life has changed in the year since the last circle. We learn a bit about who you used to be, who you wish to be, and the community tries to help you with your aspirations."

"That doesn't seem too bad," Lily lied. Her shoulders tensed as the memories of the shell of a person she was months ago flashed before her.

"But we can choose, right?" Evelyn said, her voice cold.

"As always, all you do on Samhain is your choice," Brigit said.

Evelyn exhaled and Lily recalled the stories Evelyn had told by the lakeside, about how she had used her beauty to wheedle information from powerful men.

"Shouldn't be too difficult. The change in our lives is pretty obvious. We have loads to talk about from these past three months," Sara said.

Lily's shoulders softened. Why hadn't she thought of that? Sara was right. There was no reason to tell anyone about her relationship with Liam. She hardly ever thought of him anymore and wanted to keep it that way. Lily had no desire to parade her mistake, her shame, in front of a bunch of strangers or her aunts. Despite having improved at keeping people out of her head, the anxiety of being labeled the fragile triplet still persisted. She didn't want to give them another reason to think her weak.

"It sounds nice," Sara continued, twiddling her spoon. "Besides my parents, I've never been around anyone long enough to see how they change."

Lily looked down at her plate. It was one of Sara's mindless remarks that guilted her. She recognized how easily Sara's fate could have been her own. Despite feeling unloved, transient, and isolated, Sara had risen to accomplish amazing feats. Lily doubted she would have fared as well under those circumstances.

A scrape of wood on wood filled the lull as Evelyn rose from the table, oblivious to the awkward moment.

"When will people arrive?" Evelyn asked, dropping her plate in the sink without rinsing it.

"Your aunts and Fiona will be by at five. The rest of the coven will come around seven."

"No Nora?" Lily asked, surprised. Sure, Nora had been scarce since their first ceremens lesson, but Lily thought they'd see her on Samhain.

"She's across the pond again working. Said she'd try to come back in time, but I doubt we'll see her," Brigit said, a crease forming between her eyebrows.

Lily nodded though she doubted it was the whole truth. She didn't know Nora well, but she knew she was proud of her powers. The resentment on Nora's face when Evelyn broke into her mind had been obvious. People would want to talk to them Samhain night, hear how they discovered their strengths. Lily didn't blame Nora for not wanting to be there when Evelyn regaled the crowd with her story.

"I'll be in my room preparing," Evelyn said, sashaying out of the room.

Brigit's eyebrows shot up. "She means to primp for the men? But the party doesn't start for hours."

Neither Sara nor Lily answered. The truth was they didn't know what Evelyn wanted out of the Samhain gathering. Or for that matter, pretty much ever. But if Lily had to guess, she'd say Brigit was right. The heiress had taken to frequenting Drunken Duck Tavern, the local pub that Brigit and Aoife had grudgingly agreed to place wards on once Evelyn demanded to leave the protection of Fern Cottage, claiming she needed to "let her hair down" and test her siren powers.

"Well, I guess I can't say I'm surprised. Rumor has it that young Finn Blackburn is scheming to woo her. She must have done a whammy on him. He's never been impressed by any of the local girls."

*None of the local girls come with curves that don't stop, billion-dollar bank accounts, and mythical man-enticing powers,* Lily thought, shoving a piece of toast into her mouth.

"How many people are coming tonight anyway?" Sara asked.

"About nine. Only our close friends tend to show. It's a long drive for most people. You've already met a few of them as they were your instructors. Half of the active members of the Coven of Ilargia are McKay blood now," Brigit said, beaming at them.

Sara's strip of bacon stilled between her plate and her mouth. "I read somewhere that blood bonds enhance magical capabilities. Do you think any magic we perform as a family on Samhain would be stronger than what the coven as a whole could produce?"

Brigit looked thoughtful. "We could perform extraordinary feats, especially on Samhain. Although, as you're not fully trained, I'm not sure the circle would be as strong as one composed of trained witches."

"You don't think the extra energy available on Samhain will counter our relative lack of training? Maybe if we separated from those outside our family? I was thinking for the calling of an ancestor that could really help? Maybe they'll show up if it's blood calling blood," Sara pushed.

"A strict blood circle? I don't know if that's advisable. Some of these witches wait all year to perform magic like this. They would be deeply offended to be left out. We rely on each other for the experience." Brigit's words were laden with hesitation, though Lily thought she saw a glimmer of excitement hiding in her eyes.

"Could we do the circle twice?" Lily asked, sure that Sara was right. This could be the first time in a century that the calling of an ancestor worked, and they could be the ones to do it! Not even astral travel could top that.

Brigit paused and sipped her coffee. "I'll speak with my sisters about it, see how they think the others will take the idea. It's criminal to insult a fellow witch on Samhain, especially one of your own coven. I'm sure someone will take it as a slight to their ability, so we'd have to address that first. But as most set to attend are our good friends, perhaps they'll understand. Especially if Mary makes the calls. She's the coven social butterfly." Brigit rose from her seat. "It looks as though I have some convincing to do, don't I?"

"You. Are. A. Genius!" Lily whispered to Sara, as Brigit grabbed the landline from where it lay on the counter and disappeared to her room. "You should—"

"Evelyn should lead the circle," Sara said, cutting her off as if she'd known exactly what Lily would say.

"But you came up with the idea. And you're the most powerful of us three."

"We each have our strengths, and you've heard them talk. Evelyn's a ceremens prodigy. We all know Nora's been avoiding her for weeks because she's embarrassed of what happened. And Evelyn will try harder if her reputation is on the line."

"What does mind magic have to do with anything? We're calling the dead, not butting into anyone's business," Lily said, ignoring Sara's last point, which she had no doubt was true.

"Who's to say calling the dead is any harder than pushing your mind into another person's? Both feats require that you access two worlds, your own and someone else's."

As always, what Sara said made perfect sense, in a twisted, annoying kind of way. Lily's desire to be in the circle dwindled. Evelyn would be insufferable if she led the circle and they succeeded.

Lily sighed. *Stop being so petty*, she thought, shoving back her ego.

"Alright, I see your point. So who do you think should lead with her? Brigit? Her and Aoife butt heads a lot."

Sara shook her head. "Evelyn should be alone. I think since our blood bonds are close and we know the feel of each other's magic it would be manageable."

That was the limit. Her chair clattered to the ground behind her as Lily shot up from the table. "I'm going for a walk."

The slam of the door brought forth an onslaught of memories fueled by teenage angst. How many times had she stormed out of Rena's cabin? At least back then she could claim sanctuary at Em's when the weather was unfavorable. That was a luxury she didn't have at Fern Cottage. The fall wind nipped her nose and chilled her earlobes as Lily stalked around outside, unsure of her destination.

*Unsure of a lot of things,* she thought. *I'm not even sure why the idea of Evelyn leading the circle gets me so wound up.* She had no doubt Evelyn would become unbearable after being given such a high degree of authority, especially if the circle worked. *But isn't that a small price to pay for performing magic not seen in over a century?* a small voice inside her wondered.

She stopped and assessed her surroundings. Her feet had led her to the edge of the forest, to the very spot she had decided to become unbound, a spot she had come to think of as a crossroads. Turning to face the lake, she dropped to the ground with a heavy thud. The combination of damp grass on her rear and fall chill on her skin had her wishing she had grabbed her jacket. Or better yet, that she had run to her room in huff. It was freaking freezing out here.

Unthinkingly, she pulled a few handfuls of grass from the earth before the nausea set in.

"Typical earth witch guilt. You come to realize that the little plants provide you as much power as huge trees. They'd give their whole lives if we asked. The best we can try to do is not waste them," Gwenn had explained when Lily admitted to feeling guilty about picking a bouquet of flowers from a field.

She sighed and patted the ground next to her, contenting herself with watching the ripples on the lake and smoke unfurling from the cottage chimney. *Why can't I be happy we're all growing stronger and learning? Why can't I let Evelyn have this moment? How are we going to save humanity if we can't even get along half the time?* She'd asked herself these questions over and over, but stopped short at digging deep for the answers. For the first time, she found herself seriously considering what it would be like to have Evelyn as a friend and not someone she felt she should get along with because they were related. *She's not unpleasant all the time. In fact, she can be pretty funny. Though usually by accident.*

Lily grinned as a memory of Evelyn pouring whole coffee beans straight into water and microwaving them percolated through her thoughts. The resultant mixture was revolting and, to Evelyn at least, baffling. The more Lily thought about it the more she wondered if she had been putting too much pressure on Evelyn to be normal and not the pampered person she'd been her whole life. *Normal? What is that anyways? Especially around here . . . Have I been too judgmental?*

Filled with a burgeoning sense of clarity, Lily stood and gazed out over Brigit's property. *What's one more change of heart?* She stood, suddenly determined to set her relationship with Evelyn to rights. Walking back to the cottage, Lily found herself hoping Sara hadn't given Evelyn the news yet. Perhaps they could deliver it together.

# *Samhain*

"Ahhhh Brigit! These must be your girls. So beautiful, each of them with eyes like a sparkling gem!" a plump, old woman with an exaggerated, pointed witch hat and dagger-sharp red nails exclaimed, planting a firm kiss on each of Brigit's cheeks and sloshing mulled wine from her cup.

"Happy Samhain, Mariel. Yes, these are my girls. I dare say their presence is drawing a much larger crowd than normal," Brigit said through a thin-lipped smile.

"Well, what did you expect?! We're all dying to meet them. Thought they'd be grotesque or slow, what with you sending them away and all, but look at them—they're lovely! I heard they're causing quite the stir with boys in town. And then this one!" Mariel patted Sara on the head, "I heard her talking to Morgane about a grimoire as I walked in. Dresses a bit bohemian, but whip smart. I'll never understand why you gave them up!"

"Excuse us. We must prepare for the circles," Brigit said, her voice tight. She grabbed Sara's hand and led the three of them to her room.

Shutting the door behind them, she turned to face the triplets. "I don't think our blood circle is a good idea anymore. There's at least ten witches out there I'm not sure we can trust," Brigit said, wringing her hands.

"Why did you invite them then?" Evelyn asked.

"The Samhain gathering is an open invitation to the larger Ilargia Coven. Most of the people out there are inactive members at best; I haven't seen half of them in years. Usually only family and close friends come, certainly no one outside the village. Mariel lives two hours away! Perhaps we shouldn't have warned people about the special blood circle. There was already enough intrigue with your reappearance. We never told people why we gave you up and most were too scared to ask lest they get on our bad side. Your grandfather was particularly menacing. It just seems so—"

"Fishy," Evelyn finished, her face grim.

"Well—yes, quite fishy. I'm not sure if it's wise to showcase your talents; they're sure to be enhanced tonight. What if Mariel starts gabbing outside our community? It wouldn't be the first time with her."

"Can't you ask the ones you don't trust to leave?"

Brigit stared at Evelyn. "Any other night, yes, but Samhain is a night for witches. It would be offensive in the extreme if I even insinuated they weren't welcome. Rumors would fly, and we can't have that."

A hush fell as each contemplated what to do. It was, Lily realized, the first time she'd been in Brigit's bedroom. As with the rest of the cottage, blue and green dominated the bedding and walls, while red trinkets provided warmth. She allowed her gaze to roam, taking in the details. Her breath caught in her throat as her eyes landed above the bed, where a half dozen frames filled with photos of herself over the years hung. A chubby red-headed toddler and a smiling, blonde baby, preteen, and prom queen in a crystal beaded gown hung right beside her. Brigit had been watching them grow up from afar, Lily realized. Pain shot through Lily's heart as all Brigit had given up to keep them safe washed over her. *We've missed so many moments together. I'll be damned if this is another one,* Lily thought.

"I say we do it," Lily said. "Show them how strong McKay blood is. Who would want to make an enemy out of us it we succeeded?" Her eyes sought Evelyn's, banking on her sister's pride and willing her to agree. If they succeeded word *would* get out, and right now that was exactly what Lily wanted. It was reckless but she didn't care. She should have known these women all her life. Should have known what she was all her life. Performing legendary magic with them was the only thing that mattered to Lily right then.

Evelyn stared back, her eyes a cool, evaluating sapphire blue. Only years of preparing to run a business empire could give someone so young those eyes.

Lily exhaled as Evelyn's face broke into a wicked grin.

"I'm in. Let's show them who they'll be messing with if they run off spreading rumors."

"It could cause more rumors not to do the circle now that everyone is expecting it," Sara added, her voice far more level and convincing than Lily's or Evelyn's.

It took longer to persuade Brigit but eventually, under the weight of her daughters' unyielding insistence, she caved.

They decided to save the blood circle for the finale, right before midnight, in hopes that the gathering would thin out as the night wore on.

Perhaps it was for this reason that Lily felt like time dragged. Even flying felt like a placeholder for the main event, though not so much that she didn't delight in the feeling of wind whipping through her hair as she raced through the forest on nothing but air. *That was better than any run I've ever been on,* Lily thought, arranging her windswept brown waves back into a high pony.

Sara and Evelyn were making the most of the night, too.

Lily sat resting with Mary, who had pulled out all the stops for Samhain, donning a bright purple dress and flamboyant pointy witch hat. They watched mesmerized as Sara wowed a crowd with fire magic by pulling the flames from the bonfire, transmuting them to electric pink and weaving them through the trees in the orchard. She ended her performance with a fantastic display of fireworks, creating dragons, unicorns, and gryphons as she tore the flames apart high in the sky.

"That was awesome," Lily murmured as Sara ran up to join them, her cheeks nearly as red as her hair.

"Quite impressive!" Mary agreed.

"Thanks. It felt pretty great. Aoife taught me the transmutation spell last week, but this is the first time I've pulled it off. One of the grimoires a member brought mentioned a slightly different variation and it worked!" Sara said.

Unlike Sara who'd already spent the better part of two hours reading, Lily had yet to delve into the grimoires that waited inside the cottage. The sitting room had been too crammed with people for her comfort and she'd sought refuge outside. Lily made a mental note to go in and check out the grimoires before they vanished for a year.

They walked around the gathering, meeting coven members and watching circles.

"Maybe one day I'll be willing to spill my guts like that, but not today," Lily said. They waved Mary off as she left to join the reflections circle.

"She's so open," Sara agreed. "They're probably dying for one of the McKay women to join so they can learn more about us."

"Well, they caught the right aunt then," Lily said, knowing Gwenn, Brigit, and Aoife would guard their tongues much more.

"Let's find Evelyn. I want to see what she's doing," Sara said, turning on the spot in search of their sister.

"There she is," Lily said pointing to a small circle of four in the meadow.

"Oh! I think that's the air circle! Brigit said there aren't many air witches in our coven. Evelyn must be testing herself," Sara said excitedly.

She was right. As they approached, they could see Evelyn playing with currents of air in a way none of the triplets had managed before. The magic of Samhain was indeed powerful.

Lily laughed as Evelyn launched a gust of wind at Mariel's chest, knocking the woman on her rear with a yelp of surprise.

Evelyn turned at the sound of Lily's laughter, caught sight of them, and winked.

"That'll show Mariel not to go gossiping," Evelyn muttered as she joined Lily and Sara minutes later.

"Maybe," Sara said, her left dimple deep, "Or you just gave her another tale to tell."

"Nice job getting air to work for you," Lily said. "You made it look effortless."

"Thanks. I was a little worried about draining my magic before the big circle, but let's just say the practice was necessary. I was wondering, do you guys think astral travel is a good idea after all? What if travel actually happens and we're too exhausted for the blood circle? Aoife always says it's some of the most draining magic," Evelyn said.

Sara shrugged. "Maybe we'll meet a spirit out there we can convince to show up for us? I'm still going to try."

"I'll never forgive myself if I skip out the one night astral travel may actually work for me. I mean, we've been killing it tonight! Just don't get lost, Evelyn, or we'll lose our circle leader," Lily added, grinning wide.

Evelyn smiled back tentatively.

*We're getting there,* Lily thought, *baby steps.*

An hour later, a coven member was shining a light in each of their eyes to ensure the triplet's spirits were completely present in their body. Each examination was quick, with the encouragement of better luck next time. It seemed not even the mystical powers of Samhain could release the triplets' souls from the bindings of skin.

"Hope you saved some juice for the main event, girls," Aoife growled. Her voice was deeper than usual after having returned to her body from the mountains of Appalachia. It was the farthest travel she'd accomplished all year, and a new Samhain record.

"Hark who talks, uncle," Lily teased. She ducked to avoid Aoife's playful whack on her arm, and caught a faint whiff of tobacco and smoked meat mingling with her aunt's typical scent of ginger and pepper. Aoife had returned with a souvenir.

"Have you thought about your words, Evie?" Aoife asked. She'd been the only one daring enough to give Evelyn a nickname. While Evelyn didn't seem to love it, she also hadn't forbade it.

Incantations, they had learned, were fluid. With exception of the last commanding word, a witch or wizard could customize most of a spell for maximum effect or to narrow its focus. Though many incantations had been passed down through the years for ceremonial purposes, it actually mattered little whether your soliloquy was the same as another person's or even off the cuff. What mattered most was the desire or will of the caster. Because of this, most witches chose the strongest, most evocative words they could when in a circle or casting a spell that required extra strength. Evelyn, despite learning she would lead the blood circle only hours before, had declined wordsmithing assistance.

"I have something I think will work," she said confidently.

"Good. Make sure you really feel the words. I've got to get some food in me before the blood circle, helps ground me after traveling. I'll meet you by the lake," Aoife said, heading toward the cabin.

"Do you think she's alright?" Lily said watching her aunt's unnaturally slow gait.

"I've read traveling takes a lot out of you, but Aoife wouldn't have gone farther than she could handle—not knowing what we're about to attempt," Sara said.

***

They took the scenic route to the lakeside, bumbling around the orchard and through the field, each lost in their own thoughts. It seemed their delay tactic had worked. A smaller crowd than anticipated was gathered at the lakeside. They stood in a tight circle, huddled together for warmth and, Lily was sure, gossip. Brigit, Mary, Gwenn, and Fiona were standing off to the side in their own small group.

"Are you joining us, Fiona?" Lily asked, rubbing her hands together.

Fiona shook her head. "Tonight it's you three, your ma, and aunties, all women of the same line. The closer the bonds, the better."

Brigit nodded. "We considered it. Blood is blood after all, but Aoife pointed out that Fiona may well set the elements off balance. We're already a bit risky with you, myself, and Gwenn in the circle. Too many earth witches and no one with a strong proclivity for air."

"Fiona's trying her best to keep out of the gossip," Mary added, jerking her head toward the group of onlookers. "They've been placing bets all night on how it's going to turn out."

"Aye, I'm one of the few that bet on you girls, so make sure it happens. I don't have a hundred euro to spare at the mo'," Fiona said.

"And if you did you'd pay me back that fifty you owe me, right?" Gwenn asked, eyebrows raised.

Fiona was spared the pressure of a response when Aoife appeared at her back, a healthy glow returned to her freckle-strewn face.

"Are we ready then? Let's get into our positions."

A hush fell over the night as the other witches and wizards watched them make their way to the lake's edge.

"Evelyn, stand right here. Make sure you face the water. We want you to draw as much power as you can from your strongest element," Brigit instructed. She guided Lily into position nearest the forest and Sara on the other side of Evelyn, closest to where a bonfire still raged. Brigit and her sisters took up positions at the four cardinal points, sealing the circle.

Lily looked up at the stars and shivered. The moon, reborn from a new cycle that very night, shone as a thin crescent in the dark sky. She cast her light down to all below and, it seemed, upon their circle in particular.

"Right, then. We're ready," Brigit said, raising a hand in the air. Whispers fell as the night began to vibrate with anticipation. She nodded to Evelyn.

Lily's nerves were soothed by the sight of Evelyn. Tall and regal in the center of the circle, Evelyn's blonde hair beautified everyone around her as it reflected the moon's light on their faces. A siren, a woman able to command the attention and respect of kings, popes, and soldiers with steel and surety. For the first time, Lily was grateful it was Evelyn and not her drawing the crowd's attention.

"We've come here, brothers and sisters of the craft, stewards of ancient power, to seek the knowledge of one long passed," Evelyn said, opening the circle with the ceremonial words Brigit taught her.

Evelyn raised her arms and a puff of wind skipped over the glassy lake, carving small waves on its surface as it trickled their way.

*This is why she wanted to practice with air,* Lily thought, impressed by Evelyn's foresight. The smell of damp earth and decaying leaves engulfed them as a second gust of wind rushed from the woods. Heat tickled Lily's skin as smoke from the bonfire flew forth to mingle with its sisters. The airstreams converged to form a small wind tunnel above Evelyn, tossing her hair skyward and amplifying her words.

"We seek more than kindness,
We need more than love,
We long for your answers,
The wisdom of above,
Come dine with your blood,
This dark Samhain night,
Pass through the veil,
Share with us your light."

Evelyn flung her arms above her head. The tunnel of wind followed, growing smaller and smaller until it blended into the dark clouds above.

The hairs on the back of Lily's neck stood at attention as she searched for a sign, a ghost to materialize out of thin air. But there was nothing. She frowned, the witch's blood rampaging through her veins was insisting that *something* should be happening. Whispers and one soft chuckle came from the onlookers. Lily's face burned. *Why hadn't it worked?* Hearing Evelyn's words, feeling the change in the air—the night felt ripe, ready to be taken by magic, exactly as Lily imagined calling a ghost across the veil would feel. The thought landed that whatever feeling of frustration she was experiencing, Evelyn would be feeling it a hundred times over. *I should be comforting her*, Lily thought pulling her eyes from the ground. *What the hell?*

Evelyn caught Lily's eye and smiled knowingly before bringing her hands up to cup her red lips. "Resipisico," Evelyn breathed. The word traveled from the center of the circle like a whisper on the wind.

A tornado, larger and more ferocious than its predecessor, slammed down from the sky cutting them off from all onlookers.

Lily jumped as a large rock hurled past, missing her arm by inches.

"Cast a shield!" Brigit instructed, her voice cracking as the tornado tightened around them.

"Arma," Lily yelled above the howling wind.

Evelyn reached out to grasp her hand and Lily took it instinctively. A jolt of power surged through her before evaporating. *She's draining me*, Lily realized, and suddenly Brigit grasped Lily's other hand. A jolt of power ran through Lily and she became an energy conductor, taking and passing magic through her body. She squeezed Evelyn's hand tighter to donate all the power she could. The sound of the wind grew distant as finally all seven shields knitted together to form a dome high above them. The moment the shield was whole Evelyn raised her face to the sky and began to chant once more, her words lilting and swaying in the wind's echo.

"I call on water,

Giver of life,

Restore a soul departed,

To Earth this Samhain night,

I offer her tribute,

Confidence and trust,

Drink the blood of her blood,

Shed on Earth this night."

Lily let out a sigh of exhaustion as her hand dropped to her side and Evelyn made for her waistband. Silver glinted in the moonlight and Lily winced as Evelyn ran a dagger across her palm. A thin scarlet line beaded up from the soft flesh there and Evelyn held her hand aloft, squeezing it open and shut.

"Resipisico," Brigit whispered, dropping Lily's other hand and holding her palms to the sky as Evelyn's dark red blood fell to the earth.

The motion and word was echoed by Aoife, Mary, Gwenn, Sara and, finally, Lily. The moment the enchantment was sealed a faint fog began gathering, swirling, gaining density and shape above Evelyn's small pool of blood.

From the fog an opaque, grayish head materialized, followed by a torso, arms, and legs. Lily blinked. An old woman was there, not quite flesh and blood, but very much resembling the living, sitting cross-legged in the grass in front of Evelyn. She unfurled herself with the speed and grace of a much younger body as she stood to face her caller.

"Happy Samhain, daughter. You called?" the woman asked. She was dressed in a long linen dress and a cap that resembled a bandana. The tattered dress fell loose off her skeletal frame. Her hair, the crowning glory of her otherwise haggard appearance, hung down to her buttocks in thick braids.

"Thank you for coming, grandmother. Would you like to stay for dinner?" Evelyn said, a wide smile on her bowed face.

"Thank you, but I've already eaten," the ghost said, gesturing down to the ground where Evelyn's blood stained the dirt. "Your tribute paid the way for old Florence Newton to spend another night on earth. I was skeptical about crossing the veil, but I must say it's wonderful to be back in my motherland! And on Samhain no less! I could not have asked for a better resurrection. Now do you have something particular to ask? Or shall I tell you a bit of what I see?"

Perhaps it was the unexpected chattiness of their ghost ancestor. Or perhaps she hadn't realized there would be a choice, but Evelyn appeared at a loss. She rolled her lip between her teeth and her uninjured hand clasped the other as she considered the ghost's question.

"Grandmother. Please. Tell us what you see," a voice muddled beyond recognition said.

Florence turned and her face broke into a smile. "Brigit! I've spoken to your mother recently. You must know she's proud of you, we all are. You've done right by these girls, putting their safety before your need for love."

A tear ran down Brigit's face as she stared, transfixed, at the opaque figure by her daughter. "Thank you grandmother . . . Florence."

Florence nodded approvingly at the show of tears before turning back to Evelyn. "So is that your answer then, too? You'd like to know what I see?"

Evelyn nodded, and the ghost beamed.

"You would not believe how many mortals ask ghosts the stupidest questions. But then, the women in my family line always were known for their exceptional cunning. Take me, for example! No one else in my day ever considered stealing a few scraps of paper and vanishing on the day of their trial! That's how I ended up in this part of the country, of course. I did miss the sea so far inland. But alas, Youghal could never again be home for me, not with that lot of witch hunts across the channel." She paused, taking in their shocked faces. "Right, then, enough about me. Let's see, you want to know what I know."

No one spoke as Florence ruminated. Lily thought she could hear the dim chatter of onlookers outside the shield and risked a glance. No one appeared the slightest bit shocked that a new, diaphanous family member was floating in the middle of their circle. *Can the others see Florence?* she wondered.

A cold breeze tickled her nose and Lily's gaze shifted to find Florence hovering before her. She shuddered as the ghost's eyes, which were a shade darker than her gray skin, raked over her. *Am I supposed to say something?* Lily's skin tightened and she found herself extending every blink in hopes that Florence would be gone when she opened her eyes once more. When she thought she could take no more, the ghost moved on to Sara without a word spoken between them. The experience Florence bestowed varied depending on the person in two respects: time and response. Evelyn spent mere seconds with the ghost, while Aoife was the object of Florence's attention for upwards of ten minutes. The responses never failed to reveal the subject's discomfort with Florence's gaze, whether it be the compulsive twitch of Aoife's hand or Gwenn's spontaneous humming.

Finally, Florence returned to the center of the circle, her face set in grim lines.

"I've gathered that you are a group who could use much advice. As I'm brought here to divulge one, and only one, bit of information, I have chosen to share the most urgent matter."

A stiff breeze whipped across Lily's cheeks, and Florence was before her once again.

"Your family does not know it yet, but one of their members is in danger. Only you can save her life. Her captors shall call tonight."

Lily's legs swayed. She felt her shield falter and Sara's extend to meet its cracking edges. "Who's in danger? Who will call?" she squeaked.

But it was too late. Florence, sensing the weakened shield, and her way back home, floated up past the confines of the charm and disappeared into the darkness.

***

The long grass whipped Lily's legs as she sprinted toward Fern Cottage. Her muscles burned, pushed to the point of what she recognized from years of cross-country races would likely end in collapse.

It didn't matter.

Florence's final words played in her head, matching the rhythm of her feet as they struck the earth.

"Her captors shall call tonight."

Without breaking stride, Lily burst through the cottage door. She began a frantic search for the phone, an old cordless that Brigit left laying wherever her conversations happened to end. Pillows flew and cabinets banged open as she ransacked the house.

"*Lily! Hold on!*" Sara exclaimed, as she ran through the door bent over and clutching her sides.

Lily spared no more than a glance Sara's way before resuming her search.

"Someone is going to call! I have to find the damn phone!"

"Stop running about like a crazy person," Evelyn commanded, pushing inside past Sara and grabbing Lily by the wrist to pull her to the kitchen. "Look, someone's already called." She pointed to an ancient answering machine, its light blinking a neon green number two. "Sit down, I'll do it," Evelyn said, maneuvering Lily into a chair before punching the button.

Lily's heart flew into her throat, as a familiar voice filled the room.

"Lil, it's Rena. You're probably out celebrating with your family. I wanted you to know I got a strange message tonight." Rena's voice was flat, yet Lily thought she could detect a string of worry woven through the words.

"Nothing's happened, but I want you to be careful. It was from a man . . . I think. The creepy fuck used one of those computer things so I can't be sure. He didn't make much sense, but he mentioned you and a book and that you are supposed to meet him? Be careful, honey. I'd feel much better if you stayed in the cottage. The man didn't sound sane. Call me when you get this."

The line clicked off, and Lily exhaled halfway. A creepy call was unnerving but not life threatening.

"Play the next one."

Lily's head shot up to find Brigit standing right behind her while Aoife and Mary guarded the door.

Evelyn pushed the button.

Static played, giving Lily a glimmer of hope that it was a wrong number before an exaggerated twangy Southern accent slid from the device.

"Howdy, witches. I'd hoped to catch you in person but seein' as it's Samhain, I shoulda known better. A new member of your little coven is missin' something reeeeaaaal dear to them. Bring us Seraphina's book, and my brother and I may find it in our hearts to let her live. I'm sure you'll figure out where to find us. Be seein' y'all soon." The line died and Lily shot out of her chair to replay the message.

Brigit blocked her mid-lunge, lips pulled back in a straight, thin line. "Lily, call Rena, tell her to check on everyone in the commune, specifically anyone from the South."

Lily stared at Brigit. "Why the South?"

"Because," Aoife broke in, her eyes blazing like fire, "I'd bet my right hand that was Empusa, and she sure as hell isn't from the South."

Lily's mind raced. Empusa? Wasn't she the vampire Mary said had eaten her way through ancient Greece with her brother? What was his name? They were still alive?!

"How do you know?"

"Witches have a long history with Empusa. We find it best to know as much about her as possible. I met her once when I was young. My sisters did, too, and each meeting was a very unwelcome surprise. Empusa and her twin, Amon, make a point of meeting members of the strongest witching families. They have spies who tell them who to investigate. I'll never forget the day I met Empusa. I had taken a trip to London and she cornered me on the street in broad daylight. It was terrifying. I asked about her afterward and discovered she and her brother Amon have been hunting a relic said to belong to witches for centuries. Rumor has it, in the past they even killed for it. We may have just discovered what that relic is," Brigit said, her mouth thinner than Lily had ever seen it. "Call Rena."

Rena answered on the first ring. "Lil! Are you alright? I've been so worried."

"I'm fine," Lily said. "How's everyone there? We did a circle and —something happened. It scared me." Lily explained Florence's visit and the strange voicemail, hoping to hear her mother's reassurance that everyone was home, practicing yoga, making soap, and baking. Instead she heard the vibration of air.

"Mom? Are you still there? What's going on?"

"This caller, Empusa you said her name was? She mimicked a Southern accent?"

Lily nodded, forgetting they were on the phone, before catching herself. "Yea."

"Lil . . . Em left for Portland two days ago."

"What do you mean she left?" She heard words, high pitched and trembling. *Is that my voice?*

"The women's retreat, Lil. She's speaking tomorrow," Rena spoke as if to a child. "Could I speak with Brigit, please?"

Lily passed the phone and collapsed into a chair that had materialized behind her. Em practically never left the commune, and only once a year did she travel more than half an hour away. How could they know that this weekend, out of all the weekends, she'd be gone?

"Ask if they've called Em," Lily commanded, a flutter of panic rising in her throat.

Brigit nodded but remained silent, listening to Rena. Seconds later, she placed the phone back in its cradle, not having uttered a single word.

"What happened? Did they get ahold of her? Where is she?" Lily's heart beat faster than ever as visions of Emily, bound and gagged in the back of a creepy white van, flooded her mind.

"According to Rena they've called to check on her a few times but no one's heard back. Annika confirmed she hasn't shown up to any retreat events so far. It's unusual for Emily to be out of contact?" Brigit asked, looking as if she already knew the answer.

"She was in an abusive relationship for years. Since moving to Terramar she hardly ever leaves, and when she does she makes sure everyone knows. She *always* returns calls." Tears threatened to spill from Lily's eyes as the soft pressure of hands rested on her shoulders. In her periphery, she could see Evelyn and Sara on either side of her, their touch supplying a sense of relief she vaguely recognized as a calming spell.

"We'll find her, Lil. Aoife and Mary have already started compiling a list of places they think Empusa could be. It looked short," Sara said, her voice even and reassuring.

"Very short. We've already narrowed it down to two cities," Aoife said, rounding the hearth into the kitchen, her cell phone in hand.

Brigit raised her eyebrows. "That was fast."

"A few quick calls to our sister covens living in Empusa's favorite haunts. No one's spotted her in New York, London, Paris, New Orleans, or Tokyo."

"How can they be sure?" Evelyn asked, sounding skeptical. "They're all pretty damn big cities."

"We witches have our ways. You can bet your big blue eyes that if Empusa or Amon showed up in Dublin, we'd know. It helps that she and her brother aren't much for laying low. They like to get out and have their fill, as it were."

Lily felt her stomach clench before another calming wave rushed over her.

"We're certain she's one of two places. She recently purchased vacation homes in both but had her cronies set up house in only one. Empusa never goes far without her entourage."

"Where?" Lily demanded.

"Alexandria," Aoife said, a grim smile growing on her face. "Seems we weren't the only ones doing research. She's a nostalgic bitch, that Empusa."

# *Alexandria*

Lily's head spun as she lowered herself onto a cream leather chair in the plane's cabin. In the hours it took the Locksley's private jet to fly from New York to Shannon, the witches cleared out the Samhain gathering, drove to Shannon Airport, and formulated a plan. They had decided that Lily, Brigit, Sara, Evelyn, and Aoife would travel ahead to Alexandria to investigate. The others would hedge their bets and wait for a morning flight to Venice, the other city Empusa had recently been spotted in.

"But we still don't have the book from the prophecy. Or know where it is. Or if it's even real. What are they going to do when we show up without it?" Lily tried to keep her voice level as the plane pushed back and their plan moved forward despite this glaring flaw.

"Like we discussed, Lil, there's nothing we can do about that now. Mary's spent two decades searching and come up empty handed. We'll have to try reasoning with them," Brigit said, the worry in her eyes betraying the confidence in her tone.

"We should have told the rest of the coven about the abduction. They could have had a better idea."

"None in the coven except Morgane, Fiona, and Nora know what we suspect you three are. At this point, it's better it stays that way," Brigit explained for the fourth time.

"The fact is, there were at least a dozen people in attendance tonight we know little about. Any one of them could be spying for the other side," Aoife said. "I know, I know, Brig, it's poor form to speak of our people like such, but it's the truth. Somehow the other side's figured out that you three exist and what you are. Someone's been talking. Maybe not on purpose. Maybe seemingly insignificant tidbits. Possibly they were forced to. The end result is the same: The countdown has begun."

Lily felt as if she'd been stabbed in the gut. Until that moment she hadn't realized how much she was counting on a cover of anonymity. She watched Evelyn's lips turn white and her breath grow shallow. Probably Evelyn had been relying on it, too. They both lacked confidence with many defensive spells. Sara's face was passive as she stared out the window and fingered her beaded necklace, but that didn't surprise Lily. Knowing Sara, she had considered a scenario like this before anyone else.

"Do you think it was the calling of the ancestors?" Evelyn asked, shifting in her seat.

"Now don't you feel guilty about that. No one has been able to pull that off in centuries," Aoife said.

"Besides," Brigit added, "Em left two days ago, and we know she never made it to the retreat. They could have taken her anytime in between, well before the calling of the ancestors circle."

Conversation dropped into silence as each settled into the hours with their thoughts. Lily watched Sara assume a cross-legged position and close her eyes. Within seconds her chest began rising and falling in even counts. Evelyn, too, sat with her eyes closed, though the tension in her neck and jaw screamed inner turmoil. Brigit and Aoife were attempting to lose themselves in books, though not any book Lily cared for at the moment. The only book that would satisfy her had been lost for millennia.

*Dammit, Hypatia, couldn't you have made it easier? Why couldn't Seraphina's tome have landed in Mary's outstretched prophetic arms the day we were born? Shit, right now I wish it would have landed on me! It probably didn't weigh enough to crush a baby. How do Empusa and Amon even know about the book? Why do they want it? What do they think was in it?* Aoife believed it was the story of Lilith, Eve, and Seraphina's time on Earth and the history of witches, passed down by word of mouth until someone devised to write it down. Lily wasn't so sure that was all the book was. *There must be something more to it if vampires are searching for it,* Lily thought. *No one searches for centuries just to hear a good story.*

She closed her eyes and sniffed, swallowing down the tears that threatened to fill her eyes. Her ears popped.

"We're descending," Evelyn said, breaking the pristine silence. "The pilot never announces it. Daddy forbade it. It breaks his concentration."

Lily opened the shade and saw the outline of a city rising up from the Mediterranean. The harbor was gleaming blue against the city's tall, white buildings. Small dots of yellow and red littered the water: fishermen out for their daily catch, blissfully unaware of the dangerous mythical creatures that prowled their city. The sun was already high in the sky, a not-so-subtle reminder that Lily hadn't slept in over a day.

"Do we know where we're going first?" Sara asked, opening her eyes. She looked rejuvenated, calm, and collected after her meditation.

"First stop is the Alexandrian coven safe house. Their coven is one of the longest running in history. Hypatia was a member, and it was in their archive that Mary first learned of her existence. It's possible they have new information about the book. At the very least we can get the lay of the city and devise a plan of attack," Brigit said.

*Plan of attack*, Lily thought, her stomach sinking. She realized how naive her vision of walking peacefully into Empusa's home was. Yet she still couldn't help but cling to the thread of hope that if they just explained they didn't have the book, that they'd never even seen it, Empusa and Amon would simply let Em go.

"Do they know where Empusa lives?" Lily asked.

"Aye, it's one of their members who saw her strolling the streets of a well-to-do neighborhood this week and followed her home. Vamps don't generally garner a witch's attention, but Empusa and Amon are different. They're vicious and always have been. Most witches consider it their duty to safeguard loved ones and neighbors from the pair. Others, too, if they can help it," Aoife said, unable to hide her disgust.

"Why can't the covens put their foot down and deny access to their city?" Evelyn asked.

"I hate to say it, but vampires have to eat, too, though not as often as popular tales would have you believe. Once a month is the average, much more when they're in their first two years of being a vampire. A newly reborn vampire is the most dangerous creature on Earth. They're unreasonable and answer only to their sire and blood. Their blood lust is so unquenchable they'd drain entire cities without a second thought. It takes about two years for newborns to stop acting like savages. I should mention that vampires have had to become more selective with their prey in recent years. Technology makes it harder to get away with draining a person and not getting caught. Some claim the choice is due to increased compassion rather than technology. I say it depends on the vamp. Either way, many modern vamps go for easy targets, the lowest of the low or those already in great pain." Aoife frowned. "But Empusa, Amon, and their cronies adhere to no such a code. The happier a person is, the more other people love them, the more likely Empusa and Amon are to stalk them."

Lily thought of Em's hearty laugh and wide, dimpled smile. Her heart sank.

"That's horrific," Sara said and resumed staring out the window.

Minutes later the jolt of wheels upon tarmac announced their arrival onto Egyptian soil. The plane idled into a hanger and Lily glanced at her phone. They had arrived forty minutes ahead of schedule. Their stop at customs was laughably quick. A plump man performed a cursory glance at Evelyn's passport, beamed, and pointed them in the direction of a limo arranged by Mr. Locksley's assistant.

"Is this how you always travel?" Lily asked Evelyn, who was helping herself to one of the sparkling waters stocked in the minibar.

"Usually Daddy sends a Bentley. Seeing as there are so many of us, I suppose he thought this was a better option," Evelyn said, sipping her water.

"Could you let your father know next time that I'd prefer the stretch Bentley?" Sara said in imitation of Evelyn's airy tone.

"I didn't know they made those," Evelyn replied, eyebrows knitting together.

Laughter flew from Lily's mouth. It was strange to hear such a wild, free sound after so many hours of unwavering fear.

"Thanks, Evelyn, we'd appreciate it," Lily said.

***

"We're here, girls," Brigit said, as the limo pulled to a stop a half hour later.

It was the type of home no one would expect a high priestess of one of the world's most ancient covens to live in. Stark white, edgy, and modern, the building looked more like a haunt for a rich, twenty-something Los Angeleno. They were pulling the last bag out of the trunk when the apartment door opened.

*And the surprises keep coming,* Lily thought as a striking woman approached Brigit. The high priestess was young and gorgeous with dark, smooth skin and light green eyes.

Brigit's face broke into a smile. "Bahiti, it's good to see you."

"The pleasure is all mine, Brigit. Please come in, all of you."

Bahiti decorated her home much as the exterior would suggest. The furniture was minimal, though it appeared to be custom made and the same high quality as the avant garde art hung on the walls.

"Please take a seat. I have cushions for those with younger legs," Bahiti said pointing to a small stack of large, bright pillows.

Only once everyone was comfortable, with a cup of mint tea in hand, did Bahiti deem it time to get down to business.

"I hear you seek Empusa, but I've heard of no stalkings or murders in the area. Tell me, what has she done that you would know of before I?" Bahiti said lowering herself onto the loveseat beside Brigit.

"Empusa has taken a hostage in return for Hypatia's book."

Bahiti's spine straightened.

"Which, of course, we do not have," Brigit added.

"Of course," Bahiti said, reclining once more with a small frown. "Why does she think this is possible? Very few know you've been searching. Even fewer know the reasons why," Bahiti tore her gaze from Brigit to look at the triplets, her eyes roving over each in the witchy manner Lily had become used to.

"Your daughters. I know them, but only through legend, of course."

"I'm sorry I forgot to make introductions."

"No matter. I already know. Anyone who knows the story would have to be blind not to guess, but then I say that with the benefit of already knowing. Seraphina, Eve, and Lilith," Bahiti said pointing to Sara, Evelyn, and Lily in turn. "I am Bahiti Basara, high priestess of the Daughters of Isis and a very old friend of your mother's family, your family. I am honored to meet you." She inclined her head, looking every bit a queen.

"Yes, you're quite right about the namesakes. The prophecy helped settle that, though the names we chose were a bit more modern. This is Lily, Evelyn, and Sara. It's one of Lily's relatives Empusa kidnapped," Brigit said.

Bahiti nodded. "So, Empusa has taken someone dear to Lily. I must say this comes as a surprise. I have had people stationed outside Empusa's grounds since we received word of her occupation. Aside from the day one of my sisters reported her strolling the neighborhood, I've heard no mention of Empusa's comings or goings. She seems to be content to stay at home, which as you know, is most unlike her."

"Has anyone else arrived? Amon, or any other followers we'd recognize?"

"I told my people to call the moment anyone of importance stepped foot on her property. I can only assume no one has as I've received no word."

Lily's stomach dropped. *Have we traveled all this way for nothing? Is Em somewhere else?* A vampire as old as Empusa could have at least a dozen homes all over the world.

"Have you phoned your patrols?" Aoife asked bluntly.

Bahiti's stunning features arranged themselves into one of puzzlement. "No, why would I? Their orders are to call me if something is out of place."

Aoife sighed, her face red, and tone impatient. "Oh I don't know, maybe because we're talking about Empusa here. She hasn't stepped a toe outside her own walls after a witch caught sight of her and reported her strolling about the neighborhood. That doesn't sound suspicious at all? You haven't bothered to check on your scouts? What if Empusa decided she needed a little snack before dealing with Emily?" Aoife clapped her hands over her mouth. "I'm sorry, Lil. I didn't mean . . ."

"It's—it's fine," Lily stammered, slithering off her cushion to lie flat on the floor.

"Could you check on your scouts Bahiti?" Brigit asked, dropping to the floor to grasp Lily's hand. "We will find her, Lil. I promise. Remember your lessons and how prepared you are to help. Emily needs you to be strong."

Lily nodded but was unable to meet Brigit's gaze, instead choosing to focus on Bahiti rushing out of the room to find the phone.

"We've got this, Lily. Sara will throw some crazy firepower at them and I'll get into their heads while you find Emily. Thank God you're a healer, she'll need you." Evelyn's words, though meant to be reassuring, did little to ease her mind.

Lily was saved from responding by Bahiti's breathless

reappearance.

"No one answered. I stationed four of my best scouts and they've all gone dark." Her green eyes were wide with terror as they bounced between Brigit and Aoife.

"We think Empusa wants this book quite as much as we do, Bahiti. And we all know how bad it can get if Empusa becomes desperate," Aoife said, her voice tight.

"I see that now. I never thought she'd dare attack my people. The coven has a standing arrangement for the safety of its members during her time here . . ."

"My guess is she's been searching for this book far longer than we have. Now that she believes we're connected with it, and you with us, it's safe to say prior arrangements have gone out the window."

Bahiti nodded and pressed her full lips together.

Brigit turned to Evelyn. "Will Locksley Enterprises need their jet anytime soon? We need to call for reinforcements."

***

By the time Mary, Gwenn, Fiona, and Morgane touched down on Egyptian soil, a plan was in motion. It was clear Empusa was angling to meet Lily, though Brigit and Aoife thought it possible the identities of Sara and Evelyn might still be unknown. Therefore, only Lily was to accompany them to Empusa's lair.

"She has to know we exist if she believes the tales!" Evelyn protested.

"But not what you look like, perhaps not even your names. Thanks to the wards on Fern Cottage, she's never gotten close to the place. It's obvious she knows who Lily is, where she grew up, and whom she'd risk her life for, but there may be a chance that's all she knows. Lily has no choice but to go. You, on the other hand, can and *will* remain hidden for as long as possible. I will not endanger you needlessly," Brigit said sounding, for the first time, very much like a mother setting boundaries for her child.

Evelyn scowled but remained quiet, unable to argue with Brigit's logic.

Lily, Brigit, Aoife, and Gwenn were to venture into Empusa's home while Bahiti, Mary, and Morgane remained hidden on the grounds under the cover of nightfall, awaiting a distress signal. Lily hoped it wouldn't get to that point. Their signal was neither subtle nor cunning, both qualities Brigit stressed they embody when dealing with Empusa and Amon. Only Aoife seemed to relish the idea of shooting fireballs through Empusa's walls over a peaceful mission.

"She deserves far more than that for all the stunts she's pulled over the years. You've no idea what antics our kind has had to cover up," Aoife said stoutly.

Brigit nodded, but Lily could tell that she, too, would rather not upset the vampires.

Sara and Evelyn were to wait, safe and sound in Bahiti's home, which Brigit and Aoife had placed under countless protective charms during the hours spent waiting for reinforcements to arrive.

"You can bet we'll put a sealing spell on the door when we leave, too," Aoife said, her eyes shifting to Evelyn when Lily commented on the bevy of spells used.

Sara, while disappointed to be left behind, was trying to make the best of their situation.

"Think of what we can learn from Bahiti's sisters! Egyptian magic has been world renowned for centuries." She'd been saying some version of the words since Bahiti's mention that two witches from her coven would arrive to teach Sara and Evelyn traditional Egyptian spells and a bit of lore to keep their minds preoccupied.

"Our babysitters, you mean," Evelyn huffed in response each time Sara brought this up. Evelyn simmered until the moment they were set to leave. Lily was performing one last check of her healer's kit—a small, and she liked to think fashionable, leather fanny pack filled with herbs and vials of potions—when Evelyn approached her.

"I know we don't always see eye to eye but I wanted to wish you luck tonight. I wish I was coming, and not just because I want these monsters finished and my life back. That could have been any of our families," Evelyn said, reaching out to pat Lily's shoulder awkwardly.

"I wish you guys were coming, too," Lily said, grabbing Evelyn and pulling her into their first hug. Now—when death seemed like a real possibility—was as good a time as any to drop misgivings.

Out of nowhere, a third pair of arms encompassed them, and Lily felt her and Evelyn's mutual tension soften. "Next time, we'll fight together, Lil. We won't let them hurt you or your family ever again," Sara said, her usually cheery voice thick with emotion.

Lily felt a lump in her throat threatening to rise. Months ago, she hadn't even known these girls. A day ago she'd barely been on speaking terms with one of them. Now she was offering up her life for theirs.

"Not just our lives," Evelyn said, a sheepish grin on her face, "We're in it to save humanity, remember?"

Lily grinned as her mind barriers, so prone to slipping since she'd heard of Em's abduction, clicked back into place. "All of them, too."

# *The Vampire Twins*

They arrived at Empusa's mansion as the last of the sun's rays fell upon the horizon. Bahiti split off down the street leading the emergency rescue crew along the outskirts of the house. With any luck they'd find a hiding spot near the grand hall, a large room Bahiti felt certain Empusa would receive visitors in.

"It's like a ballroom. She'll want to impress you with her power and influence. Why else would she have bought such a monstrosity? She may have even bought it for this exact moment."

Lily had never seen a home so large or luxurious. Four stories high, the mansion glowed like a white limestone cliff in moonlight. Stone lions five feet high were set on each side of the staircase leading to the front door, their teeth bared in welcome.

Aoife guffawed as they walked past them. "The gaudiest," she muttered, shaking her head.

Brigit turned to Lily. "Em may be in bad shape. Are you sure you can you handle seeing her that way? There's still time—"

"There's no way I'm leaving Em in there with those monsters," Lily said, reaching past Brigit to lift the heavy brass knocker before she could change her mind. It fell with an ominous thud.

A distinct click of heels, followed by the turning of a deadbolt, and a dim squeal of door hinges revealed one of the most beautiful beings Lily had ever seen. Tall with lean muscles, vibrant emerald eyes, light caramel skin and contrasting yet pleasing dark auburn hair, the woman smiled to reveal two rows of perfectly white, straight teeth with pronounced canines.

"Ahhhhhh, Brigeeeet," the woman purred in what Lily guessed was as a light French accent. "It has been so long. I always had a feeling about your family, you know? Such talented, strong witches and wizards, all of them. Follow me into the hall. We'll speak there."

"Empusa," Brigit said, her face stoney, as she stepped over the mansion's threshold after the vampire.

*Empusa? Where are the servants? The ambush? The display of power and fear mongering? Empusa's treating Brigit as if they're old friends.*

*Careful, Lil, she's lulling you into a trap.* Lily started at the sound of Aoife's voice in her head.

"No magic," Empusa turned, her green eyes flashing. The predatory hunch of her shoulders contradicted the sing-song tone of her voice. She caught herself and straightened. Then the gracious smile reappeared. "It's disrespectful to those of us who are not as *gifted.*"

*Message received,* Lily thought. Empusa could change tack as easily as Aoife could light a candle.

The tapping of the vampire's stilettos upon the white marble floor echoed through the cavernous hallway. With each closed door they passed, a vision of Em drained dry behind it flashed in Lily's head. *What would Empusa do if I opened one to check?* She had nearly built up the courage to turn the next doorknob when a shaft of light from an open doorway twenty paces ahead caught her eye. Instinctively, Lily knew Em would be in there, starving, perhaps beaten, or worst of all bitten. Empusa would have left it open for Lily to see. Waves of nausea swept over her as they drew closer and low moans pinged in her ears.

Then they were there. Lily gasped and bile rose in her throat. Dozens of people filled the room, each of them standing at attention and salivating as Empusa strode by without so much as a glance.

Lily couldn't stop herself from staring back at them: thin, pale to the point of death, with hollow eyes. Blood smears ran up their arms, failing to disguise the track marks and vampire bites marring their skin. Bottles, pills, and needles littered the floor beside filthy mattresses, which were a vile sort of common area occupied simultaneously by some sleeping off their poison while others engaged in more carnal outlets. Paintings of a lewd, seductive nature hung from the walls, inspiring the sexual fervor within. Here was Empusa's feeding grounds. A den of sin where she could prey upon the weak by providing the intoxicants and flesh they were unable to deny themselves.

"I trust you'll excuse the poor manners of my guests, I've been too busy to provide them any attention lately. They've become quite needy," Empusa said, her eyes trained on Lily.

"I hope that's not how you treat all your *guests*," Lily growled, her nausea flinging itself into fury.

"Oh no," Empusa said reassuringly, reaching for the handles of the elaborate French doors at the end of the hall. "Certain people get VIP treatment."

***

The doors swung inward and Lily gasped as she set eyes on a room larger than all of Fern Cottage. Dozens of crystal chandeliers hung from the high, domed ceiling. A magnificent red tiled aisle led up to the sole pieces of furniture in the room, two velvet covered thrones. Dozens of strong, attractive bodies stood at attention before them like soldiers awaiting command.

"I was wondering when we'd meet your cronies," Aoife said with a sneer as the sea of beautiful people parted for Empusa.

"You can't expect my *children* to mingle with my guests, can you? There's not enough of them for all of us to share."

*Her children? Oh shit.* A hard lump formed in Lily's throat. She had been prepared for Empusa, Amon, and a handful of other vamps, but there were at least fifty people in here. Maybe not all of them were vamps, but from what she could tell they weren't human either. Empusa, it appeared, subscribed to the belief that humans were only suitable for food and the occasional pleasure of the flesh. Striding down the aisle, Lily felt an increasing urge to vomit. *What the hell have we gotten ourselves into? And where is Em?*

"Unfortunately, we don't have enough seats for everyone at present. We just moved in, as I'm sure you're aware," Empusa said. She looked anything but sorry as she claimed a throne, leaving Lily and her aunts to stand stupidly before her. "And now, where is my brother? Amon?" Empusa's voice was silky, unconcerned, as she scanned the crowd.

"Coming, sister," a velvet baritone voice slid from the crowd seconds before a man walked out, guiding an old woman by her elbow.

Lily's heart wrenched open as all the air left her lungs. She swayed on the spot, only half aware of the hands that caught her. Squeezing her eyes shut, she willed it to be a hallucination, a mirage. *No, no, no. It can't be real*, she thought, trying to calm her racing pulse. She opened one eye, then the other, and found two stormy beacons with bright flecks of violet boring into her.

"Hello, Lily," Liam said with a devilish smirk.

Liam, her Liam, was Amon, a bloodthirsty vampire. And Amon was holding Em. Terrified, frail Emily. Her heart, still a little broken from the breakup, solidified as the depth of Liam's . . . Amon's betrayal set in. Her magic sprang to life within her and her blood began to boil.

"What have you done to her?" Lily snarled, shifting her gaze back to Empusa.

"Don't give 'em anything, Lil! I won't let you! I'm not worth it!" Emily's voice, thin as paper, cracked as she attempted to pull herself from Amon's firm grasp.

"Didn't I tell you to remain silent?" Amon asked scowling at Em, who glared back with narrowed eyes. "I can tell we won't be getting any talking done with you around, now will we? Georgina, would you show Ms. Harp to her chamber?"

A petite blonde with a southern belle air floated out of the crowd. She bestowed a slavish, seductive smile on Amon before taking Em by the elbow and yanking her toward the door.

"I swear, if you hurt her—" Lily's threats died in her mouth as Georgina spun round to face her, fangs bared.

"*Do* be gentle with our guest, Georgina," Empusa commanded.

Georgina stood down reluctantly.

Lily watched, her body vibrating with anger, as Emily vanished through a crimson door at the far side of the grand hall.

"As you can see," Empusa said, as Amon ascended to the throne next to her, "we've kept our end of the bargain. Emily is alive. No one will lay a finger on her gray little head unless we say so. That much could never be said for any other human staying in our home. Despite my stipulation that humans in the house are off limits to all but myself or Amon . . . well, accidents happen." Empusa shrugged.

"We're well aware of the 'accidents' that seem to happen when you're around," Gwenn sneered. "Is that how you're getting your fill now? Bring people into your home and lavish them with drugs and sex so they don't mind that you're sucking their life right out of them?"

"I had little choice. As you are well aware, most of the covens in the larger cities limit our hunting. They seem to think we overindulge. Those people came here on their own free will."

"We are not here to discuss your feeding habits. We are here to collect Emily," Brigit said, bringing the conversation—and Gwenn's wrath—back where it belonged.

"Where's the book? I see you have no bags in which to carry or protect it." Empusa leaned forward, studying Brigit with an intensity that made Lily's skin crawl.

"We don't have it. We never have."

"*Lies*!" Empusa screamed.

The crowd hissed behind them as the first sign of Empusa's unbridled rage bubbled up to transform her face from poised to monstrous.

"Spare us your witches' tales. We know the prophecy exists, Brigit. I heard Hypatia weaving the spell to hide the book until the three that met its specifications were born," Amon said, meeting Lily's eyes.

Lily glowered back, her repulsion for the man she once thought she loved clear on her face.

"You murdered her, you mean. I'll bet you set fire to the Great Library as well. You're why it's lost and why human knowledge is lacking. You're why we know nothing of our fate," Aoife growled, breaking their standoff.

Amon's chiseled features softened disturbingly into an expression of joviality. "It is as much our right to read Seraphina's words, the story of one of the first fata on Earth, as it is yours. Is it not? All Earth's magical creatures are descended from the same noble race. We're all family."

"*You* are nothing like us! Seems to me Seraphina didn't want you to read it, and you don't deserve to read it even if we had it." The words tumbled out of Lily in a blind rage.

Amon's face darkened and his fingers gripped his throne tighter as Lily fought back for the first time.

"I do not see how it matters what Seraphina wanted thousands of years ago. Especially when we hold such precious cargo at present," Empusa responded, having collected herself from her previous outburst. She rolled her shoulders back and stretched her neck out luxuriously. "I've always loved the taste of empaths, haven't you, brother? So much vitality in each drop of blood."

Lily seethed, but she knew it was no good. They would never convince the vampires they didn't have the book.

Lily knew Aoife felt the same when she shifted her slight frame to hide behind Lily and Gwenn. Aoife was implementing plan B. Time for a distraction.

"What do you think you'll learn in this book that you haven't managed to figure out in two thousand years?" Lily said lunging forward. Her anger would incite Amon the most and keep his eyes off Aoife. Already she could smell Aoife's familiar pepper and ginger scent intensifying as she used her power covertly. The diversion wouldn't need to last long. "If you don't know whatever it is you're seeking by now, you never will. I mean, how fucking thick are you two?"

Hisses, growls, and gasps arose from the crowd behind her only to be silenced with a flick of Amon's hand.

"Now, now, Lily love," Amon's words were laden with seduction, but for the first time Lily could hear the danger below the surface.

Her hands and shoulders tightened. How could one mention of his pet name for Lily have her feeling so disgusted and aroused all at once?

"You don't mean any of that, do you, baby?" Amon said descending the steps, his eyes narrowed and lips pursed. "You would never have said such a thing six months ago. Back then I had *all* the answers, didn't I?"

The crowd's mood shifted from provoked to gleeful. Sniggers rose as Amon swayed his hips and licked his lips.

Brigit stiffened and Gwenn gasped in horror. Lily's face burned red hot as Amon turned and ascended the steps. Taking his throne once more, he raised two fingers to his lips and blew a kiss in her direction. It was happening again: Liam, *Amon* manipulating her feelings for his own enjoyment. *I am so over this shit*, Lily thought.

"Times change, *Amon.* I've learned some things in the past few months. Like who I am. *You* always wondered that, didn't you? You knew I had secrets, power, inside me. Turns out it was just another thing you were too dim to find."

Amon's face tightened.

"Well, guess what? I've managed to figure out quite a few of my own secrets. Look what I can do." Lily raised her hands high above her.

Amon and Empusa shot up from their thrones at the motion, and the crowd leaned back.

Amon sneered, his shoulders relaxing as he took in the skin of her hands glowing dark blue, the color radiating off Lily like ocean waves, all the way out to her fingertips and dissipating into the air. "Is that all you have to show us? A useless party trick? I had hoped that your family was able to teach you—"

"NOW!" Aoife screamed, as two infernos burst from her palms. The fireballs arched high above the heads of the crowd, shattering the windows and soaring through the gardens until they fizzled out of sight.

Vampires hissed and sprinted down the hallway at an unbelievable speed, out of the way of the deadly missiles Aoife spewed from her open palms.

"Find Em!" Gwenn commanded.

Lily felt a sharp tug and turned to see Brigit racing toward the crimson door.

She caught up easily, fighting her urge to turn around and help Aoife and Gwenn with every step. A crash of glass sounded and Lily glanced back to see Bahiti, Mary, and Fiona leaping through the windows. Reinforcements had arrived. Lily stumbled over a charred body and swung her eyes forward once more. If all had gone as planned outside, Morgane would be stationed up a tree, waiting to incinerate any vampires fleeing into the darkness.

Chaos reigned. Aoife's idea to scare off the vampires, the strongest fighters in the supernatural world, with fire—one of the few infallible ways to kill a vamp—had been spot on. Empusa and Amon had vanished, and only a dozen or so of their followers remained to fight in the grand hall.

A flash of movement registered in her periphery. Lily's head swiveled to see a man, six feet tall with teeth filed into unnatural points, rushing at them.

"Brigit! Watch out!" Lily screamed, jumping away from the man, her face covered by her hands.

"Arma!" Brigit cried, shooting her arm to the right without breaking step.

Lily watched the man crumple to the ground mid-stride, a victim of Brigit's well-placed shield charm.

"I'm so sorry," Lily panted when they reached the crimson door. "I know that one, I should have—"

"It's your first conflict. Losing your head is to be expected. Come, now, let's find Em," Brigit said, wrenching the door open and pulling her inside.

# *Blood and Ash*

Brigit shut the door and muttered a charm Lily knew would prevent anyone but those with their blood from following them. The silence behind the crimson door was deafening. It was clear no one had thought to seek sanctuary here. Lily scanned their surroundings and saw this hallway was shorter than the one Empusa had led them down. There were only four rooms total, two on each side, each with its mahogany door resolutely closed. Paintings in the same lewd vein as those in the drug den hung between the doors. Unable to help herself, Lily moved closer to get a better look. She gasped. The subjects in these paintings were not only stark naked and in suggestive poses. They were also being tortured. The artist's ability to capture his subjects mid-scream, yet somehow still make them seductive, was unsettling and, Lily had to admit, a tad intriguing. Her eyes fell to the floor, ashamed by her animalistic reaction. She gasped again and lowered into a squat. Sprinkled along the marble were small drops of dark red blood.

Brigit bent down next to her. "It seems the person was struggling. It's far too random for me to get a clear read on the trail," she whispered her voice grim. "We're going to have to search each room."

Lily never thought she'd find herself hoping to see another orgy or drug den. All her instincts were screaming that this part of the house was the vampire twins' private domain. Why else would their followers avoid it? If she was right, whatever they found here would likely be far more disturbing than a drug den.

"Nothing," Brigit whispered, placing her ear on the first door to listen. Slowly, she turned the knob and peered around the corner.

Lily pulled her shirt above her nose as the stench of feces

assaulted her nostrils.

"It's empty," Brigit declared, throwing the door wide.

The room was spartan with a lumpy pillow and single blanket tossed over a twin bed, a rickety night stand, and a huge chamber pot. The decoration was minimal, but garish, with dark red velvet curtains over the windows and elaborate fleur-de-lis wallpaper patterning each wall. Meant to be grand, the overall effect was an eyesore, and Lily's attention shifted to the room's simpler aspects. She eyed the thin fleece blanket with concern. Whoever slept there must have been freezing during the cool desert nights. Anger bubbled inside her at the thought of Em huddled in this very room, shivering and frightened.

"Where do you think they took her?" Lily asked.

Brigit didn't answer right away.

Lily watched as Brigit ran her hands along the walls, before walking to the bed and examining the pillow.

"I'm not sure it was Emily who was kept here. This certainly doesn't belong to her," she said finally holding up a dark strand of hair. "We should move on."

Lily sighed, though from relief or frustration she wasn't sure. *Was Em kept in worse conditions?* she wondered.

Entering the hallway once more, Lily noted that no one, for better or worse, had managed to break through Brigit's sealing charm.

"The faster we find Em, the faster we can help," Brigit said, reading Lily's thoughts as she swung open the second door without hesitation. The aroma of rotting flesh stampeded into the hallway, and Lily's hands flew to her mouth in horror.

Corpses filled the room. Piled one on top of the other, they towered in columns above Lily's head. Her eyes latched onto a small body nearest the door. A girl no more than eight lay left to rot in a small pool of dark, congealed blood.

Brigit slammed the door shut. "Those bastards," she said, making her way toward the third door, jaw clenched and eyes hard.

"What if—?" Lily asked, her voice shaking.

"If there's more? While we'll never forget such a sight, corpses cannot hurt us. We have nothing to fear from them," Brigit answered, flinging open the door.

Three women stared down at them from the opposite wall. Unthinkingly, Lily pushed past Brigit, drawn to them. The painting was in the style of the old Italian masters, though the subjects were far more ancient.

"They're like us, but . . . different," she whispered, unable to tear her gaze from the life-like oils.

Her hair was longer in the painting, and she was pregnant, but there was no mistaking those penny-colored eyes: Seraphina, Sara's twin, sat smiling upon the grass, enjoying the sun's rays on her face as she watched children play. Eve stood to Seraphina's right, her long blonde hair flying in the wind. She alone was aware of the viewer, and her piercing blue eyes stared back at the whoever deigned to look upon her, challenging and seductive. Lily's gaze shifted last to the woman, who made her the most uncomfortable. Dark haired, green eyed and athletic looking, Lilith was leaning against a willow tree playing with branches that, even considering the painting's two dimensional limitations, seemed to dance. Each sister radiated an alien power and joy—even Eve, who alone of the three did not smile.

"The original three of Hecate," Brigit said, sidling up to her. "One look at them and you'd know. They're not of this world."

Lily nodded, shifting her attention to a candlelit altar where two other paintings hung. They were modern, monochromatic, and inexplicably mesmerizing. Only when Lily moved closer to inspect the deep navy canvas, then the pearl gold one, did she see the artist had painted a face on each. Or at least some semblance of a face, with huge round eyes, and a gaping circular mouth. Lily shivered. Beautiful as the paintings were, something about them creeped her out.

"We should go. Emily is waiting," Brigit said.

***

In the hallway, Brigit's sealing charm remained intact, though Lily thought she could distinguish the faint sounds of fighting on the other side, a sign the charm had withstood attacks and was weakening.

"Let me go first. We don't know how they've been keeping Emily. If I were her . . ." Brigit trailed off, but Lily understood. Any sort of mother would want someone else to take the brunt of their child's pain.

Lily nodded and Brigit stood before the door as if facing off with a foe.

"Arma," the shield charm whipped off her tongue to surround

them in a bubble, and Brigit threw open the door.

Lily caught herself on Brigit's shoulder as her knees buckled. Red covered every surface. Childlike images rendered in blood were drawn upon the wall. Though it smelled better than the first two rooms, the metallic scent of blood mixed with the faint stench of excrement was still revolting. Across the room, Emily lay motionless on a filthy twin bed stripped bare of sheets and blankets. Two heads—one dark, one light—were bent over her on the other side of the bed.

Brigit lobbed a fireball high over the bed and Georgina and Amon jumped back, their faces red and glistening.

"Lily love, we were wondering when you'd show up. You're a bit late, we're about done here," Amon said, grinning wickedly.

Georgina smirked and sauntered over to press her body against Amon's chest. She nipped his ear, leaving a smudge of red on the lobe that she proceeded to lick away with tremendous care.

"Get away from her," Lily screamed, stepping up against the boundary of Brigit's shield.

Amon's laugh was cold. "You are such an attractive creature, Lily. Shame you're so very dull witted. I heard Lilith was the same." His face tightened into a scowl. "Power from the weakest of the three flows in your veins. I should have guessed. How could you not have known what I am? Seen through the act I put on? Were you that desperate for someone to pay attention to you? I'm mistaken if you're not still seeing me as your little boyfriend. So tolerant of your quirks. Your prudish nature. You never could give me what I wanted. What a real woman would give." He squeezed Georgina's rear and she moaned with arousal. "Well, now you'll have to pay for that. Georgina, darling, why don't you show Lily here how a *real* woman acts?"

Georgina lunged, and Lily felt her first fireball materialize in her hand as rage burned through her to fuel the flame.

"Down!" Lily screamed, and Brigit's shield evaporated, leaving her exposed.

Georgina grinned, dodging the fireball Lily shot at her with ease.

"Flamarba," Lily said, throwing her arms wide with only seconds to spare.

Georgina jerked to a stop inches away from the chest-high line of fire that encircled Lily and Brigit. Her face contorted in anger at having been thwarted.

"Yes . . . hide behind your little flames," Georgina taunted, prowling the circle's edge. "You'll have to come out sooner or later. Unless, of course, you're hoping to witness the old one's draining." A weak groan carried across the room and Georgina's smile broadened.

Lily chanced a glance at Brigit, who twitched her head. For the first time she found herself grateful that others could read her thoughts. Wordlessly, Lily allowed her shaky hold on the flambara spell to fall. In the same instant, Brigit's flame gate rose seamlessly from the ground to cover the retracted spell. Then, Lily sprinted toward the fire.

Georgina jumped back. Her eyes widened as Lily cleared the flames, each hand poised to launch a fireball, and hit the ground running.

Without missing a beat, Brigit lifted her flame gate high over Georgina's head, trapping the two of them inside together.

Lily crossed the room in seconds and hurled herself through the air to collide with Amon, knocking him off Em's body and to the floor.

"That," Amon hissed, his quick reflexes and superior strength apparent as he forced Lily beneath him and straddled her, "was a very stupid thing to do."

His hands shot toward her throat and he began moving on top of her. "Remember how you liked this? Let's see if you wouldn't like what came next." Removing his hands from her neck he fingered her shirt buttons, his eyes locked on hers.

"GET OFF ME!" Lily screamed, trying with all her might to buck him off.

"Shhh. You're getting me *excited.* I don't like to rush through foreplay if I don't have to," Amon whispered.

Through Lily's terror, a flash of an idea. She knew it could backfire, as much as she knew it was her only chance to survive unharmed. *Please, please, please, let this work*, she thought laying her palms flat on the ground and closing her eyes.

"That's better. Nice and quiet, the way you should be," Amon growled.

Through her eyelids Lily could feel his eyes hovering over her, captivated by her, in a way he had never been before. He began to shift up and down her body. Lily sensed he was sniffing her, searching perhaps for the sweetest piece of skin to puncture.

*Well, he won't get that far*, she thought concentrating hard on the ground beneath her palms, the dark wells of the earth and pools of water held within them. Water she could use if she bought enough time.

"Liam . . . I mean Amon?" she said keeping her voice small. He had always liked it when she was shy.

He raised an intrigued eyebrow.

"I always wanted this, you know. Well, not exactly like this, but I hoped . . . could you be gentle? For my first time—please?" *Jesus*, she thought, hating herself as she bit her lower lip and blinked.

Amon cocked his head, his mouth breaking into a hungry smirk. "I'll try, but I make no promises, Lily love. We have so many secrets to discover, you and I, and I've waited an awfully long time to find out yours."

Lily waited until his body eased over hers, his warm breath swirled above her lips, and scent of sandalwood and warmed coins filled her nose. She ripped her hands from the ground. A geyser of water did what her arms were too weak to do, and Amon soared across the room to hit the far wall. She scrambled to her knees and threw a pitifully small fireball in his direction.

Amon rolled to one side, dodging it, and rose into a predatory hunch.

*Oh shit!* Lily thought, her hands trembling as she tried to generate another fireball.

"You little slut! Wait until I get my hands—"

A massive inferno flew past Lily's shoulder, missing its mark by inches. She turned to see Brigit flinging fireball after fireball at Amon as if she were a human machine gun.

"You'll *never* lay your hands on any of my daughters again!" Brigit roared, stepping through a pile of ash on the ground, her hands overflowing with hot, blue flames and a mother's fury.

Amon's face contorted in fear and in four smooth steps he leapt out the window, a thin figure retreating into the night.

"The coward," Brigit huffed. Her eyes narrowed as she assisted Lily to her feet and over to the bed where Emily lay motionless.

Em was pale as snow, save for the handful of scarlet divots that lined her neck, arms, and legs.

Lily placed her hand on Emily's cold chest. One second. Two. Three. There it was! The faintest thump of Em's heart against her hand.

There was still hope, no matter how small.

"We have to get her out of here, but how are we going to move her without hurting her?" Lily asked.

Emily rose an inch above the bed.

"Levitation charm," Brigit said, directing Emily out the door. "She's very weak. I doubt she'd survive if we carried her, no matter how gentle we were. This way I can float her above any fighting that may still be happening. No more harm will come to her."

Lily froze, her face pale. She'd been so preoccupied with finding Em and then defeating Georgina and Amon that she'd completely forgotten about the rest of her family fighting. *What if Em isn't the only person we float out tonight?* she wondered.

"My sisters are quite powerful witches, Lil—Bahiti, Fiona, and Morgane as well. I'm confident they will survive this night. Remember when we're out there, if you're unsure of what to do, cast a shield. No one can leave here until you do."

***

A list of defensive spells ran through Lily's mind as they strode down the corridor with Emily floating between her and Brigit. They were feet from the enchanted crimson door when Brigit stopped. A faint creaking of wood was coming from the first room. Bringing her fingers to her lips, Brigit tiptoed over and eased the door open.

Aoife and Mary whirled to face them, arms at the ready to duel, as Brigit entered the room.

"Brig! There you are! Will you take a look at this?" Aoife said, dropping her combat stance and pointing at the wall.

"Aoife! Where is everyone else? Are they alright?" Brigit asked, her features torn between curiosity and worry.

"Aye they're fine, I wouldn't leave them out there in need. The vamps all ran for the hills. Even Empusa once we got serious with the roasting and toasting. Haven't a clue where Amon went off to, but I know he's nowhere in the grand hall or any of the rooms we passed on our way in. The rest of their fighters were a laugh, weak daemons, fae, and witches, none with any remarkable power. A few even threw up a white flag. Said they'd been coerced. Morgane and Bahiti are passing judgment on them now. Fiona and Gwenn are patching up the humans and modifying any memories that they can. Unfortunately, most have been through too much to alter it all without erasing days of their life."

Brigit's face relaxed and she stepped closer to the wall. "How'd you find it?"

"The doorway was concealed with strong magic. It wouldn't have been noticeable to the eye or touch. The caster left only a faint trace behind. If you were in a hurry you would have missed it. I asked the room to reveal its secrets and a door opened."

A door? Lily crept closer to the wall and saw it was jutting out and taller than her by a few inches. She gasped as the wall flew in at Aoife's slight push to reveal a long, dark tunnel. Her confusion grew as Brigit began to feel the wall as she had the first time they entered the room, eyes closed and lips moving soundlessly.

Her eyes popped open. "Can you and Mary investigate this? I'll gather the others and meet you back at Bahiti's," Brigit asked, her tone urgent.

Aoife, who seemed to gather a deeper subtext, nodded. "I thought you'd say that. The witch who was kept here—"

"Or *stayed* here," Brigit added, eyebrows raised.

"The witch may be able to tell us something. Mary's been collecting hairs off the pillow for identification just in case," Aoife finished.

"Let's go find Fiona," Brigit said, grabbing Lily by the wrist before she could ask what was going on.

The grand hall was a far cry from the glittering, elegant room Lily had walked through an hour before. Scorch marks the size of tires peppered the walls as liberally as chandelier crystals covered the floor. Black piles of vampire ash dotted the ground. Five captives sat on the floor before Empusa's red throne, now occupied by Morgane. Amon's throne lay in blackened ruins next to its twin. A scrap of scorched blue velvet and an arm of polished wood was all that remained of its former grandeur. It was, Lily thought, as if an earthquake and a fire had occurred simultaneously.

Bahiti appeared at Brigit's side, her eyes alive with excitement beneath a head of wild, warrior hair. "I've called my sisters. They should be here any minute. What do you think we should do with the group who surrendered?"

"If they are innocent, they will need sanctuary, at least while Empusa still walks Alexandrian streets. Your coven has a protocol for such things, I assume?"

Bahiti nodded.

"Good. Set them up in a safe house so we can question them later. Lock the ones deemed guilty in one of the rooms through there. There's one I'm sure you'll agree they're well suited for," Brigit said, pointing to the crimson door. "Em won't last much longer without help. We'll meet you back at your place."

***

"Goddess be!" Fiona cried when they found her. Rising to her feet she rushed over to Emily, abandoning a woman in the midst of emerging from a drug-induced stupor. "Is she alive?"

"Yes, but barely. The spark of life could leave her at any moment. They were trying to their damnedest to drain her when we found them," Brigit said.

Fiona assessed Em's bite marks, cuts, and bruises. "We'll need more of everything I brought, but I have to triage a bit right now if she's to survive long enough to find supplies. She's too weak to move farther. Put her over here, Brig," Fiona instructed, throwing together a pile of dingy blankets and smoothing them.

"She'll need blood soon, won't she?" Lily asked. She watched as Fiona pulled a tonic of butcher's broom and garlic from her bag and began applying it to the bite marks.

"You've been studying," Fiona said, approval in her voice. "First we must stop the damage from spreading. Butcher's broom is the best thing we've found to prevent vampire venom from propagating in a contaminated system or feeding on any new blood that may enter it. Garlic makes it impossible for venom to further transmute the cells it may have already reached. Once that's done I'll administer this." Fiona pulled a tiny golden vial from her bag. "Hawthorn, acacia, and blood of a person descended from the fae. There are few substances more magically or medicinally potent than fairy blood. I don't usually carry it, but I had a feeling I might need it today. Hawthorn and acacia accelerate fae blood's healing properties. Vampire bites are cursed bites, so there's no guarantee, but it's the best chance Emily's got," she trailed off, looking down at the elderly women.

Fiona worked in silence and finally, after the application of the fae blood blend, sat back on her heels.

They waited.

Lily had never seen Em look so terrible. The gray tinge of her skin made Lily want to recoil, but she stayed, unable to betray the woman who had always been there for her. An image of Florence's opaque gray body popped into Lily's mind unbidden, and Lily sighed. *Even Florence looked better off than Em, Lily thought. Dead hundreds of years and yet there she was spry as can be. If Florence hadn't been misty I would have thought she was alive.* As Lily stared down at Em, the images of Florence and Em began to blur in her mind, pulsing back and forth between life and death, family of blood and family of heart.

"We should do a circle to bring her back from the brink of death, like how we brought Florence back. I know she's not blood, but she's as good as. And she's not quite dead so it should be easier right? With all our power channeled into her?" Lily asked suddenly.

After what seemed like a million years, Fiona responded.

"You're right in thinking the potions don't seem to be strong enough. Something should have happened by now. A circle could work . . . you and Em did have a close relationship. Stronger than most mothers and daughters. And since we're both healers, that would help."

"Even with cursed bites?" Brigit countered.

"I'm guessing they've been feeding on Emily since they captured her. Centuries ago, vampires would keep empaths as pets to feed on. They said it helped them feel again. Em's age is against her, but with all our power and the fairy blood, it *might* work." Fiona said the words as if testing them for the first time.

"I'll channel," Lily said, springing into action.

They knelt above Emily and Lily felt a jolt of energy like the one she experienced Samhain night as their hands clasped together. The power of blood forming a bond. *Here goes nothing*, Lily thought, as words flew off her tongue.

"I call to the forests, thick upon Earth.

I call to the winds dancing above.

I call to fire, savior of this night.

I call to the ocean which no man can tame.

Resurrect this woman.

By the power given to me,
As I will so mote it be."

Though the words had been unpoetic, Lily knew it didn't matter. Magic was, at its core, all about belief, and Lily had never believed more that what she was doing would work.

Fiona's earthy healer's touch and Brigit's prodigious mix of fire and earth magic flooded into Lily's body. She gasped as her blood began to burn, set aflame by possibilities. *I could level cities right now*, she thought. *I wish Empusa and Amon were here. I would end this conflict once and for all*, she seethed, burning hot.

*Don't let the fire run away with you.* Brigit's voice wafted through Lily's head, wrenching her focus back to Em.

Opening her eyes, Lily looked down at Em, her broken body lying on a pile of filthy blankets, last used for who knew what unsavory purposes. She loosened her grip on Fiona and Brigit fearfully. As her fingertips fell into bare air, Lily felt the power of three witches rampaging through her blood. It was immortality defined. For a split second she wondered how Evelyn had handled harnessing the power of seven. *No mortal should ever feel like this*, Lily thought as fire and earth trampled her insides, begging to be released.

Placing her hands on Em's heart, Lily worked instinctively, transmuting and siphoning off the collected power at a painfully slow pace. "Salus." She whispered the healing charm as the final stream of magic trickled out of her. Her hands trembled as she pressed hard on Em's heart, her breath hitched high in her lungs.

Then Lily felt it. Em's heartbeat thumped to life with such force Lily feared it would explode from her chest. Its rhythm, glacial at first, gained speed, surging past normal within seconds, as if making up for lost time. Elation soared within her as Em's eyelids fluttered. They had done it!

A wave of fatigue overtook Lily and she sat back on her heels. She hadn't realized how close she had been to passing out, how much power she had given. *It was worth it*, she thought, her eyes meeting Brigit's crinkled ones.

"Well done, Lil," Brigit said.

Lily smiled. She was about to ask Fiona if there were any potions they should prepare when an ethereal hiss filled the room.

A gale of wind concentrated at her chest tossed Lily backwards ten feet. She landed on her butt and a flame gate materialized around her.

*What the—oh shit*! Lily thought, jumping up to peer through the flames.

Em stood tense between Brigit and Fiona, who were circling her with hands extended and ready to fight.

*What's going on? Why are they fighting Em?* Lily wondered, jumping to get a better view.

Emily's head swiveled at the motion. Her hazel eyes were bright red.

Lily gasped.

Emily growled and leapt at Brigit, exposing very long, sharp canines.

They had been too late. Em had changed. Aoife's words from hours before flashed through Lily's mind.

*"A newly reborn vampire is the most dangerous creature on Earth. They're unreasonable and answer only to their sire and blood. Their blood lust is so unquenchable they'd drain entire cities without a second thought."*

But that couldn't be true for kind, non-confrontational Em. *I can get through to her,* Lily thought.

"Em! Em! Leave them alone! Come over here. I want to talk to you!" Lily called waving her arms in hopes of diverting Emily's attention.

"Stop Lily! She won't recognize you. She doesn't know—*oh*!" Fiona fell to the ground, her shield charm deflecting Em's forceful punch as Em ran past her to Lily.

"Em! You're alive! I'm so relieved. Now we can—"

Em hurled her body at Lily, stopping only inches from the flames, her teeth bared and red eyes wild.

"Let me through! Your fight is futile. I need blood and I won't stop until I get it," Em's voice was cruel and hard as she began to prowl the edges of the flame gate, looking for an opening.

"No, Em. It's me, Lily. You can fight it. I know you can. I love you. We can go to the hospital and get you blood so you're not hungry. If you just calm down—"

"*Blood*! Give it to me, you filthy witch! I'll suck you dry once

I get in," Emily screamed. Her eyes were distant and predatory as she stared Lily down, unrecognizing that the daughter of her heart stood before her.

Lily gasped. Her Em would never say that. She sought Brigit's eye. Her mother's body was taut, ready to fight, but tears streamed down her face. She had an open shot at Em, who was distracted by Lily, and she wasn't taking it. The reason why hit Lily like a brick to the face. *She'll protect me, but she can't bring herself to kill someone I love. My family. She won't put me through that.*

Em was salivating as she circled the flame gate at a speed human Em would never have been able to achieve. Lily shuddered as she took in Em's slinky gait, her red savage eyes as they bore down, desperate to sate her hunger. She was bloodlust embodied.

Watching her, Lily felt sure even draining all the blood from her body couldn't quench Emily's thirst. She'd move on to Brigit, Fiona, and then who knew? There was a whole city out there, and Emily's sire, Amon, was nowhere in sight. *Not that he would do anything to rein Em in,* Lily thought. *That fucker would probably delight in his protege and use her as a weapon. Em would hate that.*

Lily knew what she had to do. She couldn't place the burden on anyone else. As it always was with magic, it had to be her choice.

Her hand warmed effortlessly as two fireballs, the largest she'd ever made, grew in her palms. *Goodbye, Em,* she thought, before seeking Brigit's eye once more and requesting that her mother lower the flame gate.

# *The Tree of Life*

Lily stayed perfectly still as Sara dressed for the day. Through her eyelids she could tell the sun was managing to peek past the ever present gray clouds. She took it as a sign.

Since the abysmal rescue mission, everyone had gone above and beyond to ensure her comfort. Even Evelyn had offered to switch rooms to give Lily privacy, and while she craved solitude, Lily declined the offer. It was best for her to be around others in her state, even if she ignored them most of the time. Before, sharing a room with Sara had always seemed a minor inconvenience. Now she was thankful for every bit of warmth and vitality her sister radiated as she flitted in and out of their room.

*Today is the day*, Lily thought as the door clicked shut behind Sara. The day she emerged from their room for more than a hop across the hall to the toilet. *Maybe I'll go outside?* The idea seemed as incredible as traveling across the ocean in a canoe. *The kitchen first*, she amended, easing herself into a seated position. The scent of her unwashed body rose with her. Lily wrinkled her nose. It hadn't been as noticeable beneath the thick blanket. Her ankles popped as she swirled them in circles before touching down on the cold wood. She waited for a head rush to pass before daring to put weight on the wobbly, achy limbs that bore little resemblance to her strong distance runner's legs.

Selecting her outfit from a pile on the floor, Lily dressed herself for the first time in a week. *Thank goodness there's no mirror in here*, she thought, cracking the door open to listen. A couple minutes of eavesdropping confirmed Brigit, Sara, and Evelyn were the only ones home. *Three people I can deal with*, she thought, slipping through the door and down the hall.

Her mouth filled with saliva at the hardy scents of thyme, onion, and meat wafting through the cottage.

"Smells amazing. Mind if I have a bowl?" Lily asked, hovering at the edge of the kitchen.

"Of course!" Brigit said, eyes wide with shock as she leapt from her seat. "Pull up a chair. I'll bring it to you."

Lily lowered herself into a chair. A cozy fire burned at her back, and the rain began its daily drum at the window. A bowl of stew materialized in front of her. It would have been a perfect lazy day, if such a thing were possible any longer.

"So, what does everyone have going on this afternoon?" Brigit asked casually, as if her eldest daughter had not spent a week hiding in bed.

"Aoife is coming by soon. We're working on ceremens, projecting memories out like she does. I haven't had much luck yet, but I feel like I'm getting closer. Then I'm packing," Evelyn said.

"Packing?" Lily asked, her spoon halting midair.

"Your aunts and I decided it's best that you three be given the opportunity to spend a little time with your families. We were going to let you know today. Evelyn is leaving tomorrow afternoon. We bought a ticket for you at the same time if you want to use it."

"I'm staying here," Sara said matter-of-factly.

A sharp pain pierced Lily's chest. While a part of her yearned for her family in Oregon, another part, the part that blamed herself entirely for Em's death, feared returning. *What would life at Terramar be like without Em? she wondered.*

"Can I let you know tonight?"

"Of course," Brigit said with an understanding smile.

Lily was grateful for Sara's ability to keep a room full of life and chatter. She half listened as her sister began describing one of her recent lessons on how to shoot fireballs from her hands machine-gun style. It seemed that lessons had become more militant since their return from Alexandria. *A good idea*, Lily thought, recalling her pitiful self-defense tactic in the grand hall. If she hadn't been so enraged to see Amon sucking Em's blood, she probably never would have felt her first fireball fly from her hand.

"More stew?" Brigit asked, reaching for Lily's bowl.

Lily looked down and saw the bowl was empty. She shook her

head, ignoring the protestations of her stomach.

"I'm going to take a walk in the forest," she said as an overwhelming urge for the scent of trees and dirt came over her. She rose to discard her bowl in the sink before Brigit had a chance to serve her up another.

"Alright, Lil. Make sure to wear a jacket. There's been a chill lately."

***

*Brigit wasn't lying. It is freezing*, Lily thought, shielding her face from the wind and light rain. She considered turning around and cozying up next to the fire on the couch, but instead she kept walking forward. She needed to feel the woods, hear the wind weaving through the trees, smell wet dirt and feel her feet sink into it. She needed to witness the Earth, alive and well, even if she caught hypothermia in the process.

She began to run. Her legs were shaky at first, until the muscles recalled the feel of motion, stretching and contracting beneath old baggy sweats, warming her body from the inside in a way she hadn't felt for days. Passing the lake, Lily broke through the tree line at full speed with the sound of her heartbeat pounding in her ears. The wind, a howling banshee across the fields, faded with each step she took, dulled by the trees until it died out completely. On their own accord, her legs began to slow to a run, a jog, and finally a walk.

The trees surrounding the cottage were naked now. Their leaves covered the ground like a decaying blanket. But in this patch of wood, dense evergreens gave the illusion that summer was still possible. That turning back time was possible. The thought comforted Lily as she veered off the path she'd been on into the unknown. As a child she never feared getting lost in the woods, one fact that hadn't changed, though it seemed everything else had.

For the last week Lily's thoughts had been on a continuous loop —Liam, Amon, Empusa, Em, the book, and repeat—each one so thoroughly covered in her mind that her head ached. The one that stole most of her attention was also the one she tried her hardest to push away. The book. What if they had found it in time and given it to the vampires right away? Amon and Georgina wouldn't have fed on Em. Lily wouldn't have tried to bring her back like an idiot. Emily never would have risen as a vampire.

*I wouldn't have had to kill her,* Lily thought.

Lily kicked a pile of dirt before collapsing to the ground beneath a towering oak still clinging to the last vestiges of fall. She threw her head back, grateful for the cushion of the jacket's hood as it hit the oak's hard bark. Her mind slowed as she watched the leaves clinging to the branches above swaying in the wind and rain. Oaks had always been her favorite tree, a trait that Brigit had immediately tied to Lily's Irish blood.

"None worshipped the oak as devoutly as the Irish. Druids preferred the oak grove above others as the site of their religious rituals," Brigit said as they combed the woods for Adder's tongue on a moonlit summer evening a lifetime ago.

Lily since learned it wasn't only the Druids that felt bonded to the oak. Zeus, Jupiter, Hecate, Thor, Jumala, and Brighid all considered the tree sacred. Sara had told her that in Ireland, some believed that fairies lived in oaks, and witches danced beneath them under a full moon. Fiona considered the oak tree an ancient symbol of protection with the power to heal. *The tree of life*, Lily thought, gazing up the thick trunk past the smallest branches to the gray clouds above. She'd read once that an oak tree's roots dug as deep as the branches flew high. She imagined the roots of the oak she leaned against below her. How they wound their way through dirt. Growing through buried bodies and past treasure secreted away by men long dead. True or not, the romanticism of the idea was enough for her to love them.

*I'll plant one someday*, Lily thought, placing her hands on the cold bark. *When this is over, and life is normal. I'll name it, watch it grow, show my kids how to climb it.*

A jarring image of an oak erupting from Fern Cottage's floors past Brigit's head flashed in her mind, interrupting Lily's fantasy life.

*Yeah, that's not what I meant*, she thought, annoyance flashing as her fingers traced the outline of the bark. *Why can't I just think of pleasant things—?*

"Holy shit." Her fingers froze.

*The tree of life. A witch's tree. I grew one when I still in utero. What was it Mary said in the prophecy? Uproot? Find? Seek? What if?*

***

Lily burst through the cottage door ten minutes later, wheezing and clutching her side.

"Lily!" Brigit cried jumping up from her armchair, "What happened? Are you alright? Aoife! Mary! We need help!"

Rubbing the cramps from her side, Lily allowed herself to be led to the couch. *God, I'm so out of shape*, she thought as her aunts and sisters streamed in from various parts of the cottage, anxiety written across each of their faces.

"The prophecy. What exactly did you say, Mary?" she said sucking in air between each word.

"The whole thing?" Mary asked, looking alarmed at being asked to recite a prophecy from twenty years prior.

"Just the ending. Before you collapsed."

Mary paused for a second before answering. "Find Seraphina's tome," she said her tone confident as her eyes searched Lily's in question.

Lily slumped in her seat. *Of course. It would have been too easy . . .*

"Actually," Aoife interjected hesitantly, "Your exact words were, 'Unearth Seraphina's tome.' I've lived it often enough and I'm fairly confident that's what they were."

Mary shrugged, unconcerned with such insignificant quibbles of language.

Lily's heart flew into her throat. "Where did the oak tree grow from?"

The room fell silent. Only then did Lily realize how out of left field she must seem. Out of breath, disheveled, unbathed for days, and babbling about a tree.

"The one I grew when we were born," she explained, trying to sound as sane as possible.

"Why—" Mary began.

"Are you asking for the exact spot?" Brigit asked.

"Over here," Aoife said, grabbing Lily by the hand and leading her around the hearth. "It'd be about here," she said, stopping two feet from the dining table, "though since Brig had to have hundreds of roots pulled up and the whole floor replaced, it's impossible to be sure."

Lily's knees hit the hard floor and she winced. Placing her hands flat on the ground, she began to run them over the wood, asking the earth below for a sign. Frustration bubbled inside her, turning into a rolling boil as the minutes ticked on and no sign, not even the smallest inkling of magic, revealed itself to her. If it was there, she was sure she would feel it, as it was connected to the tree just as she was. *It had been a stupid idea anyhow*, she thought, pressing her hands into the floor to rise, defeated. Her arms shook, unable to lift the rest of her, and she sighed. She was about to ask for help when Sara dropped down next to her.

"I read in Mariel's grimoire she brought to Samhain that some books bound or hidden by magic for long periods of time have been said to . . . well, they get bored," Sara whispered, her face inches from Lily's.

Lily blinked, unsure what to make of the fact.

Sara grinned slyly, and raised her voice loud enough for the others to hear. "Seeing as they're books and can't move, they have to find a sedentary way to occupy their time. The one thing books have going for them is they know a lot of words, tone, and voice, so they sing." Sara lowered her ear to the floor, and Lily's eyes widened as she followed suit.

She held her breath, waiting, praying for the slightest noise. *Come on now, don't be shy. You've had years to practice*, she thought trying to coax sound from the ground.

All the air flew from her lungs as music rose up from the depths.

The song was quiet, timid even, as if unsure if its audience would abandon it on the first pitchy notes. Lily smiled and rubbed the wood floor soothingly. The song grew louder and stronger.

"Is that?" Evelyn whispered, her head cocked to one side.

Eyes filling with tears, Lily lifted her ear from the floor and the song followed, swelling into the room, loud enough for all to hear. It was, she thought, the most haunting of melodies. A tune from a different time and culture, whose message nevertheless rang clear.

Bring me home.

***

They found their treasure seven feet below the floorboards, attached to the fine dead tendrils of the magical oak's deepest roots. Its thirty thin pages were still stitched together and bound by a leather cover no larger than a birthday card. It was impeccably preserved, tiny pockmarks from the roots being the only indication of wear.

"How is it so clean?" Sara noted with a tone of admiration. "It's been down there twenty-one years but looks brand new."

"We know from speaking with Bahiti's predecessor that Hypatia hid the book in space and time. It appears those factors have been protecting it until the right person found it. Until Lily, the firstborn of the three, was ready to find it. Neither space nor time have dirt, sun, or even air, all of which assist in decomposition. Hypatia was a brilliant witch to have hidden it so skillfully," Aoife explained, turning the book over in her hands before holding it out to Lily. "You were fated to find it. You should read it."

Lily shook her head. It didn't feel right. If these last few months had taught her anything, it was to trust her intuition, no matter how small the moment seemed. While she had found the book, she couldn't claim first dibs on all its secrets.

"Mary should read it. She's spent the most time researching. She's the only reason we know anything at all about fata or the sisters. Will you read it to us, Mary?"

# *In the Beginning*

Written faithfully in the words of Esther,
daughter of Seraphina, witch, and
first scribe of Seraphina's tale.

Transcribed from memory by Hypatia of Alexandria
after the burning of the Alexandrian Library

***

*I, Esther, daughter of Seraphina, claim this story for the witches, progeny of humans and fata. I promise to protect and preach it for all my long years. To pass it down to my own daughters. If all goes as I intend, my family story will survive, not only through my own efforts and documentation, but whispered in the night by the softly moving lips of a mother to her child, much as Seraphina, my own mother, spoke of her homeland.*

*It took many years before I, her first daughter, realized those whimsical bedtime tales I loved so much were not only for my entertainment. My mother's secret slipped out not through her mouth, but with a look. Tears often filled her eyes when she regaled us with stories of the plants, animals, and fata of Hecate. I was nearing my fifteenth year before I worked up the courage to ask the question burning in my heart, knowing it would be improper for me to marry whilst I still believed in children's tales.*

*"Is Hecate real?" I asked my mother as we prepared the evening meal. I tried my best to act as if my heart would not break if she denied the existence of the land I'd come to love.*

*"As real as you and me and the earth beneath our feet."*

*Her answer shocked me, though why I cannot say. How did I not see that we were different? That my mother, her sisters, my cousins and I aged more slowly than the humans around us. That we would live far, far longer than any other human we knew. That we were beings of two worlds.*

*Many human lifetimes later, on the brink of my own death, I see those bedtime tales were my mother's way of handing over our history, in the only way a child naive to boundless worlds and beings amongst the stars could understand. From the day I questioned Hecate's existence on, my mother spoke plainly with me about her and her sisters' lives since journeying to Earth.*

*Alas, I digress. It is difficult not to want my own story told, but this is my mother's tale. A tale pieced together from visceral memories she inserted into my body seconds before the mist of her dying pneuma disappeared into the ether, from my own life, forever. My mother instructed me never to lose the record of her memories. To bind it to our family, our blood, and those who carry it for the day when those of Earth have use of it: When the three sisters of Hecate rise once more to defend the weaker creatures around them.*

*Always Seraphina's dutiful daughter, I do as my mother says, and pass our family story to you.*

***

## Seraphina's Tale

In the beginning, there was Hecate. Lilith, Eve, and Seraphina, my mother, were born there. They flew over Hecate's crimson forests that grew smaller with each passing year. They swam down to the depths of the lone sea, devoid of life and littered with rocks. They explored the land as if it was their birthright, because it was. They were the daughters of Dimia, the fata king of Hecate.

Dimia encouraged his daughters to use their magic regularly—a fact that displeased his subjects as much as the decree that banned all but himself and other hand-picked nobles from siring children. While Dimia's limitations angered most of his subjects, they were nothing if not practical. But how could others understand that when only Dimia and the ancient ones knew the truth? That Hecate, the fata's source of all magical ability, was dying.

This may sound strange to you. I know it did to me. How can a planet die? Life on a flourishing planet can limit your views on the matter. My mother suspected that Hecate had lost its magic due to the overpopulation of fata. You see, for every fata born, Hecate supplies a pneuma, a bit of magic from her core, so that they may thrive. Only when a fata dies can Hecate regain her power. Herein lies the problem, as the fata of Hecate live for thousands of years. Seraphina believed that Hecate had begun to cling more strongly to her stores of magic causing each generation of fata to be born weaker than the last. The fata had outgrown their home and were paying the price.

My mother, Lilith, and Eve were different. They were born strong and full of magic. Dimia spoke of how Hecate had chosen to bless them, and he saw to it they had the best of everything. Tutors were sought for each speciality of magic. Soon the triplets outpaced even the most revered ancients. Dimia enforced no limitations on his daughters, allowing them to fly or swim in domains of Hecate he had forbidden to his subjects, lest other fata discover that Dimia had been hiding the truth of Hecate's demise for fear of being overthrown.

One day, Dimia's youngest seneschal, Noro, returned from his travels. Noro had the unique ability to send forth his pneuma (what the people of Earth would call a soul) to explore the heavens, often for years at a time. It was the one attribute keeping him at The Crystal Court. Noro's travels left his dark navy body incapacitated on Hecate, and no more than a ghost on the planet he explored. Most at court thought this talent amusing for the stories it produced but largely useless, just like Noro himself.

Noro, too, knew of Hecate's decline, though not because Dimia had confided in him. Noro had practiced his talent in secret for years before begging for a position at The Crystal Court. In his years of practice, Noro had seen Hecate's dying forests and seas through his pneuma. He realized what the destruction meant and saw it as his chance for advancement. Only once he could send his pneuma successfully into the heavens did Noro approach the court. He called himself a storyteller, and upon receiving a position, promptly set out to find a new planet for the fata under the guise of collecting material for court tales. He desired for once to be a hero, rather than a joke. Decades later, he had succeeded.

In a meeting with Dimia, Lilith, Eve, and Seraphina, Noro spoke of a planet with forests full and green, vast oceans teeming with life, and thousands of creatures. It was the most Hecate-like planet he had ever found. Despite his lack of body with which to experience its limits, Noro believed the new planet, which he'd named Earth, could provide magic for the fata as Hecate once did.

Dimia recognized Earth as a chance to save the fata and his reputation. He took it.

"I am sending you three, my strongest subjects, in the hope that you will find a way for the weakest of us to survive," Dimia proclaimed in his usual sweeping manner to Seraphina and her sisters. And that was that.

Dimia and Noro hatched a plan both impressive and dangerous. Lilith, Eve, and Seraphina were to create a magical portal between the worlds, the likes of which had never been seen, and travel through it. Noro would provide directions and visuals on how to get there so that they may construct it correctly. Once they arrived, Dimia's daughters would scout Earth for a time and report their findings to Noro's pneuma, which could be seen and communicate on other worlds. Dimia hoped that in time all fata would move to Earth. If they could absorb the planet's power, they might once again equal the ancients in magical prowess.

The plan shocked the fata triplets, Lilith most of all, for Lilith loved Hecate the best. Eve proposed to leave immediately. She desired nothing more than to please Dimia. Seraphina fell somewhere in between. She adored Hecate and her fellow fata, yet desired adventure. She hoped to find it in this new place. That was, if they could even survive once they got there.

Therein lay one of the many risks. As Noro's pneuma—which, like all pneumas, can live in nearly any condition as long as the fata's body is safe and the pneuma itself is not punctured—had been the only part of him to make the journey, he was unsure if fata would be able to survive away from Hecate bodily.

Despite their reservations, the day came when they were to leave. Seraphina often said creating a portal between Hecate and their new home was more difficult than they imagined. Lilith, in a true mark of bravery, leapt into the void first, connecting the planets as she went. Eve followed, waving a merry goodbye to Dimia and Noro as she disappeared into blackness. Seraphina sealed the portal as she left, pulling the end of it with her through space.

***

The sisters' arrival was as undignified as one could imagine. The pit of mud they landed in was vast, full of the bones of small animals, and smelled of death. But they were alive and that was a good sign.

They traveled for days, stopping to examine new plants and animals. The sisters noticed that many animals could not fly, as was typical on Hecate. Most land dwellers did not appreciate their floating up to meet them, often running off before the sisters could introduce themselves. In an effort to be more approachable, the sisters adopted a mode of moving that involved skimming their bottom limbs along the ground. In this way the fata sisters learned to walk like the animals of Earth.

Mere weeks after their arrival, Lilith made a startling discovery. She had come across the first animal not to balk or run at her approach. It walked on two feet and was hairless, unlike most creatures of Earth. She had found a man named Adam. To Lilith's great surprise, Adam took to her airy green fata form, unlike any other creature. Within minutes of their meeting it became clear to Lilith that Adam could think and communicate in a manner similar to fata. After having only her sisters to communicate with for weeks, Lilith found this creature, Adam, exciting. She introduced him to Eve and Seraphina, and Adam reciprocated in kind with his tribe.

From that time forward my mother and her sisters were never without the companionship of humans. They moved across the land with them, adopted human language, and learned to take on their shape. Soon enough, they began to love them. And once the fata sisters had absorbed and familiarized themselves with Earth's magic, they discovered they could bear the children of men.

Lilith and Adam were the first to have a family of five boys and three girls. Adam proved enamored with Lilith, and Lilith loved Adam more than her own life.

My mother assumed she too would chose a man one day, but in the meantime, she spent her days experimenting with the vast magic reservoirs of Earth and developing potions. Seraphina discovered she had partiality for magic born of fire. That no such substance was known on Hecate could not have delighted her more. Eve began pulling prodigious power from the streams and lakes they passed in their travels, while Lilith connected best with the magic derived from the land itself. The more they played with the powers born of their new home, the stronger they became.

As the years passed, Eve began to feel hindered by the small tribe they'd settled with. Despite the offers of marriage that had poured forth when she crafted a human form of ample pale curves, piercing blue eyes, and gold hair out of her sapphire fata body, Eve had not found a mate in their tribe. It was because of Eve's restlessness and both Eve's and Seraphina's desires to find mates that they decided to leave the tribe.

Lilith sobbed at the news but could not deny their decision. "I wish you both to find the same happiness I have," she said, grasping Eve's hands in her own. "In truth you are doing our kind a great service by leaving. We haven't seen much, have we? Father will want to make sure the whole planet is safe before sending the fata here."

Lilith made them promise to return to her one day. Eve and Seraphina agreed, all the while knowing how flimsy their word was in this unknown land.

***

Eve and Seraphina left laden with herbs and plants with which they could make potions to trade. They walked over forested mountains and through desolate deserts, exploring the land. No matter where they traveled, the sisters never ceased to garner the attention of other humans—especially men, who seemed drawn to Eve's golden hair and sky-colored eyes.

It began the same in every camp. Eve stole the attentions of men and my mother placated their women for her sister's poor behavior by offering potions to cure their woes. Once Seraphina's potions proved successful, the women found it easier to turn their eyes from Eve's coquettish nature. Often they even shared their own healing secrets with Seraphina. In this way she became known as Seraphina the wandering healer, a designation she relished.

Throughout their travels the sisters heard tales of a never-ending body of water. They'd been on course to see it for years, stopping and living with various tribes for months at a time. What the tribes of the forests, plains, and deserts said was true: The moment Seraphina and Eve saw the great shimmering blue expanse was unlike any other in their travels.

"Here is where I will find a worthy man," Eve proclaimed, staring wide eyed at the village before the blue unknown.

Though the women on the sea's edge had no natural magic in the way of fata, they were advanced in the applications of herbs and potions for healing. A veritable cornucopia of plants grew along the water's edge, and the sea women made use of them all. Because of this, Seraphina was happy to settle along the blue expanse.

Eve was happy too, though for very different reasons, the first of which was her power. Along the banks of the sea, Eve's magic grew unthinkably strong. Her ability to pull power from the water's unknowable depths gave Eve a vitality Seraphina had never before seen in a fata, let alone her sister, who had been the weakest of the three on Hecate. The villages along the sea also supplied a great deal of happy distraction for Eve as the men here loved her more than any others. Eve frolicked and flirted shamelessly, making no attempt to hide her affairs while she searched for a mate.

To everyone's surprise, Seraphina was the first to choose a mate in the bustling seaside village. She adored Seth, my father, and he adored my mother in return. They built a joyful life and family together, until it was taken too soon by death, as all human lives are.

The day my father drowned, all my mother's happiness shattered. Seth as a man nearing forty shouldn't have been out on the water as the waves swelled above his head, but he was a provider with mouths to feed. Seraphina felt great guilt for the rest of her days for allowing him to do so. Especially as she could have called fish from the sea with a crook of her finger.

During their years in the village by the sea, Eve grew increasingly unhappy with her inability to find a mate that pleased her for longer than a day or two. She brought up the idea of seeking Lilith a week after Seth's death. It was an idea Eve had been suggesting on and off for years, and for once Seraphina agreed. My mother was no longer able to bear the familiar sights, sounds, and people that reminded her of my father.

Eve, Seraphina, myself, and my younger sisters departed two weeks later. Had my mother and Eve been human, we would likely never have found Lilith's nomadic tribe. But then, they were not human at all.

***

Lilith wept at the sight of her sisters and hugged her nieces, ecstatic to meet her newest family members.

Seraphina noted much had changed in the years she'd been gone. Lilith, like Seraphina and Eve, looked the same, but time had ravaged the faces of their friends. Lilith had become the primary provider for her family, and stress was beginning to show in her union with Adam. She admitted she and Adam had been quarreling for sometime. Neither my mother nor Lilith saw anything unusual with that but Eve was of another mind. She judged that if Lilith had not bonded herself to a man so quickly, if she'd gone to the great sea with her sisters, she'd know better how to please a man.

Eve, my mother often said, had always been envious of Lilith's ability to know what she wanted and develop deep relationships.

Days began to flow rhythmically. Seraphina became sought after as a tribe medicine woman. Eve took a domestic turn when she agreed to watch Lilith's children on the days when Adam could not hunt and Lilith went in his stead. This arrangement suited both sisters. Stress lines melted from Lilith's face. Adam, who in recent years had begun to suffer from stiffening joints, smiled more. Eve glowed with the satisfaction that having a role brings. She'd even begun to flirt less with the men of the tribe, a sure sign that watching her kin had her considering starting a family of her own.

Then Eve began to show signs of being with child.

Seraphina asked about the father daily, listing off Eve's suitors in varying orders hoping to trick her sister into an admission. She wanted to know who had stolen Eve's heart.

The day the truth emerged our family cracked in half.

It was Adam.

I remember hearing Lilith's and Adam's screams the night Lilith found out. My mother clutched me tight beneath our furs, hoping I was still asleep as I pretended to be. Though I did not know what enraged my aunt, her obvious fury terrified me.

When our household awoke in the morning, Lilith was gone and with her my three female cousins.

Adam was furious. Lilith had taken their daughters without his permission. True, he had five sons, all full grown and capable, but without any daughters who would care for him in his advancing old age?

My mother wept for Eve's betrayal and Lilith's disappearance. She wanted nothing to do with Eve, and resolved not to speak with her sister.

At first Eve took pains to appear shocked by the change of circumstances in her family, though her remorse was short lived. Even the whispers of the tribe did not stop her from moving into Adam's home after the birth of their daughter, Aya. It was only after Aya's birth that Seraphina sought Eve's company.

Seraphina was terse with her sister, happy only when touching Aya. Eve, on the other hand, was radiant. It seemed she finally had what she wanted in life. They did not speak of Lilith but rather of their original mission on Earth, as if all that had happened in the interim was but a bad dream.

Eve admitted to having been in contact with Noro in the weeks that she and Seraphina had not been talking. Noro claimed Dimia was eager for them to open the portal. Eve agreed with their father, as she always had on Hecate, that it was time.

My mother did not agree. She claimed that without Lilith, the fata most bound to earth, they would be unable to open any portal.

"How can you be so sure? We've grown in power since arriving here. Myself most of all," Eve replied defensively

While it was true Eve was far more powerful than she had been on Hecate, Seraphina still did not think it possible. Their magic on Earth was different than their power on Hecate. A portal, difficult there, seemed impossible on Earth, in this place none of their pneumas could call home. They needed Lilith, the most connected with Earth.

Seraphina agreed to speak to Dimia soon. Of the fata triplets, only my mother had mastered the ability to send her pneuma back to Hecate to communicate as Noro could, though for admittedly shorter periods. It was her most taxing skill, required days of planning, and did not please her to do it often. Though in this instance she realized it was necessary, and set to making preparations as soon as she left Eve's hut.

***

On the day Seraphina planned to send her pneuma into the heavens, she stopped by Adam and Eve's hut first. To her great surprise someone she hadn't heard from in years was there. Noro's deep voice rang from the hut. He spoke to Eve in a familiar way most of Dimia's courtiers would not dare. Seraphina knew he must have been visiting her often to get that close, sound that intimate. She listened at the door, and what she heard shocked her.

Voices filled with passion. Discussion of a new realm, one in which all fata lived as kings and humans as their pets—their slaves. Those that did not comply would be killed, of course. It was all too easy. Humans had no magic with which to protect themselves. They were powerless compared to the weakest fata. It was all part of Dimia's plan, Noro said, and Eve, always Dimia's champion, agreed wholeheartedly.

"I am already tiring of Adam's inability to care for me and Aya. He's too human. Too weak. I would welcome a new lover. A fata who could make my life easier," Eve purred.

My mother was incensed. She wondered what would happen to her children, nieces, and nephews who were half of each species? Perhaps Dimia would make an exception for them, but perhaps not. Dimia had always been a proud fata, boasting of the superiority of fata over the lesser creatures of Hecate, who were often used as pets. Seraphina felt a fool for having not seen Dimia's plan all along, and she returned to her hut determined to avoid Eve for as long as possible.

Her avoidance was short lived.

"Why have you not yet been to see father? And why do I feel as if you are avoiding me again?" Eve asked, cornering Seraphina in her hut a week later.

My mother, unable to hold in her anger any longer, lashed out. She accused Eve of going behind her back. Of omitting information Noro had given her. Worst of all, of scheming to enslave the humans for Dimia's good graces.

"You would do anything for father, no matter how wrong!" Seraphina cried. "Have you no guilt over enslaving those who took us in as their own?"

"Why do you care so much for them anyhow? They are weak, suitable only to serve more powerful beings," Eve sneered. "Is it because you have been limited all these years? Worry not sister, soon enough we will find powerful fata worthy of us. We will not have to settle."

The idea that Seth had been a sort of placeholder took Seraphina to hitherto unseen levels of fury. She threw Eve out, hurling fire at her back, and told her never to return.

***

Months passed and the sisters did not speak. Eve tried numerous times to approach Seraphina, a great folly on her part as Seraphina's anger had only grown as she considered Eve's betrayal. Eve had thrown away their relationship with Lilith not for love, as Seraphina had previously thought, but to sate her envy. The thought was unbearable, and Seraphina wished her eldest sister would return.

It was only when Eve's friend came running to our door yelling that Eve had collapsed that Seraphina thought twice about ignoring her sister's needs. She worried that the shame of being unable to fulfill their father's wishes would be enough for Eve to attempt to take her own life. Seraphina could not allow it. Despite Eve's cruelty, my mother could not stomach seeing either of her sisters in pain. The healer in her overrode the anger and she went to help.

Seraphina found Eve's hut in a state of disrepair. Her sister, it seemed, had given up the pretense of eating, allowing food to rot where it lay. Adam whimpered in the corner, pale and weak, as Aya played with a pile of dirt. Seraphina knew Adam's health had been poor but had not known he'd deteriorated so. She wondered why Eve had not called for her sooner?

Suddenly, Seraphina felt the air constrict as magic trapped her in the hut and Eve emerged from the shadows.

Eve looked terrible, having allowed her blonde human hair to grow lank and her skin to become covered in dirt.

"What is wrong with Adam?" Seraphina asked, her mind racing.

"He is dying," Eve replied, glancing back at Adam as if he were an afterthought.

"How could you let him? He is your husband. You could have called for me."

"What do I care if he dies? Unlike you sister, I have my sights set higher," Eve said scornfully.

A movement in another corner caught Seraphina's eye. She turned to see Noro, body and pneuma, float out of the darkness.

"How?"

"Eve brought me over," Noro replied. "The act nearly killed her, but I nursed her back to health." He floated to Eve and caressed her face with his navy limb.

Adam had already been replaced.

"Why did you call me here if not to help Adam or yourself?" Seraphina asked, seething. "If you brought Noro over, do the same for the rest of the fata. Bring them over one by one. Be our father's hero."

"Dimia commands you to help Eve," Noro said, his amorphous face tightening at Seraphina's tone.

"I have told Eve before, and I will tell you now, Noro. I will not be party to the killing off or enslaving of mankind."

"We thought you might say that," Noro replied, a round smile growing in his navy face.

Seraphina felt powerful magic crawl over her human skin and gasped. Eve was spelling her, binding Seraphina's magic to her human body. My mother struggled, trying desperately to fight back, but it was too late. Eve was, after all, the strongest fata on Earth.

Noro floated toward her, raising his navy arm with a look of triumph.

A magic Seraphina had not felt in years washed over her. Noro still carried inside him power born of Hecate, a magic that had become lost to Seraphina in her years on Earth. She savored the feel of her motherland for a moment.

Then, her world went black.

***

My mother knew when she awoke in an empty hut that she was no longer near the tribe. It was too quiet. She stood and went to open the door. It was locked, not by reed or wood, but by magic. Seraphina recognized Eve's spell work and knew there would be no leaving unless Eve set her free. She began to cry for help, hoping someone other than Eve or Noro would hear.

As if awaiting her call, the door flung open and Eve floated in with Noro close behind. She was in her full fata form for the first time since Lilith, Eve, and Seraphina had transformed into humans. It was a sign of her changed alliance.

"Holler if you must, Seraphina. No one but Noro and I will hear you. Sound cannot travel to or from here, nor can humans see this place," Eve said hotly.

"What of my daughters?" Seraphina asked.

"I spelled a woman to look after them while we work."

Despite her predicament, knowing my sisters and I were safe calmed my mother.

"Your plan is to keep me locked up until I help you?" Seraphina asked.

"It is," Noro answered simply, his body so close to Eve's that one could not fit a finger between their two shades of blue.

Seraphina smiled. She thought it a stupid idea.

Eve, noticing her satisfaction added, "Unless we are present, your own magic is useless here, sister. You are, in a sense, nearly as powerless as the humans you love. I have left only the power of transformation available to you here, so that you may resume your rightful fata form at any time. Only when Noro and I visit will I widen the spell's parameters. Then we will attempt to force the right kind of magic from you."

Eve's words wiped the smile off Seraphina's face.

"What do you mean?"

"Noro has learned various means of *persuasion* in his travels," Eve said, her voice full of admiration.

In time, Seraphina learned all Noro's means of persuasion, each more horrible than the last.

Eve observed as Noro worked spells that had my mother writhing on the floor, gritting her teeth in pain. She witnessed him driving sharpened twigs beneath Seraphina's nails, pouring vile potions down her throat, and forcing insidious mind magic upon her. Not once did Eve deign to help her sister, not that Seraphina expected her to. The approval of their father was at stake, and Seraphina knew Eve would do anything for that.

"You've been stubborn beyond belief, Seraphina," Noro said the first day he entered Seraphina's magical hut alone. "I've seen no one endure as much as you and for that you have my respect. However, that doesn't change what I was sent here to do. I requested Eve stay at home from now on, as I suspect even she has her limits. I sensed more primal measures of persuasion may be the only way to get through to you."

That day began a series of daily molestations. After each horrific torture session, Noro would end the day by tying Seraphina down and forcing himself upon her. Yet, still, my mother did not agree to help.

A bulge in Seraphina's belly was unmistakable within a fortnight. Floating through the door of my mother's prison, Noro's dark eyes latched onto the bump. He smiled in victory.

"I see we have succeeded in creating your first fata child. You should be proud, Seraphina. At least *this* child will be granted full status in our new realm. I'll let you rest today. I wouldn't want to strain our babe."

Seraphina's torture ceased from that day on, though Noro still visited daily to check on her growing belly.

Seraphina assumed the torture would continue once she bore his child. Either that or Noro would use the child to coerce her into doing his bidding. But why hadn't Noro already thought to use her other children as bait, she wondered. She could only assume his prejudice against humans led him to believe Seraphina wouldn't much care if they were harmed. In this instance she was thankful for Noro's bias.

"I hope I find you feeling well today, Seraphina," Noro said, floating into her hut. His eyes shone full constellations within them, a fata sign of pure elation that Seraphina had not seen since her days on Hecate.

She stared back at him, unsure if she wanted to know what it was that pleased Noro so.

"I bring you the best of news. It's of our family," Noro continued, resting on the dirt floor next to her.

Seraphina tensed, hoping he had not decided to use my sisters or me as bait.

Noro leaned in until his face was mere inches from Seraphina's.

"Eve and I are to have a child. You two will bear the first fata born to Earth! Is that not exciting?"

Seraphina spat in his face.

The stars vanished and Noro's eyes sparked with rage. In one smooth motion, he wiped the spit off with his limb and caressed Seraphina's face.

"Be grateful you are carrying our precious bundle," Noro growled as he left my mother with juices dripping down her cheek.

***

At the cusp of dusk four months later, Seraphina felt a faint pressure in her pelvic floor that could only mean one thing. Her child was preparing to greet the world. By the following day her contractions shook her beaten body with a magnitude far beyond that of any of her other pregnancies. Fear overtook her when she worked out the reason why: This child was fata. It did not know how to navigate a human body.

"Why have you not changed back already?! The child will not know how to be born. How could you be so stupid?" Noro screamed throwing open the door for his daily visit.

"I can't now," she cried, "I have no energy left to transform or even move." Her words were ragged, barely audible.

Fear flashed in Noro's eyes, though Seraphina did not think for a second it was for her.

A battle Seraphina never thought she would have to fight had been raging inside her, since she realized the consequences of choosing her human form. Would she transform and hopefully survive the pregnancy, only to have her child taken from her? Or would she allow the child to die within her, unable to find its way out, to spite the father?

"Build a fire," she blurted out before she changed her mind.

"Fire?" Noro asked.

"Argh!" Seraphina screamed as a contraction tore through her. "Have you learned nothing in all your time spying, you imbecile? Bring me wood and two flat rocks. *Now!*"

For the first time since their reunion on Earth, Noro followed Seraphina's orders.

Seraphina instructed him on arranging the sticks, then lit the fire in the human manner on the floor of her prison. She waited until the flames swelled to the height of a full-grown man before sitting back to bask in the fire's heat.

Her magic, low after the hours spent protecting her body in labor, sung in her veins as it devoured the flame's energy. With each heartbeat Seraphina grew stronger, and within minutes she was able to pull energy from the earth and water underfoot, even a bit from the stagnant air that Eve's protective spells swirled in, still as strong as the day she'd set them.

As soon as she could, Seraphina released her human form. Her magic flew from the core of her pneuma, the essence of her fata body, outward. Waves of power pulsed through each vein, muscle, and bone she had crafted, coaxing each solid bit of matter into her natural, airy form.

"Is it working?" Noro asked inching his way closer.

"Yes," Seraphina whispered. She watched mesmerized as the tinge of her human skin grew red, her natural fata color.

Suddenly, another contraction ripped through her, halting her transformation and doubling her over in pain.

That contraction was the first of many that ravaged Seraphina's half-transformed body. The speed at which they pummeled her increased, and soon it became impossible for her to continue the transformation from human to fata. She found she no longer held sway over her power. Her magic had abandoned her, instinctively rushing to guard her womb while her body spasmed uncontrollably.

"Can you finish?" Noro asked after several minutes of watching my mother suffer.

"They're coming too fast . . . too strong. I don't have full control over my body or magic right now." Seraphina's voice startled her. It held the airy quality from her years in Hecate, a resonance she had lost during her time on Earth.

"I was afraid it might come to this," Noro replied, leaving her on the ground to pace the room's perimeter.

"What do you mean?" Seraphina asked, watching him shake queerly as he floated with his back to her.

Noro spun to face Seraphina and she recoiled. His amorphous, airy arms had morphed into long, jagged protrusions. Before she could register what was happening Noro flung himself on top of her.

Her human skin opened as easily as a ripe fruit. Surprisingly small amounts of blood flew through the air as Noro's arms pushed aside what remained of her solid human heart and lungs. As he dug deeper, searching for his quarry, Noro nicked the thin membrane that housed Seraphina's pneumatic core. She gasped as wisps of red mist began pouring from her wound. Noro made no move to stop it and Seraphina began to panic. If it drained entirely, she knew she would not survive.

Seraphina kicked and screamed weakly, hoping to buck Noro off, all the while feeling the depletion of herself as the power that had concentrated around her womb followed her pneuma, its partner, abandoning her body entirely.

"If you care for our child, you will stop kicking," Noro hissed, still manhandling her insides from neck to gut. "You're making him harder to find."

Seraphina stiffened as Noro moved closer to her womb, now free from all magical defenses.

"Stop! There. Please, be careful," she pleaded, her maternal instinct overriding survival.

The sharp protrusion inside her melted into an extremity with the ability to manipulate her half-formed viscera, much like the hands of the humans Noro looked down upon. The other remained sharp, a threatening blade above her.

"I sense him! He's strong," Noro said, his face taking on a crazed appearance as he studied her anatomy, clearly wondering how best to proceed without injuring his child.

"Do you see the bulging sac near where my legs divide? It's moving."

Noro nodded, mesmerized by the undulations of Seraphina's solid, wholly human womb.

"Make a small incision near the top and pry it open. You should be able to scoop the child out." Her vision was became increasingly obstructed by tears and the growing mist of her pneuma pouring out, creating red clouds in the divide between Seraphina and the child. She knew she had but minutes left to see her final baby.

An incision, made by the tip of Noro's sharpened limb, produced a swelling of blood that pooled in Seraphina's open gut.

With his hand-like appendage, Noro reached in and pulled something from Seraphina's body. He held it up high, a round smile on his face.

Seraphina gasped and blinked.

There were two, a boy and a girl, neither of which looked like fata. These creatures were something else entirely. The pair had inherited none of the airy qualities of newborn fata. In fact, they looked almost entirely human. *Almost.* They were larger than any human babe she'd ever seen, with developed muscles and a mouth full of teeth, two of which resembled sharp white stakes. A predatory magic no human child could ever claim pulsed from the twins.

"I wonder," Noro whispered as he stared down at the children with delight. "What are they?" Seraphina croaked.

Noro's eyes shot up in surprise. He had already thought my mother dead. Cocking his head to one side Noro knelt down, cradling a child in each limb.

Seraphina froze as the children came into greater focus. Already strong and mobile, they stared back at her as they sat upright in Noro's arms. Their eyes, deep shades of green and gray-violet, began to travel the length of Seraphina's bloodied, misty body, as if examining exactly where it was they came from. Seraphina thought there could be no colder introduction of mother and child.

She was proved wrong one weak heartbeat later when the pair emitted a hiss and leapt from Noro's arms. Mouths open wide and teeth bared, the twins began to drink from the same pool of blood that bore them life.

# *The Shadow Days*

Mary closed the book with care, her hands folding to rest over the pages.

"It's just a story," Lily said, despising the tremble in her voice.

No one spoke, fueling her rage, until she couldn't dam up the feelings any longer.

"I guess I thought it would be instructions or something useful. How to create a portal. How to kill fata. Or any supernatural creature for that matter. How to become a badass witch and beat the magical alien race we're up against. Something more than a *goddamned story*!" she screamed, unable to keep her temper in check a second longer. *Em had been changed into a vampire. She died for a fucking story. We had even known parts of it. Why the hell didn't we just tell Empusa and Amon what we knew? Em could still be alive . . .*

"Lil—" Brigit said moving to take Lily's hand in her own.

Lily pushed it away, ignoring the guilt that rose with the gesture and stood, accidentally knocking Aoife's cup of tea to the ground. She stormed down the hall.

Slamming the door shut behind her, Lily flung herself on the bed. Only then did she allow her body to do what it had been begging to for days. Release. Huge, slow, tears that grew into ugly, hiccuping sobs. She didn't even care that the others heard. *Why care at all when the world makes so little sense?* Lily thought. *My whole life has been altered by a damn folktale.*

She felt Sara's presence on the other side of the door seconds before her sister filled the room with the warmth and strength that was quintessentially Sara.

"I'd be angry right now, too," Sara said, her eyes full of grief, as she perched on the edge of Lily's bed.

"I . . . I don't understand. What did I miss?" Lily said with a loud sniff.

"Mary and Aoife are looking it over now. We have to go deeper to discover why they wanted it so badly. Who knows what the vampires believe the book holds?" Sara said, reaching down to grab Lily's hand. "There's something there, Lil. I know there is. Em didn't die in vain. This isn't only a story."

*How can Sara be sure?* she wondered. *Hypatia lived in a different time. A time when information was not easily dispersed. Back when there was no web, no phone, no planes, hell maybe not even newspapers, or whatever the ancient Egyptian equivalent was. As far as Hypatia knew, Seraphina's tale would have died with her if she hadn't made the book. Maybe that simple fact would have been enough for her to risk her life and send Empusa and Amon on a wild goose chase for centuries.*

But it didn't disappear. It survived, bits and pieces of it altered and presented as myth in human tales and religion. They had already known some of what Hypatia wrote through stories knitted together across cultures and years. *But what about the details?* a small, interested, and annoying voice in Lily's head asked.

"I need to get away from all this for a few days."

Sara nodded. "That's what Evelyn said too after you left. Time at home will help clear your head."

Lily nodded. She hadn't even considered Evelyn. How awful she must be feeling. It was clear from the story whom Evelyn resembled physically and magically: Eve, the meanest of the sisters, the backstabber and man stealer. The betrayer of humans.

Lily shuddered.

"You're still staying?"

Sara nodded. "I have no one to go home to. I've already had to take a sabbatical from my studies to stay this long. I'm going to help them with the book. It has some obvious magical properties as well as historical. How else could Mary read it? Hypatia couldn't have known English. It's either under a translation charm or written in lingua primum. Aoife is talking about doing tests to determine which. If it's the translation charm, it's likely something may have even been lost in translation."

Lily's brows furrowed. She hadn't thought of that. "Historical?" she asked, desperate to hear sound reasoning to justify the cost to finding the book.

"You know the whole biblical Adam, Eve, and Lilith debacle. Lilith was Adam's first wife, her not doing what Adam wanted, so he asked God for Eve, a more submissive wife. Lilith became demonized as Satan's cohort afterwards. Then Adam and Eve were thrown out of the garden because of Eve's temptation with the apple. This could be a new take on Eve's mistake or, as the highly devout call it, betrayal. Even Seraphina's name has biblical ties. Seraphim were fiery angles in the Bible. It's not much of a stretch to think of her as one, is it? And what about those babies? Tiny stakes for teeth? Assuming the translation is correct, it sounds like we may have a record of the first vampires! How freaking crazy is that?"

Lily felt her mouth fall open. Sara was right. Growing up in a secular environment had not inclined her to reading religious text, but even she knew the story of Adam and Eve.

"That makes me feel a little better. And if this book helps us save humans from being enslaved . . . Well, I'll still be miserable without Em, but at least then I'll know in some small way her death helped us stop that. Her death will have meant something. Does that make any sense?" Lily said.

"Absolutely," Sara nodded, leaning in to hug Lily. "She'll be a hero like her daughter."

***

Lily was grateful Rena's trademark afro made her easy to spot in Portland International Airport. She ran through the crowd, not caring about people she cut off or bumped into, straight into Rena's strong arms.

"Mom," Lily said, stifling a sob as she buried her face into Rena's shoulder.

"Shhhh, you're home, baby. You're safe," Rena said, gripping Lily tight and ignoring the looks they received as people were forced to part around them.

"We can go. I didn't check a bag," she said raising her face to Rena's a couple minutes later and gesturing at the small duffle Sara had let her borrow. She had left most of her clothes at Brigit's, knowing this would be a short trip. There was still much to learn, and only the McKay women could teach it to her.

Rena put her arms around Lily's shoulders and they made their way to the parking garage without another word.

They were passing Multnomah Falls when Rena made her first attempt at small talk. "So, how are Brigit and her sisters?"

"They're fine," Lily said. It still felt a little strange talking about her new family with Rena. It was like talking to a ex about your new boyfriend. She'd only felt comfortable talking about them to Em.

"Your sisters?"

"We found the book. I did. It was buried under Brigit's cottage all this time," Lily blurted out, unable to hold in her guilt a second longer.

"Ohhhh, Lil, I'm so sorry," Rena said. Her lack of confusion solidified Lily's assumption that Rena and Brigit had been in contact. "You know, I'm not sure it would have mattered. I've never met Empusa or Amon, but I've heard of them. They have a reputation for being particularly nasty. It was probably their plan all along to hurt her, in order to hurt you."

*So much for easing in*, Lily thought, deciding on the spot that she simply couldn't keep secrets from Rena any longer.

"I also knew Amon. I dated him when I was at Bryn Mawr. He went by Liam there. Sara and Evelyn know about Liam, but not that Amon posed as Liam. Brigit, of course, heard Amon taunt me and insinuate that we had been together, but she hasn't asked for details . . . yet." The words rushed out of her like water from a spout.

Rena slammed on the brakes, and pulled to the highway shoulder, her face ashen. "You dated Amon? Did you—? Did he—?"

Lily shook her head emphatically. "I didn't know. Seems stupid now. How could I not? He was so attractive and had a certain aura to him. He knew what I was, though."

Rena nodded, relief clear on her face. "Vampires, especially very old ones like Amon, are sensitive to magic. They had to be, in an evolutionary sense, to survive when it was used against them. Your bind was loosening. We all knew it—and some of us felt it, Em most of all—though how he knew where you where, I couldn't guess. We know they've been monitoring the strongest witch families for centuries. It's why Brigit gave you to us, but we took so many precautions with you three . . ." Rena trailed off.

Lily had wondered the same thing. How, of all the witches in the world, had Amon latched on to her? She couldn't be sure, but she had her suspicions that something deeper was going on. The room with the false doorway in Empusa's mansion seemed the perfect escape route for someone who didn't want to be seen. Aoife and Mary had reported it traveling far below the ground, exiting along the Alexandrian harbor.

"We think," Lily paused, unsure how to phrase the words without sounding accusatory, "We think someone is reporting to them. A spy. We're not sure if they knew who Evelyn and Sara were, but they knew me, and who I would risk my life for."

Rena stared at Lily. "You think someone you know is a spy?" she asked thunderstruck.

"Aoife does, Brigit isn't so sure. I told her it couldn't be anyone at Terramar, but Aoife is operating under the assumption of guilty until proven innocent." Lily hated herself for saying it.

"She always was a spitfire," Rena muttered, pulling back onto the highway. "But I have to say, under these circumstances I agree with her. We've had many women come through the commune over the years, any of whom could have been a spy. Though I would like to think I'm a better judge of character than to let a fox in the henhouse."

"Wouldn't Em have known? They told me she was a decent empath. Wouldn't she have sensed anyone's ill-will toward me?"

Rena sighed. "Em tried her best to stay out of people's emotions. Even yours, though you made it so damn hard sometimes, especially as a teenager. All the hormones I guess. Even I could read your mind a little at that age, and I'm terrible at mind reading."

"I told them I thought maybe it was someone at Bryn Mawr. I met a few mean girls there that I could see being Empusa's bestie," Lily said, only half joking.

"No matter what, we'll have to keep up our guard from now on. Anyone acting suspicious or asking too many questions about you is under my scrutiny."

Lily frowned. It was nauseating to think she'd been spied on her entire life, monitored for her potential as a witch when she didn't even know witches existed.

She watched the trees fly by as they settled into contemplative silence. The green landscape of home resembled that of Ireland, her new home a country and an ocean away. How strange it was that a place could hold a paramount position in her heart after such a short time. Six months ago she would have thought it impossible. But then, six months ago she'd have been wrong about a lot of things. The Emerald Isle was a place where magic grew and thrived. People felt magic in their bones there. It was as much a part of life as breathing. The minute Lily landed in the States, she'd noticed the difference. People hurried more, thought more, and understood less. Here magic had no place in history, religion, or life. It couldn't live here like it did in Ireland. For her, there could be no returning to a place like this, at least not for long.

Rena's gentle tapping of the brakes pulled Lily from her musings as they passed the bedazzled fir tree signaling Terramar's drive. Someone, undoubtedly Rich, had left the gates open for them and Rena drove straight up to her cabin. She threw the truck into park with such finality that Lily knew it signaled a well thought-out speech.

"I want you to know no one blames you for Em's death. Without a sire to control her, Em would have killed hundreds, if not thousands of people that night. You made a noble, selfless choice, and everyone here is thankful for that. You're so strong, but you don't always have to be. We want you to know we've made your safety here our top priority. Enchantments have been strengthened at the property lines and iron fencing extended. You're *safe* here, Lil. You can relax and think."

"Thanks, mom," she said, kissing Rena on the cheek.

They hopped out of the truck and Lily heard Rena's heavy tread moving up the stairs to the cabin door.

"You alright?" Rena asked as the door hinges squealed open.

"I just need a minute," Lily answered, pulling her duffle from the truck bed.

A pause, a soft click, and she was alone.

Lily's body loosened, cascading to the damp dirt. Sitting cross-legged she leaned against the truck's tires, her head back and eyes open wide. The stars were out in their full glory that night. No matter how hard Lily tried to ignore them, they persisted, demanding her attention, her reverence. A sight once so comforting had become uncertainty itself, a sign of change, and the root of her fears. Gazing upon their indifferent glow, Lily knew that none of them were safe.

# *About the Author*

Ashley lives in Portland, OR with her husband, Kurt and their dog, Flicka. When she's not writing she enjoys traveling the world, reading, yoga, cooking, and connecting with family and friends. She's currently studying to become a yoga instructor and obsessed with poke bowls and moon water rituals. *Prophecy of Three* is Ashley's debut novel, but she already has many more planned! Look for *Reckoning of Three* Book Two of the Starseed Trilogy late 2017.

For most direct access to Ashley visit www.ashleymcleo.com where you can sign up for her mailing list. Or find Ashley @amcleowrites on twitter of Ashley McLeo author on Facebook.

Acknowledgments

*Prophecy of Three* is like Lily, it was raised by a village.

Thank you to Kurt Leopoldt for always believing in me, even when my drafts were shit, and allowing the space and time to follow my dreams. You keep me thankful for your love, unyielding compassion, and support everyday. I love you babe.

To Jennifer Roop, my editor, I'd have so many misplaced commas without you! In all seriousness, you brought my work to a new level and gave me valuable, constructive, kind input when I needed it. Thank you for caring about *Prophecy*, being open to discuss my ideas, and supportive. You're the best!

A huge thank you to all my family and friends. Especially the ones I bugged with strange but pertinent questions to make Prophecy seem more real. Thank you for indulging me. Unlike some authors I never had the experience of anyone being anything but supportive and excited for me. That went a long way in the days when I myself wasn't very excited about my work. Those days were usually when the manuscript was covered in red, and right before my novel got better. In short, thank you for the push to rise to the next level, and being willing to read my first crappy drafts with love.

To my beta readers, I *seriously* could not have written *Prophecy* to a higher standard without your input. Every one of you were wonderful to work with and brought new insight to the table. Please never leave me!

Max Tsikhach, my talented cover artist. Thank you for creating such a beautiful cover and being a delight to work with. I hope we work together many more times in our futures as artists.

Sometimes an artist needs more than critiques on their work, and that is where my Indie Author Business Group came in. Thank you to everyone in the group who helped open my eyes to a whole new world of marketing and promotion that every book needs to be successful. I learned so much in our Friday meetings.

Finally, thank you to my email list subscribers for taking a chance on a newbie author. Your support means so much, and I hope our relationships continue to grow.

With love and light,

Ashley McLeo

Made in the USA
San Bernardino, CA
19 September 2017